HOMEWARD

· · ·

· · ·

BARB HENDEE

.   .   .   .   .

Layout, eBook and Published by
N.D. Author Services [NDAS]
www.NDAuthorServices.com

.   .   .   .   .

Cover Art by
J.C. Hendee

Novels by Barb and/or J. C. Hendee

The Noble Dead Saga—Series One

Dhampir
Thief of Lives
Sister of the Dead
Traitor to the Blood
Rebel Fay
Child of a Dead God

The Noble Dead Saga—Series Two

In Shade and Shadow
Through Stone and Sea
Of Truth and Beasts

The Noble Dead Saga—Series Three

Between Their Worlds
The Dog in the Dark
A Wind in the Night
First and Last Sorcerer

ALSO BY BARB HENDEE

THE VAMPIRE MEMORIES SERIES
[COMPLETE]

BLOOD MEMORIES
HUNTING MEMORIES
MEMORIES OF ENVY
IN MEMORIES WE FEAR
GHOSTS OF MEMORIES

THE MIST-TORN WITCHES SERIES

THE MIST-TORN WITCHES
WITCHES IN RED [5/2014]

Tales from the World of The Noble Dead Saga

"Homeward" Collection including...

The Keepers
The Reluctant Guardian
Captives
Claws
The Sleeping Curse
Silent Bells

—separate works—

The Game Piece
The Feral Path
The Sapphire

Nameless ("Bones of the Earth" Collection) including...

Karras the Kitten
Karras the Cat
Karras the Nameless

"Tales of Misbelief" Collection
—separate works—

THE FORGOTTEN LORD

"SAGECRAFT" COLLECTION
—SEPARATE WORKS—

PUPPY LOVE

ABOUT THE AUTHOR

B arb Hendee is the nationally best-selling co-author of the Noble Dead Saga (along with her husband J.C.). She is also the author of the Vampire Memories series and the recently launched Mist-Torn Witches series. She has a master's degree in English and taught college for twelve years.

She was born in the northwest, later migrated to Idaho and then Colorado, but she missed the rain and the moss too much and now lives just south of Portland, Oregon in the Willamette Valley with J.C. and their two young kitties, Ashes and Cinders. Visit her website at www.NobleDead.org.

FOREWORD

No knowledge of the saga or other related works by us is necessary to read, comprehend and enjoy what you will find herein. Readers new to this world can step right into it through any of these adventures.

—Barb & J.C. Hendee

CONTENTS

THE KEEPERS

Alexi Korovich, the young vassal lord of the keep above Chemestúk village, grew more desperate each night, and Mercedes, his pretty wife, had become a shadow of her former self.

If only they could go one night... one night without being tortured by the spirit of these dank halls.

The two of them had taken refuge outside in the night air, high atop the single tower turret of the keep: one of the few places the spirit had not yet appeared.

How had everything gone so wrong so quickly?

Had it only been two moons since Alexi believed himself born under a lucky star? Had it only been two moons since the assignment to this keep, its village, and its five outlying fiefs had been dropped into his lap like a shining, unexpected gift?

As third son of a minor baron allied to Prince Rodêk of the house of Äntes in the nation of Droevinka, Alexi had often feared for his future. He was certainly no born soldier, and too often, choosing a military path was the only option for third sons. Marriage prospects were even bleaker. But to Alexi's shock, two moons ago Lord Malbek, chancellor to Prince Rodêk, had offered him the vassal lordship of

Chemestúk Keep—along with one quarter of the taxes collected from its surrounding fiefs.

Of course rumors still abounded as to why the House of Äntes had been unable to keep a vassal there for nearly twenty years. Whispers even suggested that some of the men appointed to the place had left within a moon of arriving.

But Alexi paid those rumors no heed and accepted the position... gratefully.

Almost immediately following his acceptance, he received an offer of the hand of Mercedes, youngest daughter of Baron Oblonsky, second cousin to the prince's wife. A modest dowry was involved, but it was far more than Alexi ever expected. As soon as he met Mercedes, he accepted Baron Oblonsky's offer without reservation. She was slightly plump, with reddish-blond hair, pale skin, and a friendly expression. When she smiled at him, the smile reached her eyes.

Alexi knew he was not a man to turn female heads. With a slight build, a hooked nose, and almost colorless light brown hair, he'd never have enough facial hair to grow a beard.

Mercedes did not appear to notice any of this.

Just speaking with her the first time, he thought himself the most fortunate young man in all of Droevinka. He married her as soon as the ceremony could be arranged, and the two of them—along with a small contingent of guards—had set off from the bustling city of Enêmûsk, heading for their new home and arriving on the fourth day just past dusk.

That had been their last night of happiness.

Now, they crouched together in the darkness at the top of the open turret and whispered prayers to whatever gods might listen.

But even their own guards had deserted them several nights ago.

He and Mercedes had no servants, as no one from the village of Chemestúk would agree to work here, no matter how much money was offered. Alexi and

Mercedes dressed themselves and prepared their own meals.

Had he or she eaten today? He couldn't remember, but thankfully, there was no rain tonight.

"Maybe the guards were not wrong," she whispered to him. "Maybe we should run too? My mother might believe us and counsel my father to help you gain another position?"

Was that even possible? Alexi stared at her through the dim light—for they dared burn only one small candle lantern. No matter what happened in this terrible place, he'd not once considered leaving. He'd been given the chance of a lifetime, and he'd been determined to stay.

"Another position?" he asked blankly. That had not occurred to him, especially if he failed here.

Mercedes nodded.

Perhaps she was right... and her mother might believe their wild stories and not blame them for taking flight?

"You think she would help us?" he asked.

"She might, but if she won't, I know my eldest brother will take us in. He has always protected me.... But we cannot stay here, Alexi."

A tentative hope began to grow in Alexi. Could they truly leave this dark place—was it that simple? His own father and brothers would be no help to them, so did he dare believe that Mercedes' family might be any kinder?

"Mercedes..." he began, but then the night air grew suddenly chill, until his teeth clicked together.

"Oh, no," Mercedes whispered, shivering with her arms wrapped around herself. "He's found us."

The wailing started before they saw anything, but the sound echoed faintly from the archway at the crest of the stone stairs leading downward through the tower.

Alexi quickly struggled up to his feet, realizing that in their frightened rush to hide, they'd not remembered that the top of the turret had only one way out: back through the archway and down the stairs.

The spaces between the stone "teeth" or merlons of the turret were wide enough to pass through, but then what? It was a long fall to the ground below.

They were trapped.

Mercedes' eyes widened with fear, and Alexi felt helpless to protect her. How did one fight a spirit?

Always before, when the ghost appeared, they'd had someplace to run. This was the first time they'd allowed themselves to be cornered. Perhaps they were too exhausted to think clearly?

"What do we do?" she asked in panic.

He had no answer. The air grew colder, the wailing grew louder, and Alexi braced himself for what was to come.

A semi-transparent soldier appeared in the archway. Still wailing, he floated out into the open air atop the turret. He always looked the same, with shaggy dark hair, a few days of growth on his face, and wearing leather armor and a sword.

Mercedes gasped.

The spirit—the soldier—came closer, and Alexi did the only thing he could. He stepped away from Mercedes, backing up and hoping the ghost would follow him and give her a chance to bolt for the archway.

As always, the ghost's eerie cry echoed through the night, and with a pleading expression, he motioned with his arms, trying to draw Alexi forward.

Alexi would not go, for he knew what this *thing* wanted. His mother had told him tales of the dead, and the life they sought to steal and consume from the living. Retreating farther, he was both terrified and relieved when it followed him, waving its hands in the air as if to call him back. Alexi took two more steps away.

"Mercedes!" he shouted. "Run for the archway."

He quickly pulled back even farther, hoping to hold the ghost's attention with his rapid movement. Then, too late, he felt nothing beneath his right boot heel.

Mercedes screamed as Alexi lost sight of her ever-widening eyes.

He flailed wildly in falling, trying to grab at anything in the dark as air rushed up around him. There was nothing.

Mercedes screamed again, her voicing sounding far away.

That was the last thing Alexi Korovich ever heard.

NIZHYN VILLAGE, NORTHERN DROEVINKA TWO YEARS LATER

J an was bored.

"Play something for us while we lay out supper," Nadja, his mother, told him.

He glanced at her in surprise. Although they were home, in a circular wattle-and-daub dwelling with a thatched room, they were not alone.

His mother had engaged another village girl, named Tansy, to help out around the home. Although Tansy could hardly be called "pretty," with her thick waist and stained teeth, Jan's mother knew only too well his penchant for charming any girl brought in for help. She'd warned him not to use any of his tricks this time.

Playing a forlorn tune on the fiddle was one of Jan's best, more indirect, ways for making girls fall in love with him.

Arching one eyebrow, he asked, "Truly?"

"Yes," his mother answered as her eyes narrowed. "But make it something lively and bright."

Unlike Tansy, his mother could be called pretty—even beautiful. With shimmering black hair and a dusky smooth complexion, she was lithe and slender, though well figured in her red dress tied in at the waist with a wildly patterned, orange paisley sash. She loved her jewelry, much of which had been gifted to her by her family. Often, as now, she wore a bracelet of ruddy metal that wound up her forearm in a mix of copper and brass. That adornment depicted a detailed engraving of twining birds with long tail plumes and flecks of green stone for eyes.

"I'd be delighted," he said, smiling as he lifted his fiddle and bow from where they lay on the next stool.

Tansy smiled shyly at him. She was about fifteen, and he knew he'd need to put out little effort to lure her. After all, she was already half in love with him.

At the age of twenty, he resembled his mother to a striking degree: slender, with even features and coal-black hair that hung to his shoulders in a wild, unruly mass. His dusky complexion stood out in the villages filled with milk-pale peasants. Unlike their drab clothing, he wore russet breeches with high boots and a loose sea-green shirt with the cuffs rolled halfway up his arms—and he sported three silver hoops in one ear.

He was very good with his fiddle, and the instrument's finish had long since worn away at the base where his chin so often rested.

"And what should I play, Tansy?" he asked teasingly, as he couldn't help himself. "Something romantic?"

She blushed and nearly dropped the plates in her hand.

The interior of their home was better furnished than most in the village, with white curtains on the windows, a solid maple table with matching chairs, and colorfully glazed pottery dishes. Tansy wouldn't be thanked for dropping any of those dishes.

"Jan," his mother warned, frowning at him. "Something lively... or go outside by yourself."

With little desire to go outside by himself, he lifted the fiddle to his shoulder and pinned its base with his chin. As he was about to touch his bow to the strings, his father, Zupan Cadell, walked through the door.

"Is supper ready?" his father asked without even a greeting.

Jan lowered the fiddle. His father was not a great admirer of music.

"Almost," Nadja answered. "We're just laying it out."

Cadell grunted and sat down, clearly exhausted—which caused Jan a pang of guilt. He probably should have been outside all afternoon helping to plant wheat. But Jan had inherited little by way of nature, inclinations, or appearance from his father.

Cadell, as zupan and leader of all of the villages, was a barrel of a man with pale skin, fading freckles, and cropped red hair peppered with gray flecks. He wore brown trousers and a brown shirt. His finger-nails were forever stained dark, like his boots, from working the land.

"Here," Nadja said, hurrying to him with a bowl. "I made mutton stew with potatoes and early pea pods."

Cadell nodded. "Thank you, dear." Mutton stew with early pea pods was one of his favorite dishes.

For all his gruff ways, Jan's father adored his mother and made no secret of it. His feelings for Jan were more... complicated. Attributes the zupan found desirable in a wife were quite different from those he might wish for in a son.

To make matters worse, the situation in the five fiefs surrounding the keep above Chemestúk village was growing more and more uncertain. Jan knew this weighed heavily on his father.

Due to an unfortunate mix of blight and locust in one year, followed by flooding the next, crops had been beyond poor for the past two years. Had the villagers been charged their normal taxes, many would have starved this past winter, but as yet, no one from Chemestúk Keep had come demanding taxes. From what Jan understood, no one had been assigned as vassal lord.

In part, this was a good thing. As zupan, Cadell could make judgments over small matters, such as when one peasant had sold a mule to another, claim-ing the beast was five years old, only to have the poor creature die of advanced age less than a moon later. Cadell had ordered the price of the mule be repaid. But larger matters involving land division or disputes among the farmers required judgments by the appointed lord of the keep—and there was no lord. Few vassals had ever stayed long, but eventually a new one was always appointed.

Sooner or later, Prince Rodêk would assign a new vassal lord. It seemed inconceivable that he hadn't done so before now.

Jan knew his father was pinning all his hopes on a much better crop this year, and so far, for the planting season, the weather had cooperated. Cadell cared deeply about his people and worked from dawn to dark here in his home village during the planting and the harvest. Whenever possible, he also visited the other villages to see how he might assist them.

Jan's father was a good man, and Jan often wished that he, himself, cared for the peasants here as much as his father did. But his favorite time of year was always just after the harvest. In early autumn, his mother would take him to spend two or three moons traveling with her people, the Móndyalítko, "the world's little children," though more often others called them *tzigän*—vagabond thieves. Jan lived for those few scant moons.

It was the only time he ever felt like he was home, like he belonged. Rolling through villages and towns of the land in covered wagons—that also served as home—filled him with a joy he couldn't express. For that part of each year, he made his living with his fiddle or by telling fortunes or amusing locals with card tricks that made him appear a veritable magician. It felt natural to him. It felt right. After that, returning to the village of Nizhyn left him feeling suffocated... and bored.

"How was planting today?" Nadja asked, shooing Tansy off to fetch Cadell a mug of ale.

"Good," he answered, taking several bites in quick succession. "Two fields finished... though it would have gone faster with more help." He glanced at Jan but said nothing overtly accusing.

Jan felt another sharp stab of guilt. His father never *ordered* him to do anything but rather hoped he would offer to help on his own.

He held out his fiddle. "Sorry, Father. I was practicing and lost track of time."

Before Cadell said anything more, the sound of pounding hoof beats came from outside their little home. As none of the villagers rode swift horses, Cadell looked at his wife in alarm, and then stood up and headed for the door. Jan followed.

The village spread out around them. There were about fifty circular huts with thatched roofs, a few shops, a smithy, and a sturdy log dwelling that served as a common house. All of the small buildings circled around an open central space used for market days and other gatherings.

Six riders cantered their mounts straight toward Jan and his father. Cadell stiffened slightly, though his expression remained calm. Only someone who knew him well would have seen his tension.

Five of the riders were dressed in chain armor and bright red surcoats emblazoned with the black silhouette of a rearing stallion. The leader wore no armor and was dressed in fine breeches, polished boots, a quilted tunic, and a light wool cloak. As he drew closer and pulled up his horse, Jan could see the man was in his late forties with a close trimmed beard.

Dismounting, he asked instantly, "Zupan, have I interrupted your supper?"

At least he was polite.

"No, I'd finished, Lord Malbek. How may I be of service?"

Jan nearly started. He had never before seen Lord Malbek, though he knew the name. This was the chancellor to Prince Rodêk of the Äntes. Jan wasn't even aware that his father had met such a man, but apparently the two knew each other.

Malbek gestured toward the door of the hut. "Could we speak inside?"

Cadell hesitated for only a breath. "Of course, my lord."

The politics of Droevinka were different from other nations. Rather than being ruled by a hereditary king, Droevinka was a land of many princes, each one the head of a noble house that ruled multiple fiefdoms. But they all served a single Grand Prince, and a new one was elected every nine years by the gathered heads of the noble houses. In spite of occasional clashes between houses, this system had served the country well for over a hundred years, perhaps longer. At present, Prince Rodêk of the Äntes had recently come into rule.

For Jan and his family, Prince Rodêk was more than Grand Prince of their country. The Äntes held and ruled the greater portion of the nation's northern lands, including Chemestúk and its keep and all other villages of the five fifes of the surrounding areas. The combined villages therein and unto themselves was called a zupanesta. Cadell was the zupan of those villages... which only meant he was the one with the most authority among the peasants and the first to answer to higher authorities for any problems.

He was still a slave to a feudal prince and the nobles who served that prince.

If Chancellor Malbek—now first chancellor of Droevinka under Grand Prince Rodêk—had come for a visit, it wasn't a social call.

All the guards waited outside as Cadell politely opened the door and ushered the chancellor into the hut, but Malbek appeared surprised when Jan followed.

"This is my son, Jan," Cadell said quickly and then motioned across the room. "And my wife, Nadja."

A flicker of something crossed Malbek's features as he looked over both son and wife, but he nodded politely.

"May I bring you a mug of ale, my lord?" Nadja asked.

"No, thank you," Malbek responded; he didn't bother to sit and instead turned his attention back to Cadell.

"I've come in part to apologize," Malbek began, though Jan wasn't certain it sounded apologetic. "I know your villages have been neglected these past years. The prince is aware of the situation, and I promise we are trying to rectify it. For now, he has assigned me to make the rounds and collect back taxes."

Jan glanced sidelong at his father. He saw nothing in Cadell's expression, but he knew his father's panic must be building.

Malbek waved one hand in the air. "I understand you've had difficulties. If your people don't have enough coin, we'll gladly take grain for the military instead."

He appeared to think this offer quite generous.

"Forgive me, my lord," Cadell began carefully, giving nothing away in his tone, "but the harvest has been poor for two straight years. The people have little enough grain in store to feed themselves, and they spent what few coins they had on seed for this year."

Malbek blinked. "Surely you've put something aside. You must have known someone would come to collect eventually."

"Of course we knew." Cadell nodded in agreement. "But I had also assumed by that point, the prince would have assigned a new vassal to Chemestúk Keep, and that the vassal would be the one to speak with me first, and to then act as our representative, explaining the extent of the poor harvests and striking a bargain with the house of Äntes."

Malbek stared at him.

"That is our right, is it not?" Cadell asked. "To seek protection and representation through the vassal lord?" He paused but Malbek still said nothing. "Simply give us the name of whoever has been assigned to the keep, and I will apprise him of our situation and do all correctly."

Jan stood tense. He'd wondered what approach his father might take. None of the fifes were in a position to pay two years' worth of back taxes.

Malbek still watched Cadell, while both Jan and Nadja held their breath.

"No one has been assigned to the keep," the chancellor finally replied.

"Why not?" Cadell asked.

Malbek appeared taken aback—and then affronted —by the boldness of this question. Before he uttered a retort, Cadell pressed on.

"We have unresolved land disputes... fathers dying and sons fighting over division of fields. I am not challenging you, my lord, but can you not tell me why no vassal has been assigned to our keep? There must be a reason."

The hint of anger on Malbek's face began to fade, and he sighed. "Because no one will accept the assignment, especially not with what happened to the last..." He trailed off as if surprised at himself.

"To the last lord you assigned?" Jan asked, unable to stop himself. "What did happen?"

His father silenced him with a look as Malbek glanced away.

"We'll find someone," the chancellor insisted. "But it will take more time."

No one spoke for short while, and then Jan's father asked, "Could you assign me?"

"You?" Malbek blinked again.

"The people trust me," Cadell rushed on, "and I have the skills for proper accounting. I can manage the fiefdoms attached to the keep... for my prince."

Jan thought this offer to be absurd. The Äntes would never make a vassal of a peasant—even a highly placed one who could read and write. But he studied his father, who in turn was watching Malbek, and Jan then realized the chancellor was actually considering the offer!

Even more, a strange glimmer filled the chancellor's eyes when his features relaxed, as if he'd been relieved of problem. Cadell must have caught this as well.

"But you'll have to forgive the two years of back taxes," he added quickly.

"Forgive?" Malbek repeated.

"I can begin visiting all the villages immediately, preparing everyone to pay this year's taxes, but only if Prince Rodêk will forgive the past two years and allow me time to get the people prepared and organized. If the prince insists on collecting the overlooked taxes, the people will starve before the harvest, and then there will be no taxes paid in the future. Let the villages keep what little food they have, and with a good harvest this fall, taxes will flow from these fiefs for years."

Malbek's eyes slowly shifted back and forth as he listened until finally, he looked up.

"I accept your terms for now... with one condition. If you abandon your position as vassal for any reason, the bargain is off. All back taxes of the villages will be due immediately, and soldiers will be sent to collect them."

"Agreed," Cadell said. "I've no intention of abandoning the position."

Jan glanced at his silent mother in concern. Why would the chancellor be so desperate to keep someone—anyone—at the keep?

Droevinka was a world of dark gray skies. Jan had never known anything else, so as he drove a team of horses down a narrow forest road toward the village of Chemestúk, he barely noticed his surroundings.

Old trees were dotted with moss that dangled in scant beards from a few branches. The ground was perpetually moist, and beneath the aroma of loam and wild foliage was an ever-present thin scent of decay. The thickened forest nearly blocked the cloud-coated sky above, and except for areas cleared for fields, much of the land was draped in a perpetual dusk.

Jan's father led the way, riding a tall chestnut gelding, while Jan and his mother took turns at the reins of a wagon bearing all their worldly possessions. A small contingent of guards sent by Malbek brought up the rear. Jan wondered about their new home and what it would be like to live in an aging fortress.

He hadn't known exactly what to expect, but just past dusk, as they neared their destination, he felt a stab of reservation at his first glimpse of Chemestúk. His father visited here at least twice per year, but not Jan.

Jan reined in the team of horses at the sight of a cluster of dingy huts—smaller and much shabbier than those in his own village of Nizhyn. Lean strands of smoke arose from rough clay chimneys or simple smoke holes. Beneath the scents of the forest were the smells of cow dung, soot, and dank hay. Bleakness itself seemed to linger here like a fungal stench.

Braids of garlic and henbane hung beside doorways. Strange symbols had been carved into the outer walls and doors of most dwellings, but Jan couldn't make them out in the rapidly encroaching darkness.

To the south was another clearing, smaller than the village space, in which stood weathered planks, erect stones, and debarked wood shafts sprouting from the ground. Garlands of wilted flowers hung from the tops of a few. Jan noticed a glitter of light through the tree branches there. A lantern hung from a tall pole near the graveyard's far right corner.

"Why waste good oil, especially in hard times, in lighting a graveyard?" Jan asked.

"Superstition," his mother answered. "When one of their own dies, they will buy oil before food to keep lanterns burning for as many nights as possible, all from fear of what unseen *things* the newly dead might attract."

"Truly?"

His mother didn't answer, but as his father pulled his horse up beside the wagon, his jaw muscles tightened, as if he did not wish to hear such things.

"Use that lantern to light some our torches," Cadell ordered the guards, pointing toward the graveyard. "We'll need light at the keep."

"Yes, sir."

The guards had been told to obey Jan's father as they would any other vassal, and as they complied, eyes began peering out of doorways and burlap curtained windows.

"Is that to be our home?" Jan asked, lifting his gaze.

Up the road and out the village's west side loomed a squat keep upon a rise amid the surrounding forest. Even at a distance, its dark profile looked worn and ill-kept like the village. Its upper rim was uneven, perhaps with broken stones leaving gaps. It sported a single tower rising high from one corner, like a crudely formed black spire in the early night.

Jan shivered, unable to picture his lovely mother living in such a place. She—and he—preferred small, warm dwellings or rolling, covered wagons that served as homes. What had his father done to them?

"Hallo?" Cadell called.

Nothing happened at first, and then a hut door cracked and a voice called out. "Zupan? Is that you?"

The door widened and a muscular aging man with disheveled gray hair emerged. He squinted at Cadell.

"I saw the guards and thought..." Then he called out loudly, "It's all right! It's the zupan."

"Hello, Yoan," Cadell said, climbing off his horse. "I didn't mean to startle you with these guards."

One by one, people dressed in faded and ragged clothing inched out of their huts, and Jan shivered again.

Was this to be their only company, frightened and superstitious peasants who starved their children to keep lanterns burning in a graveyard? He'd often found the villagers in Nizhyn somewhat lacking, but they were veritable "townsfolk" compared to these people.

"What *are* you doing with those guards?" Yoan asked bluntly.

"I'm not with them. They're with me." Cadell smiled. "I've been appointed as vassal to the keep."

Yoan didn't appear to understand.

"It's true," Cadell said. "We've all been forgiven the past two years taxes, and tomorrow I'll begin to organize all the villages to pay this year's taxes without starving ourselves. I am now the wall between our people and the Äntes."

Jan felt a flash of pride, realizing his father had managed something great, nearly impossible.

A buzz of voices grew all around them in the village's open space, but not all of it sounded pleased or excited by the astonishing news that Jan's father had delivered.

"You're not planning to live up there, are you?" Yoan asked, turning his eyes toward the keep.

"We must," Cadell answered.

The skin over Yoan's cheekbones drew back. "Dark things happened up there... no one can live up there... not for long."

"What things?" Jan asked.

When Yoan didn't answer, Cadell shook his head. "After two years of the place standing empty, our first battles will likely be against mold and rats." He nodded to Yoan. "We'll speak again in the morning."

Cadell mounted his horse and started up the road to the keep. Nadja glanced at Jan. With little choice, Jan clucked to the team of horses and followed his father, hearing the guards coming behind them.

Though Jan tried to maintain a sightline to their destination, the old fortress disappeared for a short while as they pressed along the road.

When they finally rolled onto the top of the rise, Jan's apprehension doubled at his first clear sight of the aging keep under the light of the guards' torches.

It was simple, barely a huge block of stone with one half tower, or turret, sprouting from a forward corner. It was more than a bit worn with age.

Moss grew between lichen-spotted stones on its lower half. To one side was an undersized stable while the other held a small abandoned barracks with a clay chimney, and nearly half the boards of that structure looked rotted through. A stone wall, decayed by the years, encircled the grounds. Judging by some of its taller sections, and the fallen stones lying about, it had lost half its height. Its gate doors were completely gone. The surrounding forest had been cleared away from the wall for some thirty paces on all sides.

With no gate to bar their way, Jan's family and the guards entered the grounds inside the decaying wall's remains and went straight up to the keep's front.

"See to the horses," Cadell ordered the highest ranking guard, who Jan believed was called Cherock, but he couldn't quite remember. Jan rarely paid attention to the names of guards.

After dismounting, Cadell took a torch from one of the men and strode toward the front doors. Although the doors were closed, they were not locked, and he opened them. Jan helped his mother down from the wagon, and the two of them hurried after. All the guards remained outside.

Upon following his father in, Jan found the entryway to be dark and dank, and it smelled so musty that he almost backed out.

"Father..." he began.

Cadell turned and his jaw was tightly set. "We've faced worse than this, boy. This is the only chance our people have for a fair hope, so we cannot fail."

Nadja's eyes were bleak, but she touched Jan's arm gently. "Your father is right. We must press on."

Steeling himself, Jan followed his parents further inside with the only light coming from his father's torch.

"I have some thick candles in my bag," Nadja said, her voice trembling slightly. "We'll light them in the main hall."

The wide passage emptied into a large, dark and damp space that had to be the main hall. Cadell held his torch higher as he stepped to the center of the floor.

Stairs circled up along the left wall and matching ones went down below to the right. The timbered ceiling was twice a man's height and less aged than the stone, likely having been expanded well after the structure had been first built. The original fire pit in the hall's center was filled in with floor stones, and a hearth large enough to stand in had been added to the back wall.

All three of them turned a full circle, taking in their new "home," or as much of it as they could see.

The filthy rushes on the floor and rotting tables and chairs and endless cobwebs caused even Cadell's expression to waver in concern, but Nadja looked up at him, and she attempted a smile.

"Do not trouble yourself," she said. "We will clean this up, and you will win the prince's trust and favor... and speak for our people."

Cadell looked at Nadja, and for an instant, all concerns drained from his face. "I am a fortunate man to have you with me."

Jan certainly agreed, and he wished he could be more concerned about their people... about helping his father. But there and then, all he could see ahead was a dreary future in a dreary keep.

The next few days were filled with industry and exploration, and Jan's mother had no compunction against ordering their guards into cleaning duties. Once the filthy rushes had been swept out, her next order of business was to decide which furniture might be salvaged and which should be burned in the great hearth. Even Jan had to admit that once the main hall had been cleaned up a bit and a fire was burning, it was not quite as unwelcome a place as it had seemed at first.

He and his mother then took stock of the rest of their new home.

In addition to the great hall, there were storage rooms and a kitchen on the main floor. The sleeping quarters were upstairs. One such room appeared to have been converted into a study, but the legs on the desk had decayed and half of it rested on the floor at an odd angle.

Almost right away, they found two large beds that were surprisingly intact, but both needed new straw mattresses and bedding to replace what had rotted away. Thankfully, Nadja had brought almost everything they owned from Nizhyn. So far, the family had been sleeping on blankets piled before main hall's hearth, but Jan knew his mother would soon make those bedrooms inhabitable. For the first few days, he worked from dawn to dark under her instruction without a hint of resentment and never touched his beloved fiddle. She was trying to make them a home, and he was determined to be some help.

To his surprise, the constant labor helped lift his spirits.

He and his mother only shared one dark moment in those first few days. They were upstairs, taking initial stock of the sleeping quarters, and they decided to go their separate ways in order to cover more ground. After thoroughly looking through two rooms, Jan had wandered back to find her, and he walked into a bedroom that appeared more recently inhabited than the rest. A dusty quilt covered the bed, and a thick braided rug—with only a few holes chewed by mice—covered the floor.

The open wardrobe across the room was filled with dresses and dainty shoes

Jan's mother stood by a completely intact dressing table, complete with an oval mirror. She was fingering an assortment of objects on the table: half full perfume bottles, silver brushes, and a string of pearls.

"She left everything," Nadja said quietly. "Whoever lived in this room... she left everything behind."

Looking around, Jan couldn't help feeling a chill.

C adell stayed at the keep long enough to help make the place at least livable. On the fourth night, at dinner in the main hall, he looked up from a simple meal of cold ham and bread.

"I'll be leaving tomorrow. I need to start visiting the villages to tell them what's happened and what must be done."

Jan had been expecting this, but his mother glanced away toward the fire in the hearth.

"You'll be all right," Cadell said, making it sound like a statement. "I'll take the sergeant, Cherock, with me but leave the other guards." He took a bite of ham. "While I'm gone, see if you can't get a girl or two to come help with the cooking and cleaning. Someone must be in need of a wage enough to overcome any silly fears of this place."

Nadja didn't answer right away, as if she was considering her words. But before she could speak, a strange sound echoed into the hall from the front passage, like a sorrow-filled wail carried in on the wind. Even with the blazing fire, the hall suddenly felt cold. Nadja's head twisted toward the archway leading out toward the keep's entrance.

"What is that?" Jan asked following her gaze.

Then there was only the distant sound of the wind outside.

"It was nothing," his father answered, reaching for more bread. "Just the wind in the hollows of this old place."

But Nadja kept her eyes on the archway, as did Jan.

C adell left the following dawn as Jan and his mother stood in the courtyard, waving good-bye. Even in early summer, the sky was dark and overcast. A thin and misty drizzle seemed to hang in the air more than fall upon the ground. Down below along the road, Chemestúk village looked as drab and decayed as the exterior of the keep. But after his father rode off, Jan was almost embarrassed by his own sense of relief.

He needed time to adjust to this drastic shift of circumstances—to his new home. He had to try to find a way to live in this place. Keeping a brave face for his father had become exhausting, and at least now, he could be himself.

As if reading his mind, his mother said, "You should take the day for nothing but amusements. What would you like to do?"

Her black hair blew in the damp morning breeze. With her exotic eyes and bright red dress, she looked so out of place in this colorless courtyard.

But he thought on her question. What would he like to do?

He had no friends here yet. Perhaps he ought to go down into the village and try to make some? But the image of the ragged, superstitious, unwashed people he'd seen upon the night of their arrival put a damper on that plan the moment he started to consider it.

The acoustics in the keep were probably good. Perhaps he should practice with his fiddle? But could he do that every day?

He sighed. He was a realist if nothing else, and he'd have to find a way to manage until after the harvest.

"I know this is difficult for you," his mother said, "and I've been grateful for the way you've hidden your worries from your father."

Jan smiled. Though she knew his faults only too well—and occasionally pointed them out—in all his life, he'd never had an unkind word from her.

"I think I can hold out until the end of summer," he said.

She shook her head in confusion. "The end of summer?"

"Yes, until you and I head east to meet up with Uncle Rosario and Aunt Doreena to wander with your people for a while. Let's stay with them for at least three moons this year."

The thought of music and card games and the laughter of the Móndyalítko brought enough ease to Jan's thoughts and heart that he knew he could put on a cheerful face and suffer the rest of summer in this dark keep. Next winter might be another story, but for now, he had something to look forward to.

Then he took a good look at his mother's stricken face, and an uncomfortable feeling settled in his stomach.

"Oh, Jan," she said. "I thought you understood... We cannot... cannot travel with my sister and your uncle this year, perhaps not even the next. Your father is now the vassal of five fiefs for the Äntes. I am his wife, and you are his son. He will need us to care for this place, to remain visible and available in this place while he travels between the villages and organizes the people. We cannot let Lord Malbek think your father has abandoned his post. His family must be here."

As his mother's words sank in, for the first time in Jan's life, he felt angry with her, almost unable to believe she had said such a thing to him.

"Not go traveling with...?" He began and faltered.

He could have faced anything so long as he knew there would be an escape to freedom and joy each year.

"No!" he shouted, startled by his voice. "I cannot live in this place for years on end with nothing else in sight. Neither can you!" Then, realizing he was shouting at his mother, he took a step back and softened his voice. "We don't belong here, neither of us."

"Jan," she said tightly, sounding like a stranger. "Your father may still call you 'boy' at times, but you are no longer a child. We do not always have the choice to do as we please. You are a man now, and it's time you acted like one."

Jan stared at his mother for a moment. Then he turned and walked into the keep, going upstairs to his room.

He stayed there for the rest of the day.

B y nightfall, Jan had considered his mother's words enough to feel some sense of shame. All of this change had to be as difficult for her as it was for him—possibly more, as she had to show an even braver face to his father.

Emerging from his room after dusk, he went downstairs to find her sitting alone in the great hall. The guards had attempted to set themselves up in the old barracks and rarely came into the keep. A single candle lantern glowed on the table beside his mother, but the hall was dim and cold, as no fire had been lit in the hearth.

"Mother," he said from the base of the stairs. "I'm sorry."

She turned her warm eyes toward him, but those eyes were sad now. "I know you are. I don't blame you for being disappointed."

Disappointed didn't begin to describe how he felt. "I'll start a fire, and maybe we can play at cards?"

They'd certainly need some amusements of their own, as he had a feeling they would be spending many evenings alone together. She smiled gratefully as she rose, which only made him feel guiltier for his earlier behavior.

"Are you hungry?" she asked. "Should I find us something to eat first?"

He was starving, but before he could answer, the eerie wailing from the night before echoed through the keep again. It swept into the hall, as if blown on a wind, and Nadja wrapped her arms around herself as the chill air turned icy cold.

"Jan?" she breathed in confusion. "Are the front doors open?"

The wailing grew louder.

On instinct, he hurried to stand in front of his mother. Somehow... he knew something was about to happen.

Though it seemed impossible, the air grew even colder.

A shape took form in the archway of the passage to the keep's doors.

A nearly transparent man appeared out of dark passage, his booted feet floating just above the floor. He drifted through the archway, and his mouth opened. Another wail echoed through the main hall, filled with the sound of anger and pain. His dark, shaggy hair whipped about his face, though there was no wind indoors, and strands of it appeared to catch in a few days of stubble on his jaw.

The man wore leather armor and a sword, like a guard or a soldier, each as translucent as his face. Jan barely noted these details as he stared in shock, putting one arm behind himself to try to shield his mother.

"Stay behind me," he said, not knowing if she'd heard him when another wail cut loose.

The spirit raised his arms, motioning to Jan to come closer. When Jan didn't move, the ghost drifted a few paces, leaving a clear path to the upward stairs. In that moment, Jan only thought of protecting his mother. He grabbed her hand.

"Run!"

Before she even moved, he bolted, jerking her along in a dash away from the soldier spirit toward the stairs.

Of all places, Jan ran to the room of the woman

who'd left all her belongings behind. He knew it was irrational, but for some reason, he felt this room might be the last place the ghost would go.

After pulling his mother inside, Jan slammed the door shut and bolted it—as if a bolt would help.

The wailing below in the keep died away.

Jan turned, and though his mother appeared shaken, she watched the door with her head tilted slightly as if listening for the wail to come again, possibly closer this time. When it did not, she turned, and Jan followed her gaze as she looked about the room and then went to the dressing table, looking down at the silver brushes and perfume bottles.

"Well, at least now we know," she said, her voice surprisingly steady. "This must be why the chancellor has been unable to keep a vassal here. I've been wondering about that, and now we know."

Jan shook his head. How could she be so calm? They'd just seen a real ghost, angry and wailing in what had sounded like pain. Then something else Lord Malbek had said occurred to Jan.

"Mother, do you remember what he said about... something happening to the last vassal, something that stopped anyone else from taking the position?"

"Yes. Have you heard something more about this?"

"No." Jan shook his head slowly. "But I'm going to find out."

J an and his mother remained in that same room all night, emerging only in the late morning to find everything as they'd left it. But that afternoon, once he'd eaten an enormous lunch, he left the keep and walked down into the village. He was sick of mysteries and secrets and vague warnings, and he was going to get some answers.

In broad daylight, the neglected wattle and daub huts looked even bleaker. A few thin hens pecked at the mud, and the villagers moved like shadows, vanishing from sight as soon as they spotted him or if he called out to one of them.

What was wrong with them that they would fear the son of their own zupan? Or maybe they just feared talking to him... or the questions he might ask about this place in which he'd come to live?

He wasn't giving up that easily.

Jan ignored the graveyard as he tried to remember which hut belonged to Yoan. While he was busy wishing that he'd paid more attention on the night of his arrival, a tallish girl emerged from the outer trees. With long, unwashed hair, she wore a ragged dress of an undistinguishable color and carried a basket. It was hard to tell, but Jan thought with a bath and a clean gown, she might be pretty.

She froze at the sight of him, like a deer spotting a hunter.

With natural ease, he flashed her a smile. For him, this was actually better than trying to question old Yoan.

"Don't worry," he said, his voice intentionally lazy. "I've just come down from the keep for a visit."

His mention of the "keep" was a mistake, and she glanced fearfully up the road, her whole body tensed for flight.

"I'm Jan," he said quickly. "I haven't talked to anyone but my parents in almost six days." He flashed another smile.

Looking back in his direction, her eyes locked onto him in fascination, as if she'd never seen anything like him before. Maybe she hadn't. She studied him from head to toe, from his dusky features and clean, bright clothes, down to his boots.

"I'm Julianna," she finally said.

"Beautiful name. Can you show me around the village?"

"No, I can't talk to you. You've been up there."

She tossed her head toward the keep, and he wondered what color her hair might be once it was washed.

"I promise I've not brought some disease down with me," he joked.

She didn't laugh. She didn't even smile.

He didn't feel anywhere near as light-hearted as he was forcing himself to sound, but he could see her taut body relaxing a little. He knew only too well that his handsome face and lithe form had won over more than one overly cautious young woman.

Without waiting, he walked toward her. He wasn't surprised when she didn't run.

"Julianna," he breathed. "I need to know why you're all so afraid of that place. My mother is expected to live up there."

"Get her out," the girl whispered.

"Why?"

"Terrible things happened there... a long time ago."

Her eyes were blue, and up close, the barest smattering of charming freckles ran across her nose.

"What things?" he asked more seriously this time.

She sidestepped away, shaking her head and looking around, as if she feared being seen with him. Pointing to a hut nestled between two trees on the outskirts of the village, she whispered. "Talk to Bieja. You ask her."

Without warning, the girl whirled and fled back into the trees.

Jan almost went after her, but then he thought better of being seen chasing a village girl. Instead, he looked toward the hut Julianna had pointed out.

Who was this Bieja?

With no other options, he made his way over and knocked on the rickety door. Loud, quick footsteps sounded, and the door was jerked inward from the other side.

"What?" a gruff voice demanded, startling Jan.

He stood face-to-face, or nearly so, with a plump woman in a faded purple dress. Her gray-streaked black hair was pulled back into a thick braid, and her lined, round face seemed to cast an expression of perpetual ire.

She looked him up and down. "Oh, no. Don't need no fortunes told by the likes of you." She began closing the door. "Off you go."

"Wait!" he said, frustrated with himself for the hint of desperation leaking, into his voice. He normally made a firm point of never sounding desperate—even when he was. "My family is living up at the keep. Julianna told me to talk to you."

Bieja stopped with the door halfway closed. She lifted her chin, her eyes widening briefly before they narrowed in another glower.

"You're the zupan's son?"

Jan decided to stop trying to mask his desperation. "Please... talk to me."

The plump woman let out a quick rumbling hiss. It was something like that of a skunk he'd once startled his youth, just before it turned in an angry dance and lifted its tail. Finally, Bieja stepped back from the door.

"Get in here... before the whole village sees you."

Jan was startled for only an instant. He stepped in, and she slammed the door, nearly clipping his heel. But the inside of the little hut distracted him.

It was neat, even homey, with a table and two chairs, and a clean hearth with an iron swing arm and hook for hanging a kettle or pot over the fire. Something savory bubbled in the pot already on that hook. This was the most comfortable place Jan had been since arriving in Chemestúk.

"So you're living up there?" Bieja asked, not as a real question but more like it was the stupidest thing she'd ever heard.

"We're trying. Right now, my father's away, and the guards are sleeping in some makeshift barracks. My mother and I are alone in the keep."

Bieja snorted again. "That's no place for either of you."

"What happened to the last vassal?" he asked bluntly, hoping to catch her off guard.

She didn't even flinch. "Threw himself off the

tower... or fell... or got pushed, as some of them out there in the village think. Yoan found his body on a pile of fallen wall stones. Sad really, such a young man."

Jan went rigid. The last vassal had thrown himself off the tower?

"Everyone keeps telling us 'terrible things' happened up there," he said, and now his voice shook, and he couldn't stop it. "What things?"

"You want some tea?" she asked instead of answering. "I think the pot's still warm. Sit down."

Uncertain what to say, Jan sank into a chair and watched her pour him a mug of what he hoped was only very, very dark tea.

"Drink that," she said, settling across the table from him. Her gaze drifted away, focusing on nothing.

"So, you really want to hear this?" she asked.

With the mug at his mouth, Jan swallowed something that didn't taste like any tea he'd ever had. With a cough, he answered, "Yes."

Bieja grew quiet for a while, and then, with a grumbling hiss like the skunk Jan had turned from and run, she began...

"A little over twenty years ago, three lords from the keep broke in here, into my home and took my sister, Magelia, ripped her from me. They took her back with them and locked her away. Strange comings and goings were seen in the courtyard... and we heard men screaming in the night." Her voice tightened. "A few moons later, I learned Magelia was with child, and my heart almost broke. I couldn't get her back, and I nearly drove myself mad wondering what was happening to her."

Jan wanted to run a hand over his face, but he didn't. "Did you get her back?"

"No," Bieja answered and then shook her head slowly, still staring at nothing. "She died giving birth, from what I heard. One of those lords who'd stolen her brought me the baby. That same night, the keep went dark. None of those so-called lords were ever seen again, and since then, no new vassal has ever stayed there long."

"But you got the baby?"

Finally, Bieja looked at him, and a smile touched the corners of her mouth. "Yes, she was my girl. My beautiful girl. My Magiere."

Jan looked all around the hut. "Where is she?"

"Gone. The superstitious lot in this village treated her like she was part of that madness up at the keep. They drove her away four years ago, when she was only sixteen. She couldn't stand it anymore... but she'll be back. I know she'll come back one day."

Bieja rose, watching him intently, as if that was all there was to say.

Jan was quiet for a long moment. "There's a ghost in the keep. I think that's why no vassal has stayed."

Her expression went blank. "My sister?" she asked. "The ghost of my sister?"

There was a panic in her voice that didn't show in her hardened expression.

"No," Jan said quickly. "It's a man, wearing leather armor and a sword." He paused. "I don't know what to do. What should I do?"

Bieja frowned. "Well, if he's still there, he must want something. Find out what he wants."

Jan emerged from Bieja's hut to find dusk was coming. He hadn't realized they'd been talking for so long. Trudging back up the hill toward "home," his thoughts tumbled with all the things she'd told him.

Twenty years ago, a young woman had been abducted and locked away in the keep... and then she'd become pregnant. He shuddered to think what must have happened to her. Bieja also said there were "strange comings and goings" and "men screaming in the night." Later, a child was born and abandoned, and the place had fallen silent. He wondered what any of this meant—or if it had anything to do with the ghost.

Foremost in his mind though, was the information Bieja passed along that the last vassal here had not abandoned his post. Rather, he'd fallen, thrown himself, or been pushed from the top of the tower.

Jan quickened his pace, hurrying up the road to reach the keep and his mother before full nightfall. As he passed through the decayed outer wall and into the bailey, he saw light seeping through cracks in the shutters of the barracks. He almost envied the guards inside there, preparing their own dinner or playing cards in company.

There were no guards stationed at the missing front gates, as there was no need. No one ever came up here.

In spite of this, upon Cadell's return, Jan resolved to speak to his father. At present, expenses at the keep were being funded by a small loan from Chancellor Malbek—until the first season of taxes could be collected. These men should at least put on a show of doing some kind of "work" up here or why bother paying them?

Perhaps the guards had heard all the same rumors and were simply trying to pass the time until Cadell gave up and fled this place like all the other vassals? If so, they were quite mistaken. Jan's father would never give up.

Although Jan was no good at planting or organizing peasants, he might yet help his father after all.

With this in mind, his resolution to follow Bieja's advice grew firm. He needed to find out what the ghost wanted—and protect his mother at the same time.

As he made his way to the keep's front doors, the evening grew darker. Once inside, he looked down the passage and saw some light in the far main hall, enough to make his way there without touching the wall as a guide.

"Mother?" he called, walking swiftly. "I'm back. Sorry it took me so long."

When he stepped into the main hall, it was empty. Several candle lanterns were lit and the fire in the hearth as well, but Nadja was nowhere in sight. Turning around, he decided to go and check the kitchen.

The first hint of a wail echoed off the walls.

The main hall grew cold.

He tensed, trying to hear where the sound came from, but it seemed to career off of every stone in the keep.

Crossing his arms, he shouted out, "Where are you? Show yourself."

The wailing ceased.

Almost instantly, a transparent form materialized near the hearth. He appeared exactly as he had the night before... shaggy hair, leather armor, sheathed sword on his hip. Only now, he wasn't wailing. He was staring at Jan.

The hall was freezing, and Jan would have been lying if he'd claimed not to be afraid, but he had to solve this, to stop this. It was the only way he knew to help his father.

"What is it you want?" he asked.

With a desperate expression, the ghost opened his mouth, as if trying to speak, but only a low wail came out. Perhaps that was the only sound a dead spirit could make without a true voice?

Closing his mouth again, he continued staring, almost as if he couldn't believe Jan had spoken to him.

Jan knew little about spirits—no more than tales and folklore—but it stood to reason that the manner of this guard's death was probably related to his reason for remaining.

"What happened to you?" Jan asked, trying to keep his voice steady. "How did you die?"

The ghost flinched visibly and floated forward a few paces. His face twisted in what looked like anger, but Jan stood his ground. Then, suddenly, the spirit rushed at him.

Jan never had the chance to step back once more. The ghost's translucent face slammed straight into his own, and the whole hall went dark.

He must have screamed. He had to have screamed, but he didn't hear it.

He was so cold inside that he couldn't feel his own body, and then something—*somewhere*—else rose out of the darkness around him.

Jan found himself in a windowless room with torches burning in iron mounts on the stone walls. He guessed it might be underground, though he couldn't be certain. When he tried to back up, his feet didn't respond. He was frozen in place as he took in his surroundings.

There was no sign of the spirit.

"Where am I?" he nearly shouted.

No answer came.

There were five crates in the chamber.

The first was made of steel-bound oak planks, and sounds of muffled rage rose from inside of it. The second was timber framed, with stained canvas stretched over each of its sides. Soft sounds of fluttering misery were barely heard from inside it. The third was cedar and silent inside, while the fourth was a framework of oak holding an urn large enough for a man to crawl into, and some sloshing sounds within it were plain to hear. That one's bulk was enough that, in being filled with liquid, it had to weigh three or four times more than the first three.

The fifth container was by far the most disturbing.

It measured less than half a man's height in all dimensions and was made of steel plates that were discolored and blackened. Steam rose around it with a sizzling crackle from the damp floor on which it rested, and erratic scraping came from within those metal walls. The frantic noise grew until a screech from the steel made Jan flinch. Then the crate sat silent.

Was there something alive in each one of them?

In the center of the room, sat a large brass vat.

"Where am I?" Jan cried out again.

He was alone except for whoever—whatever—was in those crates.

Then he heard shouting and scuffling outside the room.

"Get your hands off me," a male voice shouted.

The door flew open and two men came through it, one of them dragging the other. The leader was unusually tall and broad shouldered, with nearly colorless crystalline eyes and features even paler than the peasants of Chemestúk. His long aquiline nose ended above a wide, thin-lipped mouth. He wore steel vambraces on both forearms, and beneath his cloak was a crestless, burgundy tabard over a shirt of mail.

A nobleman.

He dragged the second smaller man—a bound man —behind himself.

Jan's breath caught, for he knew the shaggy dark hair, leather armor, and sword of the prisoner. The captor hadn't even bothered to disarm his captive, as if it didn't matter.

Jan wondered what the tall nobleman would do at the sight of him, but neither captor nor captive even noticed him, as if he wasn't even there. He had no chance to ponder this as a third man came through the door.

His long, hooded robe swirled like black oil under the torchlight as he glided across the floor with no hint of footfalls. The torchlight raised shimmers of faint symbols and strange letters on that dark fabric. Where his face should've been was a mask of aged leather that ended above a boney jaw supporting a withered mouth. But there were no eye slits in the mask.

The shaggy-haired guard in the nobleman's grip saw the crates and the vat and nearly went wild, setting his heels and trying to pull away.

"Get off me!"

Neither of the other two answered him nor did they slow down.

"Get him up over the vat," the masked one said.

With one final wild effort, the guard broke free and tried to make a dash for the door. But with his hands bound, he couldn't use his arms to help him run. Jan could only watch helplessly as the noblemen caught his quarry with one hand. His other fist cracked the jaw of his captive, and the guard slumped.

"Don't kill him, Bryen," the masked man ordered. "He must be alive."

"It is of little matter," the nobleman answered in a hollow voice. "We need but one human, and there are others, if need be."

But he did not strike his stunned prisoner again.

The masked one began chanting as he stepped in beside the vat.

Before Jan could even try to comprehend what was happening, the tall nobleman heaved the guard up and bent him over the vat's edge, holding the man there with only one hand.

The masked one pulled a curved dagger from his robe and slashed open the prisoner's throat. The captive slumped forward, gagging as his blood drained into the vessel.

"No!" Jan shouted, but no one appeared to hear him.

He must have screamed out that word, again and again, until the noise of his own voice deafened his ears... and darkened the chamber, until he saw nothing at all.

Then there was light, only a small bit at first. More came, flickering blurred yellows and reds, until he stood again in the main hall of the keep, with its candle lanterns and burning hearth.

Jan felt himself breathing hard. He tried to move one foot, and found that he finally could do so. He stumbled back, his body still numbed with cold inside, and he bumped into the wall beside the archway.

There was the ghost in the hall again, his face twisted with emotion. He began to wail, pain and suffering pouring from his mouth.

It was too much. Any thoughts of what the ghost might be seeking fled from Jan's mind. He couldn't stay here anymore. He couldn't witness anymore.

Whirling, he ran for the stairs, nearly flying up to the next floor.

"Jan!"

He heard his mother calling to him from down the passage. He didn't slow himself until he found her in the same bedroom where they'd spent last night.

Dashing inside, he closed the door.

"What's happened?" she asked, her dark eyes wide.

Leaning with his back against the door, Jan couldn't yet start to explain.

O ne of the many strengths of Jan's mother was her talent for listening. As he crouched beside her on the bedroom floor, she allowed him to pour out his entire story in fits and starts without a single question.

"Something terrible happened here," he whispered, still horrified by what the ghost had shown him. "I know Father swore we wouldn't abandon this place... but he couldn't have known. We cannot stay. We must leave here."

He had no idea about the meaning of what the ghost had shown him, and in truth, he didn't want to know.

"No," she said, finally breaking her silence. Her lovely face was intense. "We will not." She paused, her eyes shifting back and forth. "You were wise to go to one of the village women... Bieja?"

"Yes, her name is Bieja," he answered, ready to argue. "She's the only one who would talk to me. But Mother—"

"She's right, Jan. If the ghost is still here, there's a reason. We need to find out what he wants."

.   .   .

When they returned to main hall, it was empty and quiet. Of all the things Jan might have expected his mother to do, her setting up a spirit-calling from her people's ways was not among them.

For one, the ghost was hardly making a secret of his existence, so why should they bother putting an effort into calling him?

Jan told her as much.

"Because this will help him focus," she answered, putting three small candles in a triangle on the table. "It will let him know we seek to help. That we wish for him to come to us."

Jan couldn't argue with that, but he didn't like his mother becoming involved, and he feared the ghost might show her the same scene it had shown to him.

But Nadja wouldn't be swayed.

"Sit down and take my hands," she said.

Reluctantly, he obeyed.

Closing her eyes, his mother called out, "Come to us in peace now. Show us what you seek."

Jan was no longer certain the ghost sought anything at all. Perhaps the guard had simply died so violently, helplessly, in this place that his rage wouldn't let him move on. But Jan held his tongue as his mother called out softly again... and again.

And then the hall grew colder.

Nadja opened her eyes and looked toward the archway of the passage to the keep's front. Turning his head, Jan followed her gaze.

The ghost floated there, a few steps in from the archway. For once, the guard seemed calm. He motioned to Nadja with one hand, as he had done to Jan, and she rose to walk toward the spirit.

"Mother!" Jan said in alarm, jumping to his feet.

"It's all right," she answered.

As she walked, the ghost began moving, floating backward. Jan and Nadja followed him down the passage to the main doors—where he passed right through. Jan quickly opened the doors for his mother, and they found the ghost waiting for them on the other side.

Again, he began floating backward, this time toward the stables.

"Keep following," Nadja told Jan.

The calm in her voice almost convinced Jan that their actions were not so far out of the ordinary. That illusion vanished as they entered the stables, where three guards sat playing cards at a makeshift table. All three jumped to their feet in a panic when they spotted the ghost, and one of them was foolish enough to pull his sword.

"Stop!" Nadja ordered them. "It's all right."

She seemed to be saying that too often tonight.

The ghost ignored the guards and floated into an empty stall. There he stopped and, still watching Nadja, pointed down at the floor.

"Jan," she said, but he didn't need to be asked.

His fear of the ghost was fading, and he hurried over, dropping to his knees to examine the floor of the stall. The boards appeared intact, nailed down. He looked up.

"What?" he asked. "What am I looking for?"

Then he noticed the color of the ghost's eyes: light gray. Those eyes were pleading again, and the spirit continued pointing down.

With a frown, Jan used his fingers to start checking boards... until he found one with enough of a gap between it and the next one. He looked about and spotted a bailing hook. When he pointed at it, one of the guards grabbed it for him but would only come close enough to toss it into the stall. Jan picked up the hook and began prying at that one board until its nails pulled loose.

His mother hurried in as he ripped out the board... and the next one. Beneath, he found a small saddlebag. For some reason, he didn't want to open it himself. His mother knelt down and took it from him. When she lifted its flap, Jan saw something within wrapped in mildewed brown paper.

Nadja lifted out the package, and they both saw the writing on it. It was addressed simply: *To Anna of Volokán Village*

When Jan looked up, the soldier had knelt before him and his mother. The spirit brought its hands together, and then folded them apart like an opening book.

Nadja tore at the brown paper, exposing a pouch and a note. The note was written in small letters, with a neat, even hand.

My dear Anna,

I have good news. My search for work has gone much better than I ever expected, and a great lord appointed to Chemestúk Keep has hired me. Few men would take the positions offered, but he paid me a year's wage in advance.

I have enclosed the money. It is enough to pay off our entire debt and still buy food for yourself and the children until I return. If you can, buy yourself a new dress.

I must remain here for a year and finish earning the wage I was paid, but I will send word when I can. A merchant who recently delivered supplies to the keep has agreed to carry some letters and packages for the other guards here when he leaves. I'm told he can be trusted.

I know you will feel the same relief as I that our debt is finally paid. We will be free of it.

The work here is not difficult, but I count the days until I see you and the children again.

All my love, Bran

Jan finished reading and looked up, trying to sort his emotions.

This spirit—this man—had taken work here in the keep as a guard, intent upon sending his earnings home to his wife to pay off a debt and feed his children. He'd been murdered before even one coin had ever reached his wife, and twenty years had passed since then.

Jan took the pouch and the letter from his mother, and he looked into Bran's anguished, transparent face. "I'll find them," he said. "If they still live, I will find them."

Bran closed his gray eyes briefly and opened them again, focusing on Jan. He was still staring at Jan when his form began to fade.

Within moments, he was gone, as if he had never been there at all.

Two days later, Jan climbed on the back of a horse in the bailey and leaned down to kiss his mother good-bye.

The rooms and passages of the keep were quiet at night now, and Nadja had even talked some of the guards into coming inside and sleeping on bedrolls on the floor of the main hall—by the fire. It had to be more comfortable than sleeping in the shamble of the barracks.

"At least maybe I'll finally have done something Father will be proud of," Jan said. "I wonder what he'll say when we tell him?"

His mother shook her head. "We won't tell him. His burdens are already too great. Let us allow him to think the three of us could do something no one else could... and make a home of this keep."

As she finished, he knew she was right, and he nodded.

"I'll return as soon as I can," he said.

He hated to leave her alone with only the guards for company, but he wouldn't trust this journey to anyone but himself, for he was the one who'd given his word. With one last smile for his mother, he headed out along the road from the keep, beginning his journey to Volokán to try to fulfill the final wish of a lost husband and father.

But he stalled when he reached the village of Chemestúk, and, as usual, it had something to do with a pretty face, or one that might be pretty. He dismounted at the tree line where he'd first seen Julianna with her basket.

Sitting on a fallen log, he waited for some time, and finally, he saw a pale face peering from out of the woods around the side of one tree.

"You may as well come out," he said. "I'll just wait until you do."

She took a step, coming partially into view. "For me?"

Her face was a little cleaner today, and he definitely thought she might be pretty.

"What would you say if I told you the keep was now safe," he said, "that my mother and I have made it so?"

She looked at him skeptically, but took another step. "Folks here are laying bets on how long it takes before you all go running."

He shook his head. "We aren't going anywhere." Then he pointed to his horse. "But I have an errand that may take some time, and my mother could use some help and some company. I swear the keep is safe now, and she'll pay you a good wage." He paused. "She and I... we like to have people around. We like company. Will you go?"

She was close enough now that he could see her eyes were a lighter shade of blue than he'd first thought.

"You're really not afraid to be there?" she asked. "You swear it's safe?"

"It's safe. Will you go and talk to my mother?"

Finally, she nodded, "I'll go."

He smiled and then sighed.

For better or worse, he and his family were now the keepers of Chemestúk Keep. ■

THE RELUCTANT GUARDIAN

For Bieja, the whole world seemed to have gone mad. Cheme-stúk, the village where she'd lived her entire life, was on fire, and she heard screaming from all directions in the night. Once the soldiers had come riding in, she'd run to take refuge in her little wattle and daub hut, and now the sounds of horses running, flames growing, and the angry shouts of men filled her ears.

Well into her middle-aged years, Bieja had both seen and fought her share of horrors. Part of her longed to grab a pitchfork and rush out to defend her home... defend her neighbors. Another wiser part told her that would be foolish—and futile—and the village was already lost.

She dashed to the open cupboard shelves around her makeshift hearth and shoved dried tealeaves, turnips, flour, and a small bottle of cooking oil into a burlap sack. Then she hurried to her bed, reached under the straw mattress, and pulled out a little leather pouch and an overly creased letter. These she tucked into the neckline of her dress.

Cracking the door, she peeked outside at only fire and chaos. Two soldiers on horses thundered past and one threw a torch at the roof of the village smithy.

Anger flooded Bieja in a wave, but again there was nothing she could do. With a quick breath, she darted out and around the side of her hut, which had thankfully been built on the village's outskirts, and she ran into the trees.

She was not young nor lightweight nor lithe. She was solid and stout, but she was also strong. Carrying her sack of belongings in one hand, she held up the skirt of her old purple gown and kept running through the forest until the sounds of flames and screams faded behind her. Only then did she stop, lean back against a bare tree trunk, and slide down, panting and feeling like a coward for running.

"There was nothing you could do," she told herself firmly. Of late, she'd been talking to herself more and more often. "You know that."

She did know it. There was nothing she could do for anyone who'd remained in Chemestúk, and she cursed herself for not having seen this coming.

Only two days before, soldiers in the light yellow tabards of the House of Äntes had ridden through and conscripted every man in the village under the age of forty. Bieja had heard they even went up to the keep above the village and took the zupan's son, Jan. Tonight, soldiers from the House of Väränj dressed in chain armor and bright red tabards had come riding in with torches, shouting that all here were "traitors" to their country, Droevinka, and then they'd begun setting fire to the village.

None of it made any sense, and Bieja didn't even know what these noble houses were fighting over— except probably power.

Now, sitting in the darkness, leaning against a tree, her anger swelled at these selfish men who seemed bent on destroying their own nation. All that mattered to her was that her village was gone, and she was alone. In truth, she'd had few friends there, but Chemestúk had been her home... the only home she'd ever known.

The noises of destruction and anguish grew even fainter, and her anger gave way to anxiousness as she glanced about in the dark.

What now?

With a soft sigh, she reached into her dress' neckline and pulled out the creased letter and the pouch. She'd never thought to use them, but now...

Several moons ago, her beloved niece, Magiere, had come back to Chemestúk, but Magiere had not come alone. One who'd arrived in her company had roused Bieja's suspicions right away. With his nearly pointed ears and his white-blond hair, she'd taken him for an imp or changeling, some forest spirit trying to dazzle Magiere's wits.

And so, quite correctly, Bieja had gone after him with a carving knife. Who wouldn't?

Fortunately, she'd quickly been proven wrong. He was merely a half-blood, part elven, and it was obvious he loved Magiere, and she him. At first, Bieja wasn't sure what she thought of feeding supper to some pointy-eared foreigner, but her opinion of Leesil improved upon his better acquaintance.

Magiere had been taking a side-trip before heading off to the east, but before she and her companions departed, Leesil had come to Bieja and given her a letter. She couldn't read it, as it was written in Belaskian instead of her own Droevinkan, but along with the letter he'd left her six silver sovereigns of his and Magiere's new homeland. That was more money than Bieja had ever seen firsthand in her life.

Leesil asked if she would consider traveling on her own all the way to Belaski's coast, to a little port town called Miiska, to live in a tavern there called the Sea Lion that he and Magiere had purchased. He told her that if she'd wait for them there, they would finish their own journey and head back to meet her.

Though touched by his offer, Bieja had no intention of leaving Chemestúk. Dark and filthy as the place might be, it was her home. It always had been.

Disappointed by her answer, he'd still understood.

"If you change your mind," he told her, "travel to Miiska and ask for Karlin or Caleb and show them this letter. Either should recognize my scrawl, and it tells them that you're Magiere's aunt. They'll get you settled at the Sea Lion. And this isn't charity. Caleb could use the help."

By way of answer, she'd patted his leg and told him good-bye, but sitting there alone in the forest, she gripped the letter tightly.

For the first time, Bieja thought on Leesil's offer.

After a sleepless night, Bieja rose the next dawn knowing that she had to head back into Chemestúk—to see what or who might be left standing. Setting her jaw tightly, she made her way through the trees until she reached the village's edge.

"Oh..." was all she could say.

Not a hut in her line of sight was left intact. There were only smoldering remains of what had been the homes of neighbors... and her home. Nearly everything she'd owned had been inside that hut, but at least there was no sign of the soldiers.

Stepping onward, she hoped it wasn't all as bad as the first look, but as she walked through the charred and smoking remains of Chemestúk, she grew numb.

"Hallo?" she called out, trying not to wonder if only she had survived. Deeper into the village, she spotted some huts that only been half-burned. A few cook pots and other belongings had been thrown out into the open pathway. Her gaze fixed on a large piece of canvas lying in the mud.

"Bieja!" a voice called.

Whirling around, relief flooded her mouth. One of the few people she cared about ran toward her down the road from the old keep.

"Julianna!" she called back.

Long-legged and a bit gangly, the young woman wore a red dress that whipped about her ankles. She didn't slow down until she was about five paces away.

She was a lovely thing, with long, dark blond hair and freckles smattered across her small pale nose. Once, she had been an orphaned girl—both her parents having died of fever—living on the charity of other peasants. She'd been a filthy, nearly invisible ghost of a thing, but then Zupan Cadell and his wife, Nadja, and their son, Jan, had come to live in the keep here. Julianna had taken a job as a servant for them.

Nadja had grown fond of Julianna, inviting her to live up at the keep, and the girl had changed a good deal in the past few years. She'd grown into a capable young woman with little time for superstition or gossip. As a result, she was one of the few people that Bieja liked.

In appearance though, Bieja made quite a contrast. Over twenty years older, she'd grown plump inside her purple dress, which had worn thin from far too many washings. Her gray-streaked black hair was pulled into a braid, and she was well aware that her deeply lined, round face appeared to be set in a perpetual state of ire.

"Oh, Bieja," Julianna breathed, panting as she leaned forward to put her hands on her knees. "Are you all right?"

Bieja's anger returned in a flash. "None of us are all right! Look what those soldiers did here. I haven't seen anyone but you left alive."

"There are some," Julianna rushed to say. "The zupan has taken all survivors into the keep. We have food for now. I sneaked out and came down to see if I could find anyone else."

Bieja's temper softened. "You're a good girl, thinking of others. I'll help you look."

Neither spoke for another moment, and then they both began making their way down the path, trying to search between and around the smoldering huts, occasionally calling out to see if anyone would answer. Bieja knew that some here were so fed by fear in their daily lives they might have hidden inside their own homes and burned to death. She didn't say this aloud.

Julianna let out gasp as she stepped carefully between two dwellings. "Bieja!"

Grabbing her skirt, Bieja rushed to the girl, ready to fight whatever threat lingered here, but she stopped when she saw what lay at Julianna's feet.

It was the body of a steel-haired older man, still muscular, though his hair was now matted with dark red where his head had been split open.

Julianna shook her head in disbelief. "Poor Yoan... why did they do this to him?"

Bieja wasn't sure what to feel. Yoan had been the unofficial elder of the village for many years, and a superstitious old coot in her opinion. She'd argued with him often—and loudly. But he'd been a part of her life for as long as she could remember. Now he lay dead outside the smoking remains of his home.

"Bastards!" she breathed through gritted teeth. "May they all rot in the seven hells."

She wasn't even sure if she cursed the Äntes or the Väränj or both. This was all so senseless.

"Did you hear the Äntes soldiers stormed the keep a few days ago," Julianna whispered, still staring down at Yoan's face. "They took Jan. The zupan tried to stop them... but he couldn't." For the first time since her return here, she began blinking back tears.

Bieja sighed. "Don't you worry about Jan. If anybody can rescue himself and high tail his backside home again, it'll be Jan."

Those weren't just words of comfort. Bieja believed them to be true. Grasping Julianna's hand, she pulled the girl away from Yoan's body.

"We should keep looking."

As they walked, something more occurred to Bieja. "While the Äntes were in the keep, did you hear anything said about the cause of all this?"

Bieja understood the tyranny of her own country well enough, but raiding and conscription across house territories was almost unthinkable. The politics of Droevinka were different from other nations.

Rather than being ruled by a hereditary king, Droevinka was a land of many princes, each one the head of a noble house with its own province containing multiple fiefdoms. But they all served a single Grand Prince, and a new one was elected every nine years by the gathered heads of the noble houses.

At present, Prince Rodêk of the Äntes was in rule.

The unlanded house of Väränj was a notable exception to the other houses. Descended of mercenary horsemen in service to the first invaders of this region, the Väränj served as the royal guard and city contingent for whoever held the throne. They protected the separate castle of the current Grand Prince located in Kéonsk. In turn, they were denied the opportunity to put their "prince" on the throne or establish a province of their own.

The Väränj alone served as the law enforcers and the peacekeepers in Kéonsk—serving whatever prince currently held the throne. This gave them a kind of power awarded to no other noble house.

So what could have possibly led to this bloody mess?

"Did you hear anything?" Bieja pressed.

"A little," Julianna answered quietly. "A few moons back, Prince Rodêk had to leave the castle in Kéonsk and see to a matter in his family's home of Enêmûsk. He left his prime counselor, a baron called Buscan, in charge of castle affairs. While the prince was away, his counselor was assassinated. Apparently, the baron was hated by many of the Äntes, but they still accused the Väränj of allowing him to be murdered. The Väränj accused the Äntes of having murdered the counselor themselves and trying to hide their crime by casting blame on the Väränj." She fell silent for a few breaths. "I didn't overhear how it happened, but fighting broke out between both sides in Kéonsk... and it has been spreading."

Bieja shook her head in disgust. This wasn't about power but pride.

"Fools," she spat, looking at the devastation around her, and another thought struck her. "Did the Väränj go anywhere near the keep last night?"

"No, thank the gods," Julianna breathed. "They left the zupan and Nadja alone. I don't know why, and I don't care. At least we all have somewhere to go now."

"Will the zupan try to fortify the place?"

"No. He says that's impossible, as it's too worn and broken. So we're going to do what we can to make it look deserted. That's why I had to sneak out. He didn't want anyone seen this morning, but I couldn't just... I had to come and look."

Bieja crossed her arms. Zupan Cadell was no fool. Making the keep appear deserted was the best choice left to him. She also couldn't fault Julianna for coming down to look for other survivors.

"There's no one left," Julianna said in despair, turning a full circle. "We may as well go back to the keep. Nadja will be glad to see you're safe. The zupan says that if more soldiers come... if any enter the keep to search and raid, there are places we can all hide in the lower storage rooms where no one will find us. We should be safe for now."

Bieja looked around at the smoking remains of Chemestúk Village. She knew she couldn't live up at the keep, skulking like a rat and waiting for soldiers to return, and hoping none bothered with a broken down old fortress. Her home here was gone.

Julianna took a few steps back toward the center road and then stopped.

"Bieja... are you coming?"

With another sigh, Bieja shook her head. "No. I have family elsewhere who've invited me to join them."

Julianna's blue eyes widened. "What are you talking about? Bieja, you can't go walking down the roads here now. You'll be killed... or worse! Please, come with me."

If Julianna had an inkling of just how far Bieja planned to travel, the argument would have continued. Bieja was going to have to travel straight west through an apparent civil war—past Enêmûsk, the stronghold of the Äntes—to try for the border into lower Belaski. If she managed to get that far with her skin intact, she would then need to reach the coast to find Miiska and the Sea Lion tavern.

In all her life, she'd never been more than a few leagues outside of Chemestúk.

"No, my girl," she said, trying to sound kind. "You go on yourself. I'm going to gather what supplies I can find here and be on my way."

Leesil had made sure she was offered a safe home with her true family—should she ever need it. She had need of it now.

N o one had to bother telling Bieja that the roads weren't safe.

She might not be a world traveler, but any idiot knew to stay off the roads when trekking alone in the middle of a civil war. She stayed hidden among the trees to avoid being seen, trying to keep the road within her sight so she wouldn't get lost. After two days of this, she was exhausted from crawling over and through the heavy brush.

Droevinka was nearly always wet and muddy, and beneath the aroma of loam and wild foliage was an ever-present thin stench of decay. The thickened forest almost blocked the cloud-coated sky above her. Her skirt was wet from the damp leaves, and her face bore a few angry welts from snapping branches. She began wondering about traveling for even a short while along the roadside and listening carefully for hooves or feet from either direction.

She quickly abandoned that notion. Although she was certainly no young beauty to tempt roaming soldiers, she was carrying something worth more to them—six silver sovereigns. More likely she would be robbed and murdered by deserters trying to get clear of the fighting.

As she trudged, off to the right, she could hear the Vudrask River gurgling along, and she pondered trying to find a boat somewhere to simply float down the river. What a lovely thought. But again, she'd be easily spotted out there. So, she struggled on through the woods, not knowing how many days it would take to reach the border.

She'd brought a large piece of soot-blackened canvas scavenged back in Chemestúk, along with a cooking pot, wooden eating utensils, a dull knife, and a few more bits of scavenged food. At night, she used the canvas as a makeshift tent, though sometimes she had to use it to keep from sleeping in the muck.

On the third day, a new worry reared its head. So far, she'd passed two villages, both burned to the ground. She'd thought to buy food along the way, but now that seemed a remote possibility. Even so, could she have dared show such a coin as a sovereign in the hands of peasant without rousing suspicion? What would happen when her limited supplies ran out?

There was nothing she could do except press onward. She couldn't go back, for she had nothing to go back to.

At times, she cursed herself for not knowing more about the size of her own country. In her darker moments, she began to wonder more and more about her chances. What if she didn't succeed and simply vanished along the way, and Magiere never found out what had become of her?

The thought of her niece's anguish pushed her onward again.

Toward dusk that third day, she was tugging her tattered skirt loose from a patch of thistles when the sounds of grunts and snarls drifted through the trees from the road. She quickly flattened to ground and crawled through the brush. Dragging her belongings as quietly as possible to the last of the trees, she peeked out at the road.

Two ragged soldiers in filthy yellow tabards were trying to capture an enormous brown wolf. Both were shouting and swearing—and bleeding from a number of gashes on their forearms and faces. They both had swords, but one carried a net possibly stolen off some fisherman's skiff. They appeared intent upon catching—not killing—the wolf.

"Get around the back of him!" the one with the net shouted. "Try and get him to turn!"

But when the other soldier tried to do so, the wolf charged, snapping and snarling. The soldier swung hard with the flat of his sword, cutting off the beast's attack.

Hiding in the brush, Bieja shook her head. Why would two Äntes soldiers risk their hides trying to capture a wolf? Squinting, she focused on the animal as it made a dodging lunge for the far trees.

White-chested, it had strange yellow eyes, but oddest of all was a dark bracelet of some kind around its right foreleg just above its paw. And when it flattened its ears in a snarl, and then raised them again, Bieja's eyebrows rose as well.

There was a thick silver ring pierced through the base of one of its ears.

The animal might have stepped through a lost bracelet and got it stuck, but the pierced earring of glinting silver... now that didn't make any sense.

The second soldier cut off the wolf's escape and then Bieja's astonishment grew.

Suddenly the animal's fur appeared to thin across its torso and legs, and a mane of black hair began growing from its head. Its body appeared to twist and contort as it kept trying to get around the soldiers until... it rose up, grabbed the net with its hands and jerked hard, throwing the first soldier off balance.

Bieja stared in shock more than wonder at a naked, dark-haired man fighting with all the intensity of the wolf she'd been looking at barely moments ago. But she could see there was something wrong with him. He was sweating from more than just exertion, and his eyes were glassy.

"No, you don't," the second guard shouted, and he thrust his sword out between the naked man and the first soldier. "You're done, you *tzigän* deserter! So heel like a dog, or I'll cut you down like one!"

The man only snarled at him, human lips curled back. Then his body began spouting brown fur again over limbs that narrowed, twisted, and shortened... and the wolf lunged for the nearside trees this time.

Waves of anger—at the two soldiers—flooded through Bieja. The word *tzigän* was an insulting term, meaning "vagabond thieves" sometimes used against the Móndyalítko, a wandering people who lived their own way in wagon caravans. But Nadja, back at the keep in Chemestúk was Móndyalítko and Jan was a half-blood... and the Äntes had stolen Jan from his family.

Without really thinking, only letting the rage of the past few days drive her onward, Bieja grabbed a solid branch from the ground and dashed forward, swinging her makeshift weapon down as hard as she could. It cracked and shattered on the back of second soldier's head.

He dropped like a sack of potatoes.

His partner with the net froze in shock at the sight of a plump purple-clad woman wielding half a club now. In that instant, the wolf swerved around in its dash for the trees and leaped at the second soldier, going for his face or throat.

"No!" Bieja cried out. She hadn't intended to kill anyone.

It was too late. The soldier was on the ground, and the wolf ripped his throat out. A spray of blood splattered the road. The soldier's eyes were still open, but Bieja knew he was dead, and then the wolf collapsed. It simply fell on its side as if its last ounce of strength was gone... and its fur began to thin and vanish.

Bieja found herself standing beside a naked, unconscious man with a head of thick, black hair. Where were his clothes? Glancing around, she spotted something dark green across the road and she hurried to investigate. There lay a pair of brown breeches, boots, a dark green shirt... and a sheathed dagger.

Biting the inside of her lower lip, she looked back. Most male Móndyalítko she'd seen were either small and wiry or tall and slender—like young Jan. The naked man on the ground was tall with broad shoulders and developed muscles. He looked to be in his late twenties or early thirties, and his dusky-toned face bore a white scar running from the corner of his right eye down to his jaw. By what she'd seen of his glassy eyes, he was ill. He was also dangerous, willing to kill without a second thought. He was a fighter... and a shape-shifter.

She'd heard vague rumors and gossip of strange things among the Móndyalítko, but she'd never seen anything of that until today. Seeing it first hand should've stunned her, but somehow it didn't. Instead, a dim memory struck her of something Nadja had once said about blood oaths and a hard custom of a "life for a life" among the Móndyalítko.

"Are you going mad?" she asked herself.

She had no answer, and still, she had just saved this man.

Coming to a decision, she grabbed the clothing and dagger, ran to the road's far side, and tossed them off into the woods. Then she hurried back and, gripping the naked man by his bare ankles, she struggled to drag him off the same way.

As dusk settled, Bieja worked over the campfire she'd started, occasionally glancing over at the unconscious man laying on fire's other side. She'd wrapped him up in the canvas scrap she'd been using as a tent—as that was all she had with which to cover him. He was still sweating, and she knew he was running a fever.

She used her small cooking pot to make tea first and then poured the liquid into a wooden mug, also scavenged from the remains of Chemestúk. Once that was done, she boiled turnips over the open fire until they were softer than she normally liked. Just as they finished, a groan pulled her attention.

The dark-haired man was stirring, and she set down the cooking pot and grabbed his unsheathed dagger from where she'd kept it by her side. She didn't brandish it at him. Instead, she kept it low in the folds of her skirt, in case she needed the element of surprise.

His eyes opened, and he stared upward. Then he sucked in a loud breath, and panic flooded his still glassy eyes, as dark as his hair.

"You're all right," Bieja said quickly, still gripping the dagger's hilt and hoping she wouldn't have need of it.

His head rolled toward her, the fire, and cooking pot, and his expression shifted to wild confusion mixed with wariness. He rolled onto his side, trying to push himself up.

"You stay right there!" Bieja ordered. "And don't you go sprouting any fur or fangs."

He froze at her voice, peering more closely at her.

"Now you drink this," she told him, lifting the mug of tea. "I'll mash you some turnips with salt and then fry some flat bread."

She talked of food with each order she gave him, so he'd that realize she was in charge and trying to help him. To her relief, his expression relaxed as he leaned back again.

"You were there," he said quietly, looking at her dress. "I saw you."

"Yeah, I was there. I bashed one of those soldiers with a branch... and you went and killed the other."

Stepping around the fire, she slowly—and carefully —handed him the tea, but she kept the dagger in hand behind her skirt.

"Drink that," she said.

He was weakened and sick, and she needed him at full strength. To her relief, he slowly took the cup, watching her the whole time, and put it to his mouth.

She back-stepped once before turning around to finish mashing the turnips in a small wooden bowl, adding a little salt as well. When she held out the bowl, he took it and used his fingers to eat quickly. While he didn't appear to be starving, he was certainly hungry enough. That might obligate him a bit more.

"What's your name?" she asked.

He swallowed a mouthful and licked his fingers. Some of the wariness returned to his eyes. "Milôs," he finally answered.

"Bieja," she returned, and she began mixing a little oil with flour.

"What are you doing out here by yourself?" he asked.

"The Väränj burned my village."

He grunted in a way that turned to growl and dropped the bowl to lie back down. "It's all madness."

She snorted. "You'll get no quarrel from me. Why were those soldiers trying to catch you?"

He didn't answer, but he suddenly appeared to notice the canvas in which he was wrapped. "Where are my clothes?"

"There," and she pointed a few paces to left—with his dagger—and then wiggled the blade in the air. "Can't be too careful." She took in the thick silver ring in his right ear and the braided piece of black leather around his wrist. "You want me to turn my back so you can get dressed?"

Making one failed attempt to get up, he laid back down. "Not yet."

That concerned her a little. He struck her as proud, but he was too ill and weakened to even reach for his clothes. She worked quickly to fry some flat bread.

"Do you know what kind of fever you've caught?" she asked bluntly.

He was quiet for a moment, and then shook his head. "It started back in the camp... before I escaped."

"The Äntes, they... took you from your people?" When he didn't answer, she added, "You've got no secrets from me. I saw you... change back there, wolfie."

At her mocking tone, his eyes narrowed, but he looked her over. She probably somewhat resembled the women of his people—plump, middle-aged, dark-haired mothers, aunts and grandmothers cooking over an open fire along their wandering ways.

"I think they got a spy in among us... found out what I was," he said softly, lying on his back and staring up into the trees. "Seems they wanted... something like me. They set a trap and caught us on the road... me and all my family, and they said if went with them, they'd leave everyone else alone, but if I fought, my family would die. What could I do? I agreed to go with them. My mother and sisters wept. I am their protection."

Bieja said nothing to this; there wasn't anything she could say. His profile was handsome in a way, even with the white scar. Pity made her resolve waver, but she steeled herself as she brought the fried bread and crouched beside him.

"Eat."

He took it but glanced around, as if his senses were slowly coming back to him. "Did you kill that second soldier?"

"No, but don't worry. We're a good deal off the road from where I dragged you. And I'll bet he isn't going to come after us on his own."

And aside from assurances, it was another reminder to Milôs that he was deeply in debt to her.

He nodded, rolled up onto his side again, and went at the flatbread.

"So you got sick with a camp fever but managed to

escape," she echoed, "and a few of them caught up to you."

"Yes."

"How bad off are you?"

"It doesn't matter. I have to find my family."

This was the moment of crisis, and Bieja stood up. "Not yet, you're not. I saved your fury hide back there... and you owe me a life. Those soldiers may not have killed you right away, but whatever they had planned for you was probably worse."

He stopped eating and stared at her.

"Your people ever travel through Belaski?" she asked.

"Belaski?" he gasped in surprise. "Of course, but what are you—"

"I need to get to the coast, and you're taking me there.

He dropped the flatbread and pushed himself up to sitting this time. "No, I'm not. I have to find my family. They are unprotected without me."

Bieja squared off to face him, looking down with her hands on her hips. "Oh, yes you are! Much as it pains me to say this, I won't even make it to the border on my own. You owe me a life, and you're going to pay it. What would your mother say if she were here? Mmmmm? She'd tell you to honor your people's ways no matter what the cost. I need to get to the coast of Belaski, and you *are* going to take me. After that, you can find your family."

He continued staring at her with his mouth slightly open until she pointed down. "Now eat the rest of that bread before it gets cold. You'll need your strength."

She kept Milôs resting by the campfire for the next few days, feeding him water, tea, and salted mashed turnips until he stopped sweating and his eyes were clear.

They didn't talk much.

Once he was dressed, he looked striking enough. The green shirt set off his dusky complexion, and she wondered how well he could handle the dagger now on his hip. The turning point came when he finally stood up and stripped off his shirt.

"I'm tired of turnips," he said. "I'm going hunting."

She glanced at him sidelong. "You coming back?"

Those three simple words had other questions beneath them. Would he honor his people's ways and guard her life in exchange for the one she'd given him? Or would he abandon her here?

"Yes, I'll be back," he answered in almost a wolf's growl without even looking at her.

He kept his pants on, and she assumed he'd probably leave them somewhere along the way once he took to hunting as a wolf. He was gone quite awhile, but true to his word, he returned carrying two dead rabbits. Bieja didn't give him any reaction as she skinned the rabbits, though privately she was beyond relief.

She had him.

A part of her didn't like forcing him, but that passed when she thought of her Magiere. If in being alone, she simply disappeared somewhere along this journey, never to be seen again, Magiere would mourn forever, wondering about her aunt's fate.

No, Bieja had to take the chance Leesil had given her. And for that, she needed Milôs.

On the morning of their fourth day together, he inspected her scant belongings and shook his head.

"I can hunt meat, but we need better supplies than this."

"I have coin," she answered, deciding to be honest with him. "But so far, I haven't found anywhere to spend it. We'll just have to keep looking along the way."

At those words, the reality of this journey he could not escape appeared to truly settle on him. Still crouching by her burlap sack, he glowered up at her.

"I *will* take you to the coast of Belaski, but you will

have to keep up… as I plan to finish this task with all possible speed."

"Oh, I'll keep up," she answered shortly. "You ready?"

Without answering, he lifted her sack and headed for the road.

She grabbed up the piece of canvas and hurried after him. "What are you doing? We'll be spotted too easily out here."

"Don't worry. I'll hear anyone coming well before we see them."

Somewhat flustered, Bieja followed Milôs out onto the road, but she soon felt more confident about pressing him into duty as guide and guardian. He hadn't been boasting.

They traveled all day on the open road, though every now and then he'd motion her into the trees. They'd hide until riders passed and then resume their journey.

She wasn't the best judge of distance but, by evening, she guessed they'd traveled farther in that one day than she'd covered in three days on her own in the forest. Hope began growing inside her, and for the first time, she let herself speculate on this tavern that Magiere had purchased. What would it be like?

If there were any flaws, Bieja would take them well in hand, that much was certain.

At some point along the way—later, she couldn't remember exactly when—Milôs began telling her about his family and his life among the Móndyalítko. In turn, Bieja shared a bit about her Magiere and her niece's pointy-eared darling—and why she was traveling to the coast.

Perhaps he talked to her simply because there was no one else. But soon after, Bieja began to realize that she had been alone far too long, and that perhaps the end of this journey might rescue her in more ways than one.

At least she wasn't talking to herself anymore.

However, their supplies were almost gone, and they'd not come across a single intact village with a market.

One evening, Milôs stopped in the road to stare ahead. "I hear the sound of men... a lot of men." And he shooed her off into the trees.

"They coming our way?" she whispered in the brush, wondering if maybe an entire contingent was about to ride by.

"No," he whispered back. "I don't hear horses. Must be an encampment. You wait here."

"What? No, don't you dare..."

Before she finished, he was gone. She was left fuming for an alarming amount of time, but she stayed put. She started as the bush beside her rustled, and he finally reappeared as quickly as he'd vanished. His black hair was a mess from crawling through brush, and the knees of his breeches were wet.

"Don't you do that again!" she scolded.

"Shhh!" he answered.

She could see from his expression that he had news, and she fell silent.

"A whole camp of Väränj soldiers," he whispered, "hundreds of them."

Bieja felt herself flush with heat again as she thought of Yoan's split skull and how those bastards in red tabards had thrown torches without a thought for burning innocent people alive.

"I got close enough to hear an argument," Milôs said, "but I wasn't seen."

Through her anger, she glanced at him in the darkness. "Argument? About what?"

"One of their captains wants to press on to join another contingent and help lay siege to Enêmûsk. The other wants to fall back."

She blinked. "Siege Enêmûsk?"

"Word of their maneuvers got out," he went on. "Forces from other houses are rushing to assist the Äntes. A thousand men from the House of Pählen are less than two days away from the city."

"Pählen? How did they get involved?"

"The other houses won't allow the Väränj to siege the city of the standing grand prince... no matter what the provocation. If the Väränj succeed, what's to stop them from taking down the next?" He shook his head, and his voice grew more hollow and cold with every word. "The other houses will aid Rodêk because of this. They'll start killing Väränj leaders until they find one willing to submit, swear fealty, and... and everything goes back to the way it was before."

"Then it was all for nothing," she said. "The Väränj burned my home for nothing."

"Battles between nobles are always for nothing," he replied. "But the people of this land are the ones who suffer for it."

She snorted in disgust. "And you wonder why I'm leaving?"

He looked at her. "Have I ever said I wondered?"

No, he hadn't, and she glanced away.

"In truth, none of that matters for us," he continued. "What does matters is those Väränj have a large supply tent."

She turned her gaze back to his face. "How large?"

"Big enough for me to slip in the back without being seen... if you can distract the guards."

It took a moment for his words to sink in, and then she sputtered, "Distract? How in seven hells am I supposed to do that?"

Milôs smiled for the first time since she'd met him, exposing white teeth, and he suddenly looked as young as Jan.

"No matter how brutal soldiers are when ordered to attack," he said, "in camp, they long for distraction... any distraction. With the Äntes, I saw scores of women welcomed into a camp, and none were threatened or abused. The men were too glad to see them."

Bieja exhaled sharply and made a fist. "What are you saying? That I should go swinging my hips like some skirt-swishing tart into a Väränj camp?"

He held up one hand. "No. Not all the women who came through the Äntes encampments were... like that. Some were singers, players, gamesters and fortunetellers... and some were just trying to earn a bit of coin or food by offering to launder clothing. They were all most welcome by soldiers far from home. Though you're a bit pale, you look somewhat like my people. You could offer to read a few palms and tell them some tales of their futures."

"Me? Tell fortunes? You're the Móndyalítko. Why don't you do the distracting, and I'll do the sneaking?"

"Because I'm an able bodied man, and they'd conscript me on sight!" Before she could argue, he pressed on. "Your voice and expressions will hold their attention—with a little effort. Trust me. When you speak, people listen."

That sounded like a compliment, but she wouldn't be flattered. "I don't have the first inkling how to tell a fortune... especially to no torch-throwing, murdering Väränj brigands."

His smile vanished. "Well, *you* cannot live on rabbits all the way to the border."

Sometimes, he could be as moody as her, or maybe she just had that effect on people.

"I have to get into that supply tent," he said. "So you have to distract the guards and keep them out front. Can you think of a better way?"

In the moment, she couldn't.

Bieja crept beside Milôs to the edge of the tree line. She had tied their canvas tent to her back and dragged the burlap sack with their few belongings. Together, they looked out over an open field into the Väränj encampment.

Only four tents had been set up, one larger than the others. Most of the men slept on the open ground, and there were numerous campfires lighting up the night.

"There," he said, pointing to the largest tent. "Give me enough time to get around back, and then distract the guards... and I don't care how you do it."

She scowled at him, hoping he was right about these soldiers not trying anything to give her a reason to thump them. Really, just how long had he been conscripted, and how much time had he spent in an Äntes camp?

But as she watched him slip away, her thoughts turned back to the other problem. No matter what Milôs had said about her, she couldn't see herself telling anyone wild tales of good fortune. That took a mix of flattery and bold-faced lies, neither of which came naturally to her. Perhaps she could offer to do some laundry... and then throw a raging fit over what they offered to pay her?

That was more like it. She could manage that.

However, even the notion of speaking to any Väränj was almost more than she could stomach, but she knew she'd better think of something quick.

A tall man stepped out of one of the other tents. He was cleaner than the others, and his hair was combed. The soldiers before the bigger supply tent showed him respect, standing upright with sharp nods, and Bieja remembered what Milôs had said about there being two captains here.

The tall one looked about a moment longer, ducked back inside, and Bieja spotted a small, unattended campfire beside that tent. That gave her a notion.

Slipping through the trees, she got as close to the captain's tent as she could, though it was still a good twenty paces out from the trees. She took out her dull kitchen knife and cut a piece off the canvas tent. Then she cut a thinner strip and used it to tie the bigger piece around the head of a small branch she found lying on the ground. Pouring the remaining cooking oil over the branch's wrapped end, she had herself a makeshift torch.

When the path was clear of any soldiers, she took a breath and hurried from the trees as quickly as her stout legs could carry her. She tried to stay low in the dark as she rushed to the unattended campfire, lit her torch, and tossed it at the side of the captain's tent.

Oh, that felt so good.

To her astonishment, the tent burst into flames far faster than she'd thought it would. She dashed back for the tree line and nearly dove into a bush, hoping that no one had spotted her.

Within a few breaths, shouts exploded in the camp, and she saw men running for the flaming tent from all directions. Quite a commotion followed as futile buckets of water were thrown, and Bieja couldn't help a vicious little smile in the darkness.

"We'll see how you like your having home burned," she whispered, wishing she could say it to the captain's face.

She lay there in the dark, hidden by heavy brush, watching the tent burn, until a soft voice sounded behind her.

"It's me."

Jumping slightly, she turned to see Milôs crouched beside a tree behind her. "How did you find me?" she whispered, crawling back toward him.

"You have a distinct scent, like turnips and salt."

Bieja lost all her glee as she hissed at him, "Don't you say a word about me setting that tent ablaze! I'm no fortune-teller or panderer, and I couldn't think of anything else!"

His dark eyes widened in surprise. "Scold you? No... setting a captain's tent on fire was good thinking. I wouldn't have thought of that." He held up a bag tall enough that it would reach his thigh when he stood. "Come and look at this, Bieja. We're well stocked now."

She crawled closer and peeked in the bag's top, but it was too dark to see inside.

"Jerked beef, smoked trout, lentils and onions," he began, "more tea, flour, and cooking oil. I even stole a jar of honey and some oatcakes."

Bieja's anger faded at the realization of a successful—though small—raid on a camp of butchering Väränj soldiers. A moon ago, had someone told her she'd be crouched in an unfamiliar forest with a shape-shifting Móndyalítko after raiding supplies, she'd have boxed such a liar upside the head.

"Do we have enough food now?" she asked, still uncertain how many days it was to the border. Milôs hadn't been able to gauge their distance so far, as he was unsure what they might encounter along the way.

But he nodded. "Yes."

"All right then," she whispered.

The following morning, Milôs told her they couldn't travel by the road for a while.

"Why not?" she asked, more from curiosity than disagreement.

"We're getting too close to Enêmûsk, and that's where all the fighting will take place. There'll be too many soldiers on the road. We have to circle wide to the south around the city."

And so, they left the open road and struggled through the trees and brush yet again. For all his earlier threats about her keeping up, he let her set the pace this time. They encountered no one in the forest, and that night, as they made camp up a hill from a gurgling steam, he looked up at the stars, appearing relieved.

"We'll be all right. By late tomorrow, we can risk the roads again."

They ate well that night on a supper of beef jerky, oatcakes, and a pot of lentils boiled with onions.

Bieja looked up at the stars in some wonder that they were the same ones she'd seen for well over forty years from outside her little hut in Chemestúk.

They seemed so different here.

"I'm sorry I'm keeping you from your family," she said quietly to Milôs, who sat on the other side of the campfire. "But I have to reach Miiska."

He took a bite of jerky and didn't answer. But she hadn't expected him to. He would not openly forgive her, nor say anything to help ease her conscience, and she couldn't blame him.

The next morning, Bieja rose stiff and aching, rubbing the small of her back as she stood up. "I'll go and fetch some water for our tea."

Rubbing his eyes, Milôs nodded. "I'll get a fire started."

As they had no bucket, she picked up the cooking pot and headed down a hill for the gurgling creek below their camp among the trees. As well as being stiff, she felt especially grimy this morning, and she glanced back over her shoulder and upslope, gauging the distance from the camp.

Upon reaching the creek, she decided to head downstream a little ways—so she might have some privacy to wash a bit more thoroughly. Setting the cooking pot down, she knelt by the water and rolled up her sleeves... debating on removing her dress for a more proper bath. But the morning was chilly, and she decided to just attempt to wash up while clothed.

The cold water felt surprisingly good after its first shock. She scrubbed her face with her hands as her thoughts—her imaginings—drifted to notions of living on the edge of an actual ocean, which she'd never seen in her life, and helping to run a tavern of all things. The idea had begun to appeal to her more and more. Of course, her real goal was to reunite with Magiere, so that her beloved niece—her only kin—would know she hadn't perished in another pointless civil war.

Still scrubbing her face, she froze when a branch cracked behind her.

Milôs didn't step on branches when he moved in the forest.

Slowly, she turned her head to look behind herself, and her heart skipped a beat.

Three filthy, ragged, and starved-looking men were standing ten paces upstream, staring at her. They wore no colors, so Bieja could only guess they were the lowest form of conscripts, not even worthy of a tabard by the side who'd conscripted them. Now... they were escaped deserters.

She cursed herself for not having brought her dull knife, but she stood up and tried to make her voice sound light—which was difficult for her as she was naturally gruff.

"Plenty of water here, boys," she said. "Come have a drink."

Her words were intended to make herself sound friendly, like someone from their own villages—who should not be attacked. But again, sounding friendly was not one of her strengths.

Not one of them even acknowledged she'd spoken.

"She ain't got food," the shortest one said, wiping his nose with a dirty sleeve.

"She's got a cook pot," another said, and Bieja noticed he was missing his left hand.
"So she's gotta have food somewhere."

The one standing furthest away was tall and boney. His eyes looked almost dead, as if he'd stopped feeling anything anymore.

"See what she's got inside her dress," that one said. "Women always hide anything of worth inside their dresses."

Bieja drew a quiet breath through her nose with furtive glance among the trio for any sign of weapons. She had Leesil's letter and the six silver sovereigns stashed inside her bodice, and she wasn't giving those up to anyone.

As the shortest man took a step, she dropped to a crouch and grabbed a sharp heavy rock. When he saw she was going to fight, he dashed at her, grabbing for her arm. She sidestepped and then slammed into him with all her weight, knocking him into the stream. But before she bashed him over the head, the tall boney one grabbed her from behind.

The one-handed man ran in and gripped the neckline of her dress.

"Get off me!" she shouted, trying to shove back against the one behind her.

A sudden low growl made the boney one behind her stiffen, but the one-handed man still pulled down on her bodice, trying to tear the front of her dress. And then he was gone amid snarls and the blur of a brown bulk.

Over the splash in the creek, Bieja heard a scream and savage snarls before she could even look. On the creek's other side, a huge wolf stood over the motionless man lying with his feet in the running water... his throat bloodied and torn open while his eyes were wide, unblinking as they stared up toward the sky.

"What in the..." whispered the tall man behind Bieja

He let go of her and scrambled backward. The wolf turned and snarled, drawing its jowls back to expose long canine teeth.

The short man in the stream struggled to get up, his expression panicked. "Run!" he shouted, scrambling backward and then fleeing.

In the same instant, the wolf lunged at the tall man so fast Bieja could barely see it move.

"Milôs, no!" she yelled, "There's no need—"

It was too late; he leaped onto the back of the tall deserter, knocking the man face first into the water. The choking and splashing of the man ended and the creek running by Bieja's feet began to turn red. The wolf lunged off the dead body to go after the third man.

"Milôs! Stop!" she shouted.

This time, the wolf stalled, half turning in middle of the stream to look back at her.

"Let him go," she ordered, dropping her stone. "They were just looking for food."

With a final growl, the wolf crouched in the water and its fur began to recede. Black hair sprouted from its head, and its shoulders began to widen. A breath later, she stared at Milôs—his expression half-mad. But as he looked at—*saw*—her, the rage on his face vanished was replaced by fear. Stark naked, he ran back to her with his jaw and mouth still covered in blood.

"Are you are all right?" he rushed to ask, exposing more blood in his teeth. "Did they hurt you?"

His manner—and lack of clothing—caught her off guard.

"I'm all right," she answered, glancing once at the bodies. "More than I can say for them."

It sounded judgmental, even to her, but did he have to kill them?

A muscle of his jaw twitched. "They'd have slit your throat for anything you carried."

They might have.

"Where are your clothes?" she asked.

He didn't answer and just crouched at the stream. She looked away as he began washing off and spitting out all the blood. Only as they headed back up the hill did she think about the expression on his face after he'd turned back into a man. He'd been in a genuine panic at the idea of her being hurt. Not at all like some obligated, indebted guardian.

Instead of making her feel better, that only made her feel worse.

Two days later, they crossed the border from Droevinka into Belaski. In short order, the whole world seemed to change. The roads were smooth and well maintained, and Milôs no

longer shooed her into the brush if he heard someone coming. In part, she couldn't believe she'd made
it this far... that she'd left her homeland and
reached a new country.

In the late afternoon, they walked into a small
town with neat rows of wooden dwellings and shops
and a bustling market square. A few of the townsfolk
going about their business glanced her way—with a
brief pause—and Bieja realized how dirty and
bedraggled she and Milôs must look.

Milôs, however, didn't seem to notice. Instead, he
pointed to a white two-story building.

"That looks like an inn, so we'll sleep indoors
tonight. If you give me one of the sovereigns, I'll get
you settled and then find a stable to bargain for a
pair of horses. That way, we'll reach the coast
faster."

Though she trusted him now, Bieja didn't relish the
idea of letting anyone bargain with the money Leesil
had given her. "Why can't I buy the horses?" she
asked.

"Because you don't speak the language."

She blink once and then stared at him. Of course
she'd *known* people spoke a different language here,
but she'd never given it much thought until now.

"And you do?" she asked.

"Of course I do." He seemed surprised by the
question. "My people are travelers. We must be able
to communicate."

For some reason, instead of making her feel safe
and relieved, this annoyed her—but perhaps the annoyance was aimed at herself. He'd known how to
speak Belaskian all along, and he could have been
teaching her by the campfire at night. She'd been a
fool not to think of this sooner.

"I'm coming with you," she said, hands on her
hips, "so you might as well lead on."

Without waiting for an answer, she reached inside
her bodice and pulled out the pouch, gripping it
tightly. He scowled, but then started off down the

clean, cobbled street. The thought of finally reaching the coast, and soon, was a relief, but she felt she ought to tell him one thing.

"Mind you," she said, "I've ridden a mule or two in my day, but I've never been up on a horse."

"We'll find you a gentle mount." He glanced down at her. "With a broad back."

Bieja cast a narrow-eyed glare up at Milôs. Then again, he was probably right.

A few moments later, they walked inside the open doors of a wooden building near the outskirts of town, and Bieja breathed in the scent of sweet hay. Harnesses, bridles, and pitchforks lined the walls, and directly ahead, she could see a row of stables.

"Hallo?" Milôs called out.

Apparently, people used the same greeting anywhere. A stocky man in a leather apron and over-sized canvas shirt came out of a stall and looked Milôs up and down before glancing at Bieja. When he spoke, the words ran together like some guttural music... so very different than Droevinkan. Milôs responded in kind, and Bieja couldn't follow a word of what they said.

She didn't like that, but the stable master turned and headed toward the back stalls, gesturing to the second from the end. Milôs cocked his head, studying a tall light gray gelding and a stocky mare. Bieja liked the look of the dark brown mare with gentle eyes and a white blaze down her nose. And she didn't need to speak Belaskian to know when Milôs set to haggling with the stable master.

"How much does he want?" she finally interrupted.

"Five silver pennies a piece," Milôs answered. "More than I like, but he says he can make change for a sovereign."

"Five a piece?" Bieja snapped. "That could buy six mules back home! Talk him down."

When he stalled, she huffed and faced down the stable master herself. "No," she said in Droevinkan, shaking her head furiously. "Too much!"

The stocky man appeared unimpressed and only raised one eyebrow as he crossed his thick arms.

"Things cost more here," Milôs explained in a low voice, "and these are good horses. You have plenty of money, and it's even coin of this realm. There's no bank or money-changer here, and we may not find many who can change out a sovereign in this small place."

When she pursed her mouth, thinking hard, Milôs added. "The sooner I get you to the coast, the sooner I can look for *my* family. Take the offer."

"Oh, very well," she grumbled. "But if any inn-keeper here wants more than a penny, we're sleeping outside!"

As they rode west through Belaski, Bieja badgered Milôs almost every waking moment to teach her enough of the local language that she might get by on her own. Sometimes his patience wore thin, but he seemed to know which words or phrases would be most useful to her. In spite of the different sounds of the Belaskian, some terms were nearly the same as in Droevinkan. And traveling under an open blue sky instead of a dank, dripping forest was a relief she'd never imagined before.

But, as she'd never ridden a horse in her life, much less for entire days, her backside and thighs soon grew more sore than she could've imagined as well. Still, she didn't complain. Milôs had been right, and they made good time. The mare was gentle, and Bieja took to calling her "Mistress Brownie."

Milôs asked directions at several villages along the way, and then one afternoon he sniffed the air and turned in his saddle, as he'd been leading the way. There was a glint in his dark eyes.

"Bieja, hand me your reins and close your eyes," he said.

"What?"

"Just do it. There is a surprise ahead." For reasons she later never really understood, she did as he asked, and he began leading Mistress Brownie ahead.

"Keep them closed," Milôs insisted.

Feeling a fresh breeze on her face, she almost disobeyed him.

Then he said, "All right. Open your eyes."

She did.

Stretched out before her, as far as the eye could see was a body of blue-gray water. Foaming waves crashed against a sandy shore. Tall, tan grass waved in the breeze.

She stared. "Oh, Milôs."

He smiled that rare smile of his, making him look so young. "I suspected you'd never seen it."

They dismounted and walked into the sand. She couldn't take her gaze off the endless water. For once, he didn't seem in a hurry to press her onward.

Two days later, in the mid-afternoon, they rode into a large port town with shops, taverns, countless dwellings, another open-air market, and at least two wooden structures toward the shore side that were bigger than any Bieja had seen in her life.

"This is it," Milôs said. "This is Miiska."

A knot formed suddenly in Bieja's stomach. Leesil had made it plain that he and Magiere wouldn't be here yet. They had their own journey to complete and would return when they could. She knew no one in this strange, foreign port town.

Milôs raised his hand to stop a young man walking down the main path and asked him a question. Bieja picked out the words "Where" and "Sea Lion." The young man pointed toward the town's far end and a little towards the shore side with a polite answer, but Bieja didn't even try and listen.

The knot in her stomach just kept tightening.

Milôs led the way on his gelding, and Bieja clucked to Mistress Brownie to follow. Almost too soon, he stopped and waved a hand at a newish-looking building of two floors with a sign hanging over the door.

"This is it," he said.

She frowned. "You sure? It looks... too new, like it was built a year or two ago."

Magiere hadn't said anything about buying a *new* tavern.

He nodded. "The sign says the 'Sea Lion.' This has to be it... you're home."

As he said this, a rush of emotion hit her, a hard awareness that she would never have made it alive to the Droevinkan border without him, and even if by some miracle she had, she certainly wouldn't have been able to find this place, not knowing the language and not being able to ask for a single direction.

Perhaps he just honored the "life for a life" custom of his people, but she wanted to do something more for him.

Climbing off Mistress Brownie, "Get down."

"What's wrong?"

"Just get down."

He dismounted with a confused expression. "I thought this was what you wanted?"

She said nothing to that and reaching inside her dress to pull out the pouch of coins. Most of what Leesil had given her was still there, as they hadn't been able to spend much before reaching Belaski.

"Take this," she said, "For the journey back. Maybe you owed me a debt, but your family didn't. I owe them this—and my thanks—for the loan of you."

He looked at the pouch and took a step back, shaking his head. "No. You have no idea what you're going to find here or what life will be like. You may not be happy... you might need that money for my mother calls a 'nest egg'. I will not take all that you have and leave you in a strange place."

Her eyes began to sting, but she damn well wasn't going to start bawling.

"I was supposed to be saved by you," he went on. "After my time among the Äntes, I had... changed... seeing everyone but my own kind as not worth the air they breathed. You... you made me see the world as I used to." He glanced away. "I can make my way back easily enough, but I would like to keep the gelding, at least to get through Belaski."

"Of course," Bieja answered gruffly. She didn't know what else to say.

He tied both horses to a rail, and his gaze turned to the tavern's door. "We should go in."

"You're coming?" she asked in surprise.

"Yes, I want to make... I want to make sure."

Her eyes still stinging, Bieja followed him toward the door.

K arlin Boigiesque stood inside the Sea Lion— amid an array of mismatched tables and chairs—with his arms crossed, engaged in a familiar argument with a stooped, aging man.

"Caleb, there's nothing wrong with the bread I baked this morning," he insisted.

"I'm just saying... if you bake it in the morning, it's already hard by evening, and I don't like serving that my patrons."

Karlin sighed. Though he was one of few bakers in town—and never short on business—he was fond of the old tavern caretaker left to tend the place by its owners.

Old Caleb was half a head taller than him, with straight ashen hair pulled back at the neck of his plain muslin shirt, which was always as clean as the well-swept floor. His face was wrinkled but smooth of expression around steady, dark brown eyes. Karlin, on the other hand, was stocky, muscular, bald, and wore a flour-covered apron nearly everywhere he went.

"I'm not firing up the ovens in the late afternoon just for you," he shot back. "Bakers bake in the morning! If you think my bread is too hard by time you open for business, take your patronage to someone else."

It was a hollow threat, and they both knew it. Magiere had made arrangements with Karlin before she'd left, and neither Caleb nor Karlin would do anything to go against her wishes. Just then, the tavern's front door opened, and both men turned to look.

The place wouldn't be opened for a short while yet, and normally, Caleb had no compunction against turning people away until he was ready for business. But Caleb's gaze locked on the stranger who stepped in the door.

Karlin went still and silent as well. Though he was easy-going by nature, something about the newcomer put him on guard.

The man in the doorway was dusky-skinned and broad-shouldered. His hair and eyes were black, and his clothing was tattered, as if he'd been on a long journey. His face bore a thick white scar, and he wore a silver ring in one ear.

His only weapon appeared to be a dagger on his hip.

But none of these things bothered Karlin. He dealt with rough, scarred sailors almost every day of his life. No, there was something else.

Although the man's face was calm, there was a hint of savagery underneath it, a suggestion that right or wrong or the laws of men were nothing to him. He moved carefully, even gracefully, as he entered, but still somehow gave the impression he might rush the room without warning.

"Can I help you?" Caleb asked. "We aren't open for supper yet."

"Help?" said a gruff female voice behind the man. "No help us. I... help you."

Karlin's wariness turned to confusion as a magnificent woman came through a door. Her purple gown was a bit tattered, but she was plump and strong looking, with gray-streaked black hair. Her face was pale—and familiar somehow—and she held herself like a queen overseeing her court for the first time.

He couldn't take his eyes off her.

"Yes, yes," she said in a thick Droevinkan accent as she pushed past her scarred companion and continued looking over the room. "Good."

Karlin came here nearly every day for one reason or another, but he looked around now, trying to see it as she did.

From where she stood, the bar on her left was long and made of stout oak. Behind it was a curtained doorway that led to the household kitchen and stockroom, and at the bar's far end was a narrow stairway that led up to the second floor and the living quarters.

The hearth stood near the room's center, its backside open like the front, so that patrons could circle around it or nestle close to either side for a little extra warmth in winter. Most of the tables and chairs had been purchased second hand, so nothing matched, but that only added to the place's charm.

Karlin finished his own survey of the room, and when his eyes came back around, the woman was watching him. He couldn't help but smile at her. However, Caleb appeared far less impressed by two overly early patrons.

"You can come back just before dark," he said.

"We need to find either someone called Caleb or someone called Karlin," the dark-haired man said, still by the open door, and his accent was barely noticeable. Though his voice was soft, like his face, it carried an undercurrent of something wild.

Karlin grew more intrigued. "Well... I'm Karlin, and that's Caleb, so what's this all about?"

The woman pulled a piece of paper out of the neck of her dress and strode over to bar. Karlin had been a widow for some years, but he could not remember a woman ever affecting him like this before. Her presence seemed to fill the entire room.

Caleb took the letter, scanned it, and he went slightly pale.

"What?" Karlin asked in alarm.

"She's..." Caleb trailed off and, after a swallow, began again. "It's a letter from Master Leesil in his own hand. He says this woman, Bieja... she's Mistress Magiere's aunt."

Karlin's surprise was mirrored on old Caleb's face.

"She's come to live here... and help run the place," Caleb finished.

Karlin found this quite a lot to take in, but it suddenly made sense. Of course this was Magiere's aunt, for she had Magiere's eyes—and ways.

"Is she welcome here?" asked the man in the doorway.

Karlin frowned in confusion. "What do you mean?"

"Is she welcome? Does she have a home here? You'll let her stay, and you'll look after her until her niece returns?"

The woman called Bieja hardly appeared to need "looking after." She ran her fingertips down the bar's top, looked at them, and then scowled as she held one finger up in front of Caleb's face.

Caleb's jaw tightened, and the letter crinkled in his grip.

Karlin wondered how much of the conversation she was following, but she appeared to speak at least some Belaskian already.

"Yes, of course," Karlin answered the man, without consulting Caleb. But there was no need. This woman was Magiere's aunt. "Of course she has a home here."

Bieja walked with purpose toward the stairs and both Caleb and Karlin followed her with their eyes.

"Bedrooms?" she asked, pointing up. "I... go... see."

This came out like an edict, but then she looked towards the front door and her expression changed to a mix of surprise and loss. Karlin glanced back quickly to find the open doorway empty.

The scarred man was gone, and Bieja looked distressed by his sudden absence.

"It's all right," Karlin said quickly. "You are home."

She turned back to him, studying his face with interest. Then she nodded once and repeated. "Home." ■

CAPTIVES

Three days after Chemestúk village nearly burned to the ground, Julianna walked through the wreckage with Nadja, the village zupan's wife, as they scavenged for anything left that might still be of use.

"Oh," Nadja breathed. "How could this have happened?"

None of the huts still smoldered, but the few that remained partially upright were little more than blackened shells. Julianna couldn't allow herself to mourn yet—or to feel much of anything. But she was glad Nadja had come down here with her.

At the old stone keep up above the village, Nadja's husband, Zupan Cadell, had gathered all the survivors in attempting to ensure their safety. But he'd given Nadja and Julianna permission to make a quick trip down to see what they might recover.

A few bodies with smashed skulls still lay within sight, but so far, it had seemed too risky to send enough people down—who'd need to spend a good deal of time out in the open—to bury them.

Julianna looked away from the blackened huts to her companion.

In her mid forties, Nadja was still a beautiful woman. With shimmering dark hair and a dusky smooth complexion, she was lithe and slender though well-figured in a red dress tied at the waist with a wildly patterned, orange paisley sash. She was of the Móndyalítko, a vagabond people who traveled the land living in wagon-homes. But back in her youth, Nadja had married Cadell before he became the local zupan, and she now helped him oversee the keep and its five attached fifes.

Julianna adored her.

In contrast, Julianna had recently turned twenty. She viewed herself as too tall and gangly, with long straight hair a shade somewhere between dark blond and light brown. She'd been orphaned as a girl, and later, Nadja had taken her in. Julianna now often wore red dresses—but only because she admired Nadja so much.

It was strange how the color of a dress had mattered only a few days ago.

"I don't think we should enter any of the half-burned dwellings," Nadja said. "A number of villagers are still unaccounted for. They might have hidden inside during the raid and burned to death."

Julianna didn't see how charred bodies could be any worse than those with smashed skulls. Closing her eyes, she quickly opened them again for fear of picturing those remains or the horrors that had taken place here while she had been living safely up at the keep.

For now, she simply tried to make sense of what had happened here... and why.

From what she'd pieced together, about a moon ago, Prince Rodêk of the House of Äntes—the current reigning grand prince of Droevinka—had left the royal castle in Kéonsk to see to a matter in his family's home in Enêmûsk. He'd left his prime counselor in charge, a baron called Buscan; while the prince was away, Buscan had been assassinated.

No matter which of the noble houses was currently in power, soldiers of the House of Väränj always guarded the royal castle and grounds at Kéonsk.

Apparently, Baron Buscan was hated by many of the Äntes, but they still accused the Väränj of allowing him to be murdered.

The Väränj were proud, and in turn accused the Äntes of murdering the counselor to bring shame on them and distrust from the other houses. Fighting between these two houses broke out inside the city of Kéonsk and began to spread.

Of course the villagers of Chemestúk knew nothing of these events—nor did they care about pride or power struggles between the noble houses. Then five days ago, soldiers in the light yellow tabards of the Äntes had ridden through and conscripted every man in the village between sixteen and forty. They even entered the keep and took Nadja and Cadell's son, Jan—who was in his mid-twenties and a state of fine health.

Just the thought of Jan trapped into conscription made Julianna want to weep. At the time of his abduction, she'd thought nothing could get worse than the prospect of Chemestúk losing most of its men... and what awaited those men.

She was wrong.

Two nights later, soldiers from the House of Väränj dressed in chain armor and bright red tabards had come riding in with torches, shouting about the people here being "traitors" to the land. They began setting fire to the huts and killing people at random.

Between the conscriptions of the Äntes and the following massacre launched by the Väränj, a village of over two hundred people was now down to forty-seven, consisting of women, children, and aging men.

"I don't see much of use," Nadja said, looking at the charred rubble that marked another lost home. "And I can see this is upsetting you."

"I am well," Julianna answered, trying to sound as if she meant it. "And if we can scavenge a few more cook pots, we'll be able to fix larger meals in the keep's kitchen."

In spite of everything around them, Nadja smiled. "My strong girl. We'll keep looking."

Julianna followed Nadja's advice and didn't enter any of the half-burned dwellings. After digging through rubble until nearly dark, they found only one usable teakettle and two cast-iron pots.

"We should start back," Nadja said, "or Cadell will begin to worry."

Carrying their meager finds, the two women turned to follow the road up the forested dome hill to their home. The old fortress disappeared from sight for a short while as they pressed along. When they finally reached the top of the rise, Julianna was glad for the sight of the solid keep.

The surrounding forest had been cleared away for some thirty paces on all sides of the decayed stonewall encircling the grounds. Judging by some of the wall's taller sections and fallen stones lying about, it had lost half its height. Its gate doors were completely gone.

The keep was simple, barely a huge block of stone with one half tower, or turret, sprouting from a forward corner, and the place was more than a bit worn with age. Moss grew between lichen-spotted stones on its lower half. To one side of the grounds was an undersized stable while the other held a small barracks with a clay chimney.

Julianna knew most people would look at this place with utter dismay, but for her it offered safety and food and warmth and love—things she had once lost and never thought to regain.

To her, the old keep was a haven.

"What did you have in mind for dinner?" Nadja asked as they trudged toward the broken gate. "I think the children are growing tired of lentil soup. Perhaps we should cut into one of those hams we've been saving?"

Julianna didn't answer. Instead, she held up one hand, half turning and looking back. She thought she'd heard something.

"What was that?" she asked.

Nadja fell silent in listening. The sounds came

again... the voices of men coming up the road behind them, numerous voices.

Looking back toward the keep as if gauging the distance, Nadja whispered, "Run!"

J an was thirsty.

He and the other men taken from Chemestúk were kept in a tight group surrounded by Äntes soldiers as they'd slowly been moving west. The soldiers stopped at every village along way, taking men wherever they saw fit. They gave no thought or pity to the women, children, and elders left behind.

Due to his attire and coloring, Jan stood out like a bright stone in a stream of gray pebbles. He resembled his mother to a striking degree: slender, with even features and hair that hung to his shoulders in a wild, unruly mass. His dusky complexion contrasted with the milk-pale men around him. Unlike their drab clothing, he wore russet breeches with high boots and a loose sea-green shirt with the cuffs rolled halfway up his arms—and he sported three silver hoops in one ear. As a zupan's son, on the day of his conscription, he'd been allowed to gather a few belongings, so he now carried his violin in its case.

Evening began setting in as the sun dipped low.

"Make camp!" called out a voice from the front of the line of marching men.

Jan breathed in relief, hoping that meant a ration of water. Over the past few days, he'd paid attention to anything said around him, learning what he could. The men in charge were a Captain Oakes and a Lieutenant Braeden. Apparently, they'd been appointed with the task of gathering men to be taken back to Enêmûsk to reinforce the city's forces in case the Väränj decided to lay siege.

Oakes was a stocky man in his late forties, with peppered hair and a long moustache. He was business-like in his manner and appeared determined to fulfill his current task to the best of his ability. Braeden was younger and clean-shaven, tall and well built, and sported a perpetually arrogant expression, as if his current assignment was well beneath him.

Both men wore chain armor, swords, and the light yellow tabards of the Äntes.

By Jan's count, over a hundred and fifty conscripts had been taken. He and the others with him were herded into an open meadow and allowed to crouch down. Some of the soldiers began building fires and setting camp, but a number of them were left to watch over the conscripted men. Looking around, Jan searched for a possible way to slip away and vanish into the trees before anyone noticed him gone. He could not stop thinking about his father and mother... and Julianna left alone, without him, back at the keep.

He had no intention of being taken to Enêmûsk and trapped inside a walled city—so he had to get free before getting that far. As of yet, he'd seen no chance to escape.

"Have you seen Cherock?" someone whispered beside him.

Turning his head, Jan realized he was crouched beside one of the keep's guards who'd been taken along with him back in Chemestúk. He thought the man's name was Klayton.

"Cherock?" Jan scanned behind them. Cherock had been the man in charge of the keep's few guards and been with Jan's father for years. Jan knew him well. "No... I don't see him. He was near the back earlier."

Just then, a commotion pulled his attention left toward the tree line, and three Äntes soldiers emerged —two of them dragging a man by his arms.

Jan rose a little, trying to see what was happening. The man being dragged was Cherock.

"Get your hands off me!" Cherock was shouting. "You've no right!"

The soldiers kept dragging him until he was close enough that Jan could see the mix of fear and anger etched on his face. Lieutenant Braeden came striding toward them.

"What is this?" he demanded.

One soldier holding Cherock answered, "We caught him trying to escape, sir."

Braeden looked Cherock up and down in open disgust. "A deserter?"

"I'm no deserter," Cherock argued. "My place is in Chemestúk. I was assigned there by Lord Malbek himself."

Braeden didn't acknowledge that Cherock had spoken. Instead, the lieutenant glanced around until his gaze stopped near a wagon and fixed on a small upright log and an axe that the soldiers sometimes used to split wood.

"Bring those over," he ordered, pointing.

Jan went cold, and Cherock went wild, fighting to break the grip of the men holding him. He failed.

A stout Ántes soldier carried over the axe and the log, setting the log upright on the ground.

"Execute him," Braeden ordered.

"No!" Klayton shouted, straightening up next to Jan.

No one even looked their way, and Jan held his tongue. He needed to get himself out of here, and there was nothing he could do to help Cherock.

The lieutenant finally turned to address everyone watching. "Your prince is at war," he called out. "Desertion is a crime and will be treated as such."

Jan realized he was setting an example.

Cherock was dragged over and forced to his knees. His head was barely pushed down on the log's upward end when the axe swung high and came down. Cherock's head rolled off in the meadow's grass as blood spilled over the log's top.

Lieutenant Braeden walked away, as if to see to his next duty, having finished with this one.

Jan was struck hard by the reality that slipping off into the woods and trying to run was no longer an option.

. . .

J ulianna's legs were longer, and she ran ahead of Nadja, reaching the keep's doors first and opening them.

"Inside, quick," she whispered as Nadja caught up.

Both women were soon inside and running for the main hall, skidding to a stop in the archway. The hall was a large, open space taking up nearly half the keep's main floor of the keep. Stairs circled up along the left wall and matching ones went down to the right. The original fire pit in the hall's center was filled in with floor stones, and a hearth large enough to stand in had been added to the back wall.

Zupan Cadell stood by the blazing fire, a barrel of a man in his late-fifties with pale skin, fading freckles, and cropped red hair flecked by gray. He always wore brown trousers and a brown shirt.

"Cadell," Nadja panted. "There are men coming toward the keep."

"Soldiers?" he asked in alarm. "How many?"

"I do not know," she answered, leaning forward and trying to breathe. "We only heard their voices."

"I know," another voice said from the archway.

Looking back, Julianna saw young Gideon standing there. He was about twelve and quite skinny, with crooked teeth and hair that stood up in the front. But Julianna had always found him quick witted.

"What did you see?" she asked.

"I was up on the wall," Gideon answered, "and I saw about twenty men coming with swords and axes. But they aren't wearing tabards of any color."

Zupan Cadell was already striding toward the archway. "Nadja! Julianna! Get everyone below. You know what to do."

Indeed they did, and as the two women quickly and quietly spread the alarm, all the villagers now living in the keep made a run for the kitchen.

As there was no way for the walls or gate to be rebuilt or reinforced, Zupan Cadell had decided to try and use the decaying state of the keep in their favor. The downward stairs in the main hall led to a cellar of seven good-sized storage rooms, along with what had once been a prison hold.

Anyone invading the keep would almost certainly go down and search there. However, the kitchen was positioned near the back of the main floor. At the back of the kitchen, just inside a short passage leading to the back doors, was a narrow door that opened into an equally narrow stairwell. This led down to a few small storage rooms once used by the cooks here—in the days of the keep's glory, when noble vassals had entertained guests.

Cadell's plan was that should any band of soldiers or deserters come to plague the keep, everyone here would hide in these less obvious lower storage rooms. He'd had food and water and a few weapons stored down there.

When he'd first explained this to Julianna and Nadja, he expressed that any raiders would believe the old place abandoned. With luck, they would ransack the main floor, the upstairs, and the main cellars and then leave. Cadell was gambling on them not paying attention to a narrow, non-descript door near the back beyond the kitchen.

Of course this plan had several flaws—and risks—but it was still better than remaining openly visible and attempting to welcome any invaders in a friendly fashion or to try and fight them, as either of those options would most likely result in Cadell, the boys, and the few aging men being killed and the women being abused.

Besides, Julianna had not come up with anything better, and no one was willing to abandon the keep. Everyone here had been informed of exactly what to do. As a result, it took a surprisingly short time to get everyone through the kitchen and then into the narrow stairwell, descending below.

In addition to Julianna, Nadja, and the zupan, there were forty-seven people to hide. Julianna found herself toward the front of the group in following the zupan's lantern while Nadja brought up the rear. The stairs emptied into a small rectangular space.

Zupan Cadell stopped to take a lantern from the wall and light it from the flame of his own before handing it to Julianna. After that, he stepped onward, making room for everyone to follow. The space contained a door to the left and to the right while the wall straight ahead appeared to be a dead end.

Julianna opened one door and Cadell the other. Silently, villagers filed off the stairs and entered one room or the other. Julianna took refuge through the door on the right. Blankets, water, dried foods, and several crossbows had been stored along the walls.

This far down, it was nearly impossible to hear anything in the keep above.

"Now what?" Julianna asked.

Nadja entered and took a place beside her. "We wait."

Later that night, as Jan crouched by a fire, he tried to keep apart from the other Chemestúk captives. He wasn't going to be able to help them, and he didn't want any false expectations raised.

After watching Cherock so callously beheaded, he could only think about himself... and his parents and Julianna. Closing his eyes, he pictured himself in the main hall of the keep, eating warm bread and drinking tea and teasing Julianna.

When she'd first come to live with them, she'd been a gangly girl in a filthy dress who had been living on the charity other peasants. Nearly five years later, she'd grown into a lovely young woman with silky hair and an endearing matter-of-fact countenance.

In all his life, Jan had only possessed two real skills: playing the violin and making women fall in love with him. He was very good at both.

Julianna had refused to fall for his wiles and, after a time, had become his... friend. He'd never once thought of her like a sister, but he'd come to care for her. She was the only woman he couldn't charm, though she saw him every day. For some reason, this meant more to him than he could explain. He missed her so much his chest ached.

And with all the chaos in their world right now, Jan's family needed him.

No matter what he had to do or who he had to hurt, he was getting away from these Äntes soldiers.

Looking around, he noticed Captain Oakes nearby, overseeing the final touches of the men setting up his large tent.

"Captain," Jan called, standing up.

Several guards posted near the conscripts turned in surprise, and one dropped his hand to the hilt of his sword.

Captain Oakes, however, squinted through the darkness and came walking over. By the light of the campfire, he took in Jan's green shirt, longish hair, and silver rings. Without waiting to be addressed, Jan held up his violin case.

"Do you think the officers would enjoy some entertainment with dinner?"

Oakes glanced at the violin. "You're the zupan's son from Chemestúk, the tzigän?"

Jan kept his expression still, not wincing at the verbal slight. "Tzigän" translated into "vagabond thieves." His mother's people called themselves the Móndyalítko—"the world's little children."

Somehow, he managed a smile. "I can play music, do card tricks, read palms... and I'd much rather entertain you and the officers inside the tent than crouch out here in the cold."

To his surprise, Oakes smiled back and motioned him forward. "Come on, lad. I don't blame you. This is all a nasty business."

Jan blinked. Were those last words some kind of apology? Did the captain regret tearing men from their homes and families? If he did, he'd made a good secret of his feelings so far. Not an able-bodied man had been left behind. Or perhaps as the son of the vassal of Chemestúk, the captain simply thought Jan deserved better treatment?

Jan didn't care. He had caught the captain's attention and, once inside the main tent, he might win some trust to make himself appear as nothing more than a Móndyalítko entertainer who required little supervision. He wasn't certain what he might be able to do with that trust... but it was a start.

Oakes led the way through the open tent flap.

"I've brought some entertainment," he announced.

Inside, Jan saw Lieutenant Braeden and five other men. With the exception of Braeden, he didn't know their ranks or their names.

The youngest man looked pleased upon seeing the violin case. "Music?" he asked. "Are you any good?"

"My mother seems to think so."

Except for Braeden, the men laughed, but their tone was good-natured.

Jan almost couldn't believe the friendly treatment he was receiving, as if these men were in denial of their actions... in denial of Cherock being thoughtlessly killed for nothing more than trying to return home.

A few regular soldiers carried in a table and chairs unloaded from a wagon outside, and Jan realized the captain and lieutenant meant to dine in some style. Within moments, goblets of wine were poured, and a plate of fruit was carried in and set upon the table, and Captain Oakes handed Jan a goblet.

"Have a drink first. Then play us something lively."

The wine was good, and Jan drained the goblet. Something lively? In only a short time in here, he could see these men—except for Braeden—wanted to laugh. They were eager for their own escape... to pretend they were not destroying families and condemning a large number of men to death should it all come down to fighting the trained soldiers of the Väränj.

If his actions could win their trust, Jan was only too glad to oblige them.

He spotted two daggers on the table near the fruit plate. Perhaps later, he could pocket one without being noticed. Opening the case, he took out the violin, raised it to his shoulder, and retrieved the bow with his right hand.

More food was carried in as the officers sat down to dine, and Jan began to play.

The first song was a jaunty piece more suited to a large room occupied by people who wished to dance. However, it was complicated, requiring a good deal of finger work, and Captain Oakes watched him work the bow and strings, eventually nodding in approval.

Jan kept this up until the men nearly finished with dinner and then added his voice to the strings. He sang a bawdy tale about a village strumpet who found herself "with child." Each stanza recounted her unsuccessful efforts to pin the deed on yet another man.

By the time he finished, Captain Oakes was laughing out loud, along with the other men—except for the lieutenant. Braeden sat with a politely pained expression, as if the entire evening was beneath him.

"Very good!" Oakes called, still laughing.

"Can you do card tricks?" another man asked.

"I can."

In truth, this suited Jan, as it got him closer to the table. He pulled a tattered deck from the violin case, and he had a feeling these officers would prefer something simple. For a while, he just played "hide the queen," by placing three cards face down—including one queen—and he moved them around on the table, letting the men take turns trying to keep visual track of the queen and pick her out. Sometimes he palmed and replaced the card. Sometimes, he left it in and allowed one of the men to point her out, to keep them from being discouraged. No money changed hands, and he focused more on keeping the men entertained.

"Can you show me how you do that?" one asked.

"Ah, no," Jan answered. "I'd be giving away the secrets of my mother's people."

Captain Oakes just watched, but he appeared grateful for the diversion. Jan was offered food and more wine.

The earlier soldiers who'd delivered the table and chairs returned and started clearing away the remnants of dinner. The officers got up and made room for them. Jan remained seated as the men he'd just been entertaining began talking amongst themselves.

However, one of the regular soldiers came close, eyeing him in a less friendly fashion than the officers.

Jan swept his hand across table, and the fanned out cards slid smoothly together. While the soldier looked on in brief astonishment, Jan had already swept one of the daggers away behind his sleeve with his other hand. When he dropped the deck back into the case with the violin, it was easy to slip the blade up his sleeve.

The dinner gathering began breaking up and the officers left the main tent. Captain Oakes glanced at Jan with an expression of mild regret.

"Sorry, lad, you'll have to sleep outside with all the others."

"Of course," Jan answered. "Thank you for the wine and chance to play."

Oakes waved his thanks away. "I should be thanking you. It was good for the men. As I said earlier, this is a nasty business."

Indeed, Jan thought dryly as he took up the violin case, careful not to let the dagger slip out of hiding. On the walk back toward one of the campfires to sleep on the ground, he wondered what he had really gained tonight. Besides stealing a dagger and possibly winning the captain's appreciation, he was no closer to getting away from these Äntes soldiers than he'd been at dusk.

Surely, he must possess some skill, some talent he could use to escape. But what?

His mother's people had trained him in their ways, and he was a decent pickpocket. However, a palmed dagger wouldn't do much good against trained soldiers with swords.

He was adequate at card trick and reading palms. He was highly skilled at playing his violin and making women fall in love with him, but surely there must be something more? He'd always thought well of himself, and he could not be boiled down to those few capabilities.

Had he been lazy?

Mulling over his pathetically limited skills, he could see no way to use any of them to help him escape before the Äntes reached Enêmûsk... where he would find himself trapped inside a city wall.

After spending the night and the next day in a crowded storage room below the keep, Julianna wondered what their next step might be. She was on the verge of asking when Zupan Cadell pushed through the crowded little room to the door and stepped out into the open passage.

"We need to find out what's going on above," he said.

There were about twenty people in the room, including Nadja and young Gideon, and everyone listened in silence. When Nadja rose to join her husband, Julianna followed.

"What if all the men are still here?" Nadja asked, "and maybe one or more happen to be in the kitchen when one of us steps out and is instantly seen? We will have given ourselves away."

Julianna knew she was right, but they couldn't stay down here forever. Sooner or later, someone needed to check the main floor.

"Perhaps..." Cadell began, hesitating. "Perhaps someone can go up without being seen."

Nadja shook her head. "What do you mean?"

Cadell sighed and glanced away. "There is a hidden passage inside the keep, down here. It leads up into a dead end... with a spy hole looking into the main hall."

Disbelief flooded Nadja's lovely face. "And you never told me? Did you tell Jan?"

He shook his head once.

"How did you know?" Nadja went on, her dark eyes moving back and forth while absorbing this information. Julianna kept silent for now, just listening.

"Lord Malbek knew and he told me," Cadell answered, sounding deeply embarrassed. He and Nadja did not keep secrets from each other. "I'd almost forgotten, as I never thought we'd have need of it. When we first arrived, the place was so bleak and dark, I didn't think to burden you with any more secrets about this place... and as time went on, it didn't seem important."

"Well, it's important now," Julianna put in to move this along. "One of us needs to use this passage to see what's happening."

"I'll go," Cadell said.

"You?" Julianna breathed.

The zupan was aging, his waistline thickening, and he sometimes puffed when climbing stairs. Nadja was still slender, but Julianna knew that she was beginning to have to problems with her knees—pain and stiffening. Either one certainly *could* take the passage up to spy on the main hall, but Julianna saw another option.

"I could go," young Gideon suggested.

Julianna turned to him, noting his crooked teeth and cow-licked hair with fondness. He was brave but just a boy, and upon seeing the situation upstairs, comprehending all aspects of the situation would require adult thinking and adult decisions.

"No, I will go," Julianna said. "I can do this without being heard or noticed and bring back a report."

Nadja went pale. "Should you be caught... I cannot... I cannot think of what might happen to you."

"I won't be caught," Julianna insisted. "How could I be? Not if this passage works the way the zupan says. I'm quiet and quick on my feet, and you need someone old enough to understand anything seen."

The zupan was silent for a moment and then picked up a lantern. "Come with me."

Nadja appeared to bite back further arguments as Julianna followed Cadell down the rectangular passage toward the dead end. Upon reaching the wall, she expected him to stop, when—to her amazement —he appeared to walk into the wall.

But he didn't vanish. He stood there in plain sight, *inside* the wall.

"Come, my girl," he said. "There's no real trick."

As she drew closer in following him, something strange caught her eye. The dead end wall appeared to separate from the sidewalls, and she found herself looking through an opening beyond which the zupan stood.

The stones of the wall beyond the zupan had been perfectly lined up with those of the passage's sidewalls to create the illusion of a solid wall blocking the way. She now saw the side passage ahead to the right beyond Cadell.

He stepped out, and she stepped in.

"I don't think you're in any danger," he said, handing her the lantern. "But keep quiet when you reach the top, and leave the lantern on the stairs. You'll be at the back of the main hall. There is a small hole that looks like only a crack between the stones from the outside."

She nodded. "I won't be long."

Gripping the lantern's handle, she turned in and made her way up the stairs. The climb felt long, but she stepped slowly and lightly, hearing the voices of men before she even reached the top.

"I told you I'd find us a good spot," a deep voice growled. "What could be better than this? The kitchen's well stocked and the ale casks are full."

At the top of the stairs, where the passage leveled out, she set down the lantern and crept toward a spot of light ahead. There at the hole, wider on her side than the crack in the pocket of stone, she leaned in to peek through the wall.

Exactly as the zupan had described, she was at the back of the main hall with a full view of the room. What she saw made her stop breathing for an instant.

About twenty filthy men had taken all the bedding and blankets down from the upstairs rooms—including her own—and spread them in front of the great hearth. Hams and wheels of cheese and a cask of ale had been taken from the kitchen and placed on the long wooden table.

As Gideon had mentioned, the men wore no colors of any house, but they were armed with short swords or cutlasses or axes. Unshaved and unwashed, one of them tore off a piece of ham with his fingers and shoved it into his mouth.

Resentment bubbled inside Julianna. She and Nadja had been saving those hams.

The largest man sported a shaved head and a full beard. He wore a leather hauberk and a sword, and he swaggered when he walked, going to the ale cask and drawing himself a mug.

"Didn't I tell you?" he challenged, and she recognized the same deep voice from a few moments before. "I found us a right good spot."

"That you did, Argyle," answered the man chewing the ham. "We can live like lords here. No sense in us trying to go home now. I got nothing to go home to."

Julianna went cold. They planned to remain, to *live* here? They were probably deserters who had once been conscripted. She counted the hams and cheeses on the table, knowing there wasn't much more food in the kitchen. Once that was gone, these men would start looking for more. Sooner or later, someone was bound to open the narrow door behind the kitchen and see the stairwell.

At present, these men had everything they could want at their fingertips, but how long would that last?

They weren't ransacking the place for valuables. They were moving in.

Turning, Julianna hurried for the stairs, grabbed her lantern, descending quickly to tell Cadell and Nadja what she'd seen.

After a long day's forced march, Jan stumbled behind the man in front of him, as the contingent entered a village. Women, children, and elderly men scurried aside to let Äntes soldiers and their conscripts pass.

Jan assumed their younger men had already been taken. He expected Captain Oakes to lead the way out the village's other side and find an open spot down the road to make camp.

Instead, the captain took them down a side path, through about a hundred paces of trees, and stopped in front of a large two-story manor surrounded by a wall. Guards at the gate opened up, and to Jan's surprise, the soldiers began herding the conscripts through. He found himself walking through a vast courtyard of light-colored tan stone.

The manor was constructed from the same tan stone, and as Jan had never seen anything like it before, he assumed the stone had been shipped in from elsewhere long ago. The courtyard was so large that even with all the soldiers, their horses, and the conscripts, there was plenty of room to move about. An unfamiliar man beside him began to breathe heavily, as if in fear.

Jan looked at him. "What's wrong?"

"This is the lieutenant's family home. We're only one day from Enêmûsk. What do you think they will do with us there? Put us up on the wall to take the first round of arrows?"

Jan had no intention of finding out.

He watched Captain Oakes and Lieutenant Braeden dismount and pass off their horses. Carefully, he moved through other conscripts to get as close to the manor as possible. The front doors opened and four women in fine gowns came out. A middle-aged woman with a kind face nearly ran to the captain, gripping his hands in affection.

"Brother," she said, smiling. "I heard you were coming through here, and I came to visit Gisele in the hope of seeing you."

The captain pulled his hands from hers and embraced her with both arms, lifting her feet off the ground in a most undignified manner. "Margareta. What a surprise. But you shouldn't have risked the roads right now."

Two of the other women greeted two other officers, but Jan's attention shifted sharply to the fourth woman. A lovely creature in a pale blue gown, probably not yet twenty, she had shining red-gold hair hanging to the small of her back. Her eyes were the same pale blue as her gown, and her skin was flawless.

With her slender, white hands clasped against her stomach, she walked to Lieutenant Braeden and bowed her head. "My lord."

He nodded in return and didn't touch her.

"Is all ready for tonight's banquet?" he asked.

"Yes, my lord."

Captain Oakes walked over and grasped one of her hands, raising it to his mouth. "Ah, Gisele. I always said Braeden would marry the most beautiful woman in Droevinka."

Her face broke into a smile, as if hungry for his approval—or perhaps any approval.

As opposed to being offended by the captain's familiarity, Braeden's expression shifted to one of pride. Jan was good at reading faces, and he understood the situation instantly. The lieutenant had no love for the girl, but he was proud to have her as his wife, as a possession.

And with that thought, Jan saw a way to use one of his talents to set himself free. It was risky, but in being only one day outside of Enêmûsk, he was willing to try anything.

How could he gracefully get himself inside to entertain at the banquet?

His mind was racing when Captain Oakes spotted him and solved the problem.

"Oh, Jan, come here," he called.

Jan did.

"This one is quite good with that violin he carries," the captain told his sister, and then he turned back to Jan. "Would you to consent to play for us? If you do, I'll try to find you a place to sleep inside."

"It would be my pleasure," Jan answered.

Glancing towards the lieutenant, he found Gisele staring at his face. She looked away and then couldn't help looking again.

Braeden frowned.

"What do you say, lieutenant?" Captain Oakes asked. "Should the ladies have some music tonight?"

"Whatever you wish, sir," Braeden answered tightly. "I am your humble host."

The lieutenant was hardly humble, but Jan didn't care. With access to Gisele, the next part would be easy, and anything after that was up to fate.

Down in a storage room below the keep, Julianna reported what she'd seen in the main hall. Zupan Cadell went pale and Nadja's mouth was tight as they both listened. Everyone in the room heard the truth, and Gideon's mother, Sari, took in the news with bleak eyes.

"Will this never end?" she asked.

She was young to have a twelve-year-old boy, and when he was born, she probably hadn't been much older than he was now. Her husband had been conscripted by the Äntes.

"Perhaps..." Zupan Cadell began, "perhaps it is time we slip upstairs, go out the back, and abandon the keep, at least for now."

Sari looked up sharply. "And live in the woods like animals? Sleeping in the cold?"

"Nizhyn Village is only a two day walk," he answered. "We could head there."

"And what if it no longer exists?" Nadja asked quietly. "What if the Äntes conscripted men from there, and then the Väränj burned it to the ground. We'd be little more than victims out on the open road, and we might arrive in Nizhyn to find nothing waiting for us."

Cadell fell silent. Nadja was right—on several counts.

"We have to find a way to make the men upstairs leave," Julianna said suddenly.

Everyone looked at her.

"How?" Cadell asked.

"I don't know... but for twenty years, this place had such a dark reputation that the Äntes couldn't get anyone to remain as vassal." She looked into Sari's eyes and added, "We all remember."

Sari nodded. "The ghost."

Cadell frowned, as if they were wasting time. "What ghost?"

Julianna glanced at Nadja. There had been a ghost in this keep, the victim of horrifying events over twenty years past. Nadja had managed to get rid of the ghost while Cadell was away, and she'd never told him about it. Neither had Jan or Julianna.

At the time, their zupan had had more than enough on his plate.

"Just stories, of course," Nadja put in quickly, "but there were a few unexplained deaths, including a young lord throwing himself from the tower. The place was said to be haunted."

Julianna sighed, wondering why she'd even brought this up. "Well, we can't conjure up a ghost."

"We don't need to," Nadja said. "We only need make those men upstairs believe."

Listening intently, young Gideon asked, "You mean dress someone up in torn sheets and paint their face white? Have that one wave their arms and scream and scare the men? I'll do it."

Nadja smiled at him. "No, that isn't quite what I meant."

The zupan appeared put off—almost annoyed—by this entire discussion, as if he wanted to start planning something serious, but then Nadja began to speak again, pouring out the threads of an idea that caused him to put his hand to his mouth while listening.

Julianna felt her heart beating faster. Could it work?

"We need to do more than frighten them," she said. "They have to believe themselves in true danger."

Still hesitant, Cadell finally sighed. "I might be able to help with that."

Julianna inched in on Nadja, speaking as quietly as possible. "You'll be the one up the secret passage, inside the room with the spy hole. Will your knees be all right if you need to move quickly?"

For the first time ever, Nadja looked at Julianna in something akin to anger. "My knees are *fine*."

Julianna glanced away, sorry she'd asked.

"So... if we do this," Sari began, "how do we start?"

The other villagers in the room looked to Cadell for an answer. Once a decision had been made, he was never long in taking action. Stepping between a few of them, he picked up two burlap bags of apples and dumped out their contents, leaving only the empty bags in his grip.

"Gideon, get a few of the boys to come help me search the rooms, around, behind, and inside any crates. We need to start hunting."

Jan played nothing lively that night at dinner. Inside the main hall of the manor, he walked around the table where the officers and their sisters or wives ate and he kept up a string of beautiful, slow songs, filling the place with a haunting, melancholy air.

Every time he passed Gisele, he could see her struggling not to look at him, and he timed each pass near her with the most heart-aching strains of a tune. Throughout the meal, Braeden all but ignored her, except when he chastised her choice of brook trout instead of silver salmon for the fish course.

She apologized.

As dinner ended, one of the lower officers suggested a game of cards, but the captain hesitated.

Motioning Jan over, Oakes asked, "I think the men would like to play cards on their own for a while, so they can place bets. Would you mind entertaining the ladies? Maybe show them a few of your tricks?"

The man was probably not remotely aware how condescending he sounded, but Jan couldn't have been happier. This was easier than he'd expected.

"Of course. Tell them I'll read their palms."

"Oh, my sister would enjoy that. Thank you."

Not long after, Jan was seated near the hearth with Margareta, Gisele, and the other two women—whose names he quickly learned were Brenna and Camille. The latter two were married to Äntes officers and had traveled here with the captain's sister. Jan thought it would be easy to grow fond of Margareta, who possessed a warm spirit. He didn't think on this for long, however, as Gisele was his target.

"And have you actually traveled with the Móndya-lítko?" Margareta asked him, leaning forward in her chair.

"Nearly every autumn of my life. My mother and I join her sister's family, and we roll through the towns and villages putting on shows."

"How romantic," she sighed. "I'm sure most of the village girls swoon at your feet."

Jan blinked at her honesty. Most women of her rank didn't pay such compliments to men of his status. But he recovered quickly and flashed her a smile. "I fear they do."

She, Brenna, and Camille laughed. Gisele only smiled nervously, her eyes still moving over his face.

"So, can you tell us our futures?" Margareta asked.

"I can. Who would like to go first?"

He hoped it would not be Gisele, as he wanted her to continue watching him in action for a little while. She was starved for love and approval, and he needed to make her aware of her hunger.

"I will," Camille said, pulling her chair closer to his. Then suddenly, she seemed to grow hesitant and asked, "Can you really tell the future?"

For the first time, he took her in. She wasn't as young as Gisele, but she was only in her mid-twenties, with rich brown hair and a round face.

"I've been told I have a gift," he said, avoiding a direct answer.

She lowered her voice. "Can you tell me... will I have a child soon? I have been married two years, and nothing has come of it. It is... painful for me. I so want a child."

Despite everything, Jan forgot the room around him. For a few moments he even forgot Gisele. He could see what Camille's question had cost her to ask in front of the other women.

Reaching out, he grasped her hand, running his finger lightly down the inside of her palm. "I see a boy," he said. "A young boy with brown hair like yours, running to you. You are a good mother to him, and he loves you."

She put her free hand to her mouth. "Truly?"

Jan nodded once.

Normally, when pretending to read palms, he was nowhere near this specific, but this situation was different. He needed to put on quite a show, and she was clearly in pain. Perhaps believing the child would come might help ease her mind... and a child would come. He hoped so.

Margareta was watching him with a thoughtful expression. "Gisele," she said. "You go next."

Turning his chair toward Gisele, Jan extended his hand. "May I?"

Trembling slightly, Gisele held out her hand, and he took it, turning it over and running his fingers slowly and lightly across her palm. She drew in a quick breath at the sensation.

"Do you have a question?" he asked, leaning closer to her.

"No... I... No, just tell me what you see."

He kept moving his fingers lightly over her palm. "I see great love in your future and adventure, a life you never thought possible, with joy in every day."

"Oh," Brenna said. "Perhaps the lieutenant will take you with him on his next assignment? I wonder where you will go."

Gisele's face clouded at the suggestion.

Jan could see that she barely knew her husband and didn't care to know any more. Women of her station were usually viewed as chattel by their parents, bargaining chips in marriage to strengthen alliances between families. As a result, they were guarded carefully until such a marriage was arranged. This poor girl had been sold off to the cold, arrogant Lieutenant Braeden.

Jan knew that what he had planned for this night would greatly injure her—and possibly ruin the rest of her life.

But that didn't stop him.

"You see love?" she asked.

"Yes," he breathed.

Across the hall, the men were still playing cards.

L ate in the night, with Gideon right behind her, Julianna paused at the top of the stairs where the closed door emptied into the kitchen. Nadja had already taken the secret passage from below and was heading upwards in a different stairwell. Julianna and Gideon's part in the plan was more dangerous—and somewhat distasteful—but they'd both agreed.

Each one of them carried a wriggling burlap sack, and Julianna tried not to think about what was inside.

Putting her free hand to the door's latch, she whispered, "Ready?"

"Yup," Gideon answered from behind.

They'd waited until this late hour in the hope that the invading men had consumed enough ale to fall asleep by the fire in the main hall. Still, Julianna cracked the door slowly and peeked out, both looking and listening.

"Seems clear," she whispered.

Stepping into the small passage, she turned left into the kitchen. It was empty of people, but a cask of ale sat atop a butcher-block table, causing her to breath in relief. The men hadn't taken it yet.

Passing off her wriggling bag, she told Gideon, "Hold this for a moment."

"What are you doing?"

"Something Nadja asked me to do."

Finding a heavy knife, Julianna pried off the cask's lid and drew a good-sized pouch from her pocket. Opening the pouch, she dumped its dried, powered contents into the cask and then replaced the lid, making more noise than she wished by pounding it in place.

"What did you put in there?" Gideon asked.

"I don't really know. It's a ground herb Nadja gave me."

Taking back her wriggling bag, she led the way onward, deeper inside the keep until they reached the archway of the main hall. Careful to remain outside, Julianna peered around the edge. All the men were sleeping, snoring at various levels, their bodies scattered about on the floor, on top of the bedding they'd dragged down. Asleep, they didn't look quite so fierce.

Both she and Gideon knew not to speak and give themselves away. Their part in this was simple but critical, and they had to wait for the exact instant. So they crouched, listening to the snores in waiting —and waiting. Julianna was beginning to worry that something had gone wrong on Nadja's end when the first wail rang out.

It was loud and long and like nothing she had ever heard before.

Gideon flinched beside her, glancing about in alarm.

The second wail rang out, and the men on the floor began stirring, rolling onto their hands and knees.

"What the...?"

The second wail faded, and a voice carried through the air, hollow but filled with a mix of pain and rage.

"Out, defilers!" the voice cried. "This place belongs to the dead! The last lord who refused to leave finally flung himself from the tower."

The bald leader was on his feet, looking all around, but even Julianna—who knew—could not tell from which direction the voice was coming.

It sounded nothing like Nadja.

"For your crime of invading this haven of the dead, you will be punished," the voice droned on. "You will be plagued by rats, and your food will never pass through your stomachs. It will be expelled from your bodies until you die."

The eerie quality of the voice was so unsettling that Julianna found herself wanting to run, and Gideon's eyes were wide.

All the men were on their feet now, hands moving to weapons, but it was still impossible to tell from where the voice came.

"Rats!" it cried. "You will be plagued by rats."

Upon hearing their cue, Julianna and Gideon leaned out as far as possible without being seen and dumped the contents of their bags. Around twenty panicked rats ran from the archway into the hall, straight for the men—who began shouting.

"Rats!" one of them called.

"Over there! More! Get 'em off the blankets!"

A few men swung with their weapons, trying to hit the racing rodents.

Julianna and Gideon did not stay to see the rest. Gripping their emptied bags, they whirled and ran for the kitchen. She reached the door first, pulled it open, and shooed Gideon inside. Only when she'd followed and pulled the door closed did Julianna take a full breath.

She heard no one coming after them.

"Down," she whispered.

Gideon didn't need to be told twice and hurried down the stairs.

At the bottom, Julianna stopped him. "Tell the zupan what happened. I'm going to Nadja."

Without waiting for an answer, she ran to the dead end wall and passed through. Halfway up the stairs beyond, she began to pant but kept pressed onward until she reached the top.

Nadja knelt on the floor before the peephole, her red dress spread all around her legs. Looking back at Julianna, she held a finger to her lips. Julianna crept forward and knelt down. Nadja's expression was distressed, and she tilted her head toward the spy hole.

Julianna peeked through.

A few rats lay dead on the floor, but the others had scattered, and the men were arguing.

"I say we leave now," a wiry man with no armor insisted. "I've heard of this place. I'd forgotten, but I have. A young lord threw himself off a tower some years back in these parts... and folks say he was plagued by the dead."

"By the dead?" Argyle scoffed. "So you're going to let a few rats run us off at some voice, likely a skulking peasant?"

"More than rats," a middle-aged man in chain armor put in. "We've been over every inch of this place. There's no one here... alive, that is. I say we pack up."

"We stay!" Argyle roared and, putting one hand on the hilt of his sword, he waved the other about the hall while slightly lowering his voice. "You want to leave this keep and go back to robbing beggars on the road? I don't care if the place is haunted or not. I won't let some screaming voice and a few rats chase me out of here. What about the rest of you?"

Almost shamefaced, the other men began agreeing with him. One cut off a fresh slice of cheese, and a few others began bedding down again.

Julianna sat back in near despair, whispering, "We failed."

"Not yet. You put the herbs into the second cask of ale?"

"Yes."

"Good. They should break into that by tomorrow night. Then they'll have bigger problems than vermin."

A s the men continued playing cards in the manor's hall, Jan approached the captain and leaned down.

"Might I go outside and answer the call of nature?" Jan asked. "I swear I will return straight away."

"Of course," Oakes answered.

This was hardly a kind concession, as even if Jan should try to run, he'd never get past the courtyard gates.

"How are the ladies doing?" Oakes asked him.

"Well, I think. When I come back, I'll show them some card tricks they might enjoy."

Oakes nodded and turned back to placing a bet.

Jan started for the archway out of the hall, but Gisele stood to one side of it, stretching her legs and watching him. As he passed her, he slowed long enough to whisper, "Make an excuse to leave and meet me outside the kitchen door."

Though he hadn't seen the kitchen, most manors such as this always had a back door for deliveries. At this point in the game, he wasn't worried.

Gisele's blue eyes flooded with shock and then excitement—just as he knew they would—and she nodded almost imperceptibly.

He walked out of the hall and stopped a serving girl coming toward him. "The kitchens? I've been sent on an errand."

She pointed down a passage. "That way."

With a nod of thanks, he followed the passage, walked through the kitchen—ignoring the surprised faces of two cooks and three scullery maids—and went out the back door. The night air was cool but not cold, and he waited, though not for long.

The kitchen door cracked open, and Gisele stepped outside.

He'd chosen this meeting place because now five people had seen him walk out, only to be followed moments later by the mistress of the house.

Gisele walked toward him—lovely and sheltered, naïve and lonely—and he had to push down all regrets over what he was about to do.

"Jan," she breathed in wonder as she stepped close enough for him to touch.

He took her hands in his own and whispered back, "You are so beautiful... and kind and gentle. I can see so much in your eyes."

Her expression filled with longing, as if she wanted him to keep talking, to go on lavishing praise and approval upon her. Braeden must be a blackheart to have done this to his young wife.

Instead of saying more, Jan leaned in slowly, giving her every chance to pull away. He gently pressed his mouth to hers. Though she flinched at first, her mouth then moved clumsily against his, as if she'd never been kissed with any kind of softness.

Pulling back, he said, "Come away with me, tonight. My father is the vassal of Chemestúk Keep. You won't ever have to do without. I can take care of you, and in the autumn, when my mother and I go to travel with the Móndyalítko, you will come with us. She will love you as I do."

He saw the effect his words had on her as she pictured a life with him—someone who praised her and thought well of her, with a mother-in-law who would love her. Adventure for a few moons of the year on the open road with the Móndyalítko... and best of all, she could leave behind the hollow life she currently lived.

"Will you?" he asked.

"How will we get the guards to open the front gates?"

That was a more intelligent question than he expected.

"You are the lady of the manor. Have your husband's guard not always followed your orders?"

She blinked several times, thinking and then nodded. "Yes... yes, they have."

"Then order them to open the gates."

Jan knew full well that the guards would never allow Braeden's lady to leave the grounds in the middle of the night with some dusky stranger wearing three rings in his ear. But he had no intention of ever taking her that far. As long as she believed it was possible, that was all that mattered.

"All right," she said, as if waking up from a dream. "I'll come with you... anywhere with you. Take me away from this place."

Jan faltered for an instant, but his parents and Julianna were alone in the middle of a civil war.

"Would you give me something to keep close to my breast?" he asked.

"What?"

"A lock of your hair."

Tears sprang to her eyes, and she kissed him again.

Crouching down, he pulled the dagger from where he'd been keeping it inside his boot, and he cut off a small lock of her hair, holding it between his fingers.

"Go pack," he said. "When you return, we'll find horses. Don't let your husband or the captain see you."

With a joyful nod, she ran back into the house.

Jan waited long enough for her to get upstairs, and then he re-entered the manor himself, walking past the shocked kitchen staff again and continuing on to the main hall. The men were still playing cards, and he went to the lieutenant and leaned down.

"A word out in the passage," he said quietly.

Braeden frowned, but didn't appear eager to be seen arguing with someone of Jan's rather uncertain status here—not quite a servant and not quite a guest. Rising, he followed Jan out into a wide passage where the stairs to the upper floor were a few paces to their right.

"What do you want?" Braeden asked, as if uncomfortable even speaking to Jan.

"I've just talked your wife into running away with me. She's upstairs packing."

Braeden's expression flattened in shock and quickly hardened with rage as he stepped backward. "You dare you make such a—"

His words broke off as Jan held up the lock of red-gold hair.

"A number of your kitchen staff saw me walk outside," he said. "Lady Gisele followed, and they saw her re-enter... shortly followed by me." He dropped his voice even lower. "Take me outside *right now*, order your guards to open the gates and let me go, or I swear I'll make sure everyone here knows your wife agreed to run off with some tzigän scum rather than stay here with you. You'll be a laughing stock."

Braeden's face turned ashen. There was only an ornately sheathed dagger on his belt, and he pulled the weapon.

"Unless I kill you here."

Jan still held his dagger by the hilt, its blade flat against his forearm. In a quick back-step, he spun it point-out before himself.

"No doubt you'll best me," he said, "but not before I yell loud enough to bring everyone running, and I'll make sure they know why we're fighting." He paused. "And your lady is about to come down those stairs with her bags packed."

The muscles in Braeden's jaw were twitching as he stared in Jan in hate, but Jan could also see his mind working. The one thing Braeden could not abide, could never allow, was a wound to his pride. He cared nothing for Gisele, but he would probably rather die than have word get out that she'd agreed to run away with Jan.

"All you need do is let me go," Jan added, "and no one will ever know what happened tonight except you, me, and Gisele."

"Don't say her name!" Braeden hissed, but he glanced at the stairs nervously.

He believes me, Jan thought. *He knows she'll be coming down any moment.*

With another hiss through his teeth, Braeden tilted his head toward the front doors.

"After you," Jan whispered, for he wasn't about to let the man get behind him with a dagger.

Together, they left the manor and headed for the gate. A few soldiers straightened at the approach and passing of their lieutenant, but not one of them would say a word without being spoken to first.

"Tell the captain you took pity on me," Jan said. "I have a feeling he might understand."

"Don't speak to me."

As they reached the gates, a sound from behind caused Jan to turn. Gisele came running around the side of the manor and stopped cold at the sight of her tall husband by the gates with Jan. She wore a cloak and carried a traveling bag.

She stood staring.

At the sight of her, Braeden's face filled with hatred again, and Jan tried not to think of what would happen to the girl later... and over the following years. Instead, he pictured Julianna's face.

"Open up," Braeden ordered his guards.

His men obeyed.

Without looking back, Jan ran through the open gates and down the road.

The following night, Julianna and Nadja crouched inside the secret room, taking turns watching through the peephole in the stones. In the main hall beyond, the new cask was on the table, and the men had been drawing mugs from it.

"Not long now," Nadja whispered.

"What will it do to them?" Julianna asked.

She knew Nadja would never poison these men— or at least not kill them. Nadja was no killer, no matter what the situation.

But the answer never came.

Instead, as Nadja watched from the peephole, she said, "One of them is turning green. It's time."

Taking a long breath, Nadja let out a wail.

Julianna could barely believe the sound, loud and long and otherworldly.

"Get out! This place belongs to the dead," Nadja cried in that voice too deep to be her own. "Your food will no longer sustain you."

An instant later, Julianna heard the retching begin below.

Pulling back, Nadja motioned Julianna to the peephole. Looking through, she saw a number of men on their knees, vomiting all over the floor and the bedding, and she realized Nadja must have used a purging herb. Julianna had heard of such, but she herself had little knowledge of herb lore.

More of the men began retching violently.

Then Julianna saw that Argyle was not bent over. He was not even tinged green. Had he not tasted from the new cask yet? He stood looking around in anger and suspicion.

"Someone else is here," he mouthed so quietly that Julianna only read it on his lips.

Turning, he strode from the hall.

Where was he going? Would he start searching again? If so, how long before he opened the door beyond the kitchen?

Standing quickly, she whispered, "I'll go tell Cadell this has started. You stay and watch. Hopefully, they will leave this time."

She fled down the narrow stairs, but upon coming out at the bottom, she ran across the rectangular space between the storage rooms. Everyone down here was still hiding inside the two rooms with the doors closed. No one saw her as she dashed up the stairwell to the kitchen, desperate to reach the upper door before Argyle.

At the top, she didn't hesitate and slipped out the door, going straight for the butcher-block table and picking up the heavy rolling pin that she and Nadja used to make pie crust.

With the rolling pin in hand, she hid behind the archway between the kitchen and the inner passage. Her plan was half mad, but it was all she could think of. When Argyle walked through, she'd swing hard, hopefully cracking his skull with the first blow. She was no trained fighter, but the rolling pin was as solid as a cudgel, and she was fairly certain she could crack a man's skull with so heavy a weapon.

After that... well, she'd think about that later. Zupan Cadell could come up and help her drag the body downstairs. Argyle would simply vanish. Without him, the other men would leave.

Swift footsteps were coming, and she pressed her back against the wall. She'd only have one chance at this, and she knew it.

His wide form passed through the door, and she took a step forward and swung. Unfortunately, he'd been walking faster than she calculated, and she only clipped the back of his head, hard enough to hurt, but not do much damage.

Roaring in surprise, he whirled around, and they locked eyes. Up close, his shaved head was filthy, and his beard was flecked with bits of food. His shoulders were broad inside his leather hauberk, twice as wide as her own.

He had not drawn his sword, and it was still sheathed on his hip.

Though he'd been momentarily startled, that passed quickly, and his upper lip curled back.

"A girl," he spat in derision. "I knew it. That was you calling through the wall somehow?" His deep-set eyes moved up and down her red dress. "I'll make you sorry for poisoning my men."

Panic flooded through her. Sucking in a loud breath, she wailed at him, trying to pitch her voice exactly as Nadja had done, and a loud, unsettling sound exploded from her mouth.

It startled him, and he stepped back.

Knowing she had only an instant, and still gripping her rolling pin, she dashed through the kitchen for the back door of the keep, shoving it open and nearly flying outside into the night air. She could hear him coming behind her.

A part of her knew this was foolish—running blindly—but she could think of nothing else, and her long legs had served her well in the past when she'd needed to escape.

She ran around the corner of the keep, and then around the side of the single turret, scrambling over the rocks, unsure where she was even trying to go.

To her horror, she could hear him gaining.

And then... she heard a grunt and a thud.

Juliana didn't stop. She only slowed in glancing back and then slowed more.

Argyle lay among old fallen wall stones long covered in creeping weeds, and he was struggling to get up. He didn't know the grounds as well as she did in living here for years, and he must have slipped on or tripped over some of the rubble.

Instinct took hold, and she ran back at him.

Just as he saw her coming, and his eyes widened...

Juliana slammed the rolling pin with both hands against the side of his head.

This time she heard a loud crack on impact. She drew back to bash him again—and she missed as he flopped to one side. Quickly retreating, before he could grab her ankle, she thought to turn and run again. But he only lay there, not moving, and she finally crept closer.

When she saw his open eyes, even in the dark, she almost bolted, but his eyes didn't blink. They stared across the damp earth the other way.

He was dead.

Julianna stood there panting for a few moments, trying to come to grips with the fact that she'd just killed a man. Then she wondered what to do with the body.

A thought struck her, and she raised her eyes to the top of the turret. From where he lay, it looked as if he'd fallen... or thrown himself, just as that last young lord who'd refused to leave this place. Stepping back, Julianna left him there and she walked back inside, slipping through the door leading to the storage rooms below.

Sometime in the night, the men must have found Argyle's body, because Nadja came down to announce that they had all packed up and left.

The days passed quickly, and Jan almost never stopped moving as he headed east. He rested no more than he absolutely had to, thinking only of his parents and Julianna. Along the road there was little to eat, and he drank water from streams, or even puddles.

When he realized he was less than half a league from Chemestúk, even in exhaustion, he broke into a jog, finding strength in the knowledge that he was almost home.

As the edge of the village came into sight, he slowed, first in disbelief and then alarm.

The sight of a blackened hut filled his vision, and he kept walking forward until he could see it all.

The place had been burned and two bodies with smashed skulls lay out in plain sight. No one had buried them... suggesting there was no one left.

Looking up to the keep, he whispered, "No."

He broke into a run.

.　　.　　.

J ulianna walked through the courtyard of the keep, still trying to come to terms with the fact that she had killed a man. Worse, she wasn't sorry, and if she were given that night to do all over again, she'd have acted the same. Perhaps that bothered her more than anything.

Life at the keep was returning to normal in a sense, but everyone was worried about their lost men, and she couldn't stop thinking about Jan, about what might be happening to him, what he might be suffering.

The zupan had announced that tomorrow, they would all go down into the village and begin the clean-up... and to bury their dead. He'd been so set on keeping everyone hidden, on protecting them, but now he seemed to realize it was time to move forward.

Julianna wondered if it was even possible to move forward.

With a sigh, she was about to walk back inside the keep, when movement caught her eye. Looking out through the broken gate and down the road, she saw someone running toward her. She froze, ready to sound the alarm... when she noticed the green shade of his shirt.

"Jan?" she said to herself.

Running through the gate, she closed the distance rapidly. He slowed, and she stopped when they were barely a few paces apart. She wanted to throw herself into his arms, but they had never even touched that much before. He looked terrible, thin and filthy. Worse, his eyes were bleak, and more, they were haunted. She'd never seen him like this.

"Oh, Julianna," he said, even his voice sounded different. "Are my parents...?"

It hit her then that he must have come through village, and he'd been taken before the massacre.

"They're all right," she answered quickly, closing the distance one more step. "Both are inside, along with... what's left of... everyone. Your father has been hiding those who survived."

Then it truly sank in that Jan was back—and safe—and she looked down the road beyond him.

"Did you... did anyone else escape with you?"

He dropped his gaze and wouldn't look at her.

"No," he choked. "I was only able to... and I had to do something... awful... to get free."

She'd done something awful too, that she didn't want to tell him.

A voice spoke from behind. "Whatever you did, you did what you had to do."

Julianna spun around.

Nadja walked out the broken gate, taking in the sight of Jan with an expression beyond relief. "My son." Her gaze turned to Julianna, "And my girl. You are both safe, and that is all that matters to me." Motioning them toward the keep, she said calmly, "Dinner is ready. Both of you come and eat."

Julianna found this statement absurd. Jan had just returned, and Nadja had hardly welcomed him or asked him anything. Although Julianna could not, Nadja should be hugging him, holding him.

Then again... perhaps Jan did not want to be hugged or questioned? Maybe he simply wanted to be with his family again and let everything else wait?

Jan's expression was unreadable, but he reached out for Julianna with his right hand. For once, he wasn't trying to charm her or use his wiles for his own amusement. He seemed desperate for something to hang onto.

Reaching back, she took his hand, grasping it firmly, and led him after Nadja into the keep. ∎

CLAWS

Jan was restless. He stood on the outskirts of Chemestúk, watching his father, the zupan of the village, give orders to shabby, threadbare peasants working to rebuild their wattle and daub dwellings before autumn set in.

Earlier in the summer, the village had been caught between two factions in a civil war and burned to the ground. Well over half its occupants had either been conscripted or killed. Now, the survivors were furiously attempting to prepare for autumn.

"No," Zupan Cadell called to two people on top a roof. "That thatch must be tighter or you'll never keep out the rain." He strode forward toward a rickety ladder leaning against the new hut. "I'm coming up."

Jan's father was a barrel of a man in his late fifties with pale skin, fading freckles, and cropped red hair peppered with gray flecks. He always wore brown trousers and a brown shirt. His fingernails were forever stained dark, like his boots—as he was a hardworking man.

Jan, in contrast, was not.

Neither did he resemble his father, but rather had inherited his appearance from his mother's side. At the age of twenty-five he was slender, with even features and coal-black hair that hung to his shoulders. His complexion was smooth and dusky. Unlike the drab clothing of the people of Chemestúk, he dressed in russet breeches with high boots and a new cerulean blue shirt with the cuffs rolled halfway up his arms—and he always wore three silver hoops in one ear.

He had dressed in a similar fashion for as long as he could remember.

Yet, in the past few moons, on the inside, he'd felt himself somewhat... changed. Before, he had viewed himself as carefree, light-hearted, and someone who preferred to enjoy life as opposed to working hard.

Recent events had forced him to take a hard look at himself and instead of "care-free," the word "lazy" now came to mind. He didn't like this change and would have given almost anything to go back to viewing himself as he had before.

"Julianna!" his father called from above. "Are you there?"

"I'm here, Zupan," a voice called back.

Jan's gaze moved toward the direction of the voice. A slender, leggy young woman came around the side of the hut, and he continued to watch her. Her dark blond hair hung loose down her back. Her pale face was narrow, with a light smattering of freckles across her nose. Normally, she wore brightly colored gowns like his mother, but today she wore a dress of gray wool. The skirt only reached her shins, and she was wearing a pair of boys' breeches beneath. Even in such drab clothing, she was lovely. Once, she'd been a half-starved orphan, but Jan's mother had taken her in, and Julianna had bloomed over the years. Now, Jan's parents depended on her, as she was quite... capable.

Again, unlike Jan.

"What is it?" Julianna called up to the roof.

"I need my good hammer," Cadell answered. "Can you fetch it for me? I left it near that hut closest to the road."

"Yes, I'll go and find it."

Julianna's long body was like a coiled spring, and she broke easily into a run, hurrying toward the road. A few moments later, she came back, carrying the hammer. As she spotted Jan, she slowed and smiled hesitantly before hurrying on, and this only made him feel worse. For years, she had been the voice of his conscience, and only a few moons before, she would have stopped to berate him for not helping and probably shoved the hammer into his hand and shooed him up a ladder.

Now... she treated him like an invalid, and he didn't need to ask her why.

A few days before the village had been burned, Jan —along with other men from Chemestúk—had been conscripted and pressed into a forced march. He'd seen men from this village beheaded for trying to escape. He'd seen things he wished he could erase from his mind. He'd done something he considered unforgivable in order to escape himself, and he'd returned here thin and ill. Both his mother and Julianna had taken care of him. Now, his body had filled out again, and he looked like his previous self.

But he wasn't his previous self, and Julianna seemed to sense this. At times, he wished she would berate him the way she used to.

Upon reaching the hut where his father was working, Julianna scaled the ladder easily while carrying the hammer in one hand.

"I wish I had a portion of her energy," said a voice from behind him.

Turning, Jan watched his mother, Nadja, approach from behind, her affectionate gaze still on Julianna. The two women were fond of each other.

"Yes," he agreed. "She and father could probably rebuild the entire village by themselves."

In her mid-forties, Jan's mother was still beautiful. Today she wore a cerulean dress—that matched his new shirt—tied in at the waist with a red paisley sash. She loved her jewelry, much of which had been gifted to her by her family. Often, as now, she wore a bracelet of ruddy metal that wound up her forearm in a mix of copper and brass. That adornment depicted a detailed engraving of twining birds with long tail plumes and flecks of green stone for their eyes.

However, lately... he had sensed a change in her as well, though different from himself. He wore his scars on the inside.

Once, Nadja had been as quick and lively as Julianna. In recent days, her movements had begun to slow, and he'd occasionally noticed a shortness of breath if she walked too far. It worried him, but whenever he asked, she waved him off.

"Your eyes look so far away," she said, smiling. "What are you thinking?"

In truth, for several days, his mind had been occupied with a thought that had nothing to do with Julianna or his mother or the village, but he'd hesitated to bring it up.

"Do you really want to know?" he asked.

He and his mother were open with each other—to the point of sometimes expressing when they didn't wish to speak of serious matters.

"I do."

Both of them turned back to watching Julianna and Cadell up on the roof, wrestling with the thatch.

"Summer is over," he said. "Soon, Aunt Doreena and Uncle Rosario will be rolling through to fetch us. I find that... I almost cannot wait. I wish they would come today."

Jan's mother was of the Móndyalítko people, "the world's little children." Since he was a boy, his mother had taken him to travel with her sister's family for several moons in the autumn. In his youth, Jan had lived for those few scant moons.

Later, once his father had become the vassal of Chemestúk, Nadja and Jan had been forced to skip several years—as they had responsibilities here. But for the past two autumns, they'd resumed their tradition, living in covered wagons and breathing in the freedom of the open road.

This year... with the village in a shambles and everything that had happened, Jan's greatest fear was the prospect of having to remain at home. A part of him was certain he might be able to recapture himself, his real self, if he was set free among his mother's people again.

Turning, his eyes searched her face, seeking an answer, but her expression was unreadable. The last thing he wanted to do was cause her pain or demand that she assure him they would be able to go, but he was desperate to know.

"I know your aunt will be here soon," Nadja whispered. "I know."

She said no more, and he couldn't bring himself to press her.

That evening at the keep, Julianna got back from a hard day's work and headed upstairs to wash her hands and change out of the filthy clothes she was wearing—so that she could go downstairs and start supper.

She was pleased with the progress of the village and believed they would have proper shelters in place for everyone well before winter set in. Yet... other worries preyed upon her mind. She'd been so happy to see Jan standing on the edge of the village, watching, and she'd hoped he would come in and offer to help.

He had not.

Then—as he loved to tease her—she hoped he might at least come and tease her for trying to lay thatch like a man.

He had not.

Something inside him had changed since he'd returned from being conscripted, and nothing she did seemed to help. All she could do was hope that a little time and a little peace might bring the old Jan back, as this new one was a stranger.

Stepping off the landing, she strode down the passage toward her room, and then slowed as another door opened and Nadja stuck her head out.

"My girl," she said. "I thought I heard you."

Julianna never minded that Nadja called her "my girl," even though she was twenty years old and hardly a girl anymore. She adored Nadja and secretly hungered for these small words of affection.

"Do you need me?" Julianna asked.

"Yes, come in."

Entering the room, Julianna glanced around at the bedroom that Nadja and Cadell shared. It was a pleasant mix of them both, with painted hangings on the walls and piles of bracelets and Cadell's muddy boots and well-worn tools scattered around.

"I have something for you," Nadja said, motioning toward the bed.

Julianna looked over and drew in a sharp breath. There... on the bed lay a new dress, the color of rich scarlet. She loved red dresses, and owned only one —which had come to her second-hand with threadbare seams.

"Oh," she breathed moving closer to the bed. "How long have you been working on this?"

The dress laced up the front with a v-neckline. The sleeves were long and slender and hemmed without cuffs. The waistline was cut perfectly for Julianna's slight figure and the skirt was full, but not so full as to be cumbersome. A purple paisley sash lay beside it.

"I wanted to surprise you," Nadja said, and something her voice sounded pained.

Forgetting the dress, Julianna turned. "What's wrong?"

Nadja didn't answer or take her eyes from the gown. "This isn't a bribe. It is a gift, with my love, but I'm going to ask you something, and I beg that you will not refuse."

"You know I'd do anything for you. You need not make me such gifts."

"This is different," Nadja said, and the pain in her voice increased. "Listen to me carefully."

As she began to speak, Julianna's eyes grew wide...

J an stood in the main hall of the keep, facing the fire, knowing his parents and Julianna would join him soon, and they would all have dinner together. He liked their custom of gathering each night for dinner, no matter what else was going on. It helped him feel... grounded.

"Jan," a voice said from behind.

For the second time that day, he turned to see his mother approaching.

"Does Julianna need me to help her carry dinner from the kitchen?" he asked. Normally, if she made a soup or stew, he would carry it and she would bring the bread.

"In a moment," Nadja answered quietly. "I want to talk to you." Her expression was serious, almost strained.

He crossed the floor of the hall so that she wouldn't need to.

"About what?" He feared she was on the verge of giving him news he didn't want to hear.

"As you said earlier," she began, "your Aunt Doreena will be arriving any day now."

"And we're not going with her?" he whispered, already sinking into despair, but fighting not to show it.

"No... I know you need to go. I know how the road and life with my people call to you."

He froze, uncertain what to say, uncertain what she was about to say.

"I cannot... cannot go with you this year," she continued. "I need to stay and help your father with the villagers. But in my heart, I am afraid to send you alone without a solid piece of home to guide you back." She paused. "Julianna has agreed to go with you."

"Julianna? But she... she knows nothing of the Móndyalítko."

"She will learn."

"And how do you think she will respond to my cousin, Rico?"

"She is a sensible girl who understands there is more in this world than most people realize. She will respond just fine to your cousin, Rico."

A part of him was overjoyed that he would soon be rolling down the road in the company of his extended family, but he was still attempting to get his head around the idea of Julianna having agreed to this. He was also surprised at the excitement growing inside him at the prospect of her company all through the autumn. There was so much he could show her.

However, did his mother truly fear that he might not return and that Julianna would act as his anchor? That bothered him more than he cared to admit.

Besides, Julianna handled a good deal of the household by now.

"Don't you need her here?" he asked.

Nadja sighed. "Just the thought of you both being gone at the same time pains me, but my decision is not just for you. She has seen nothing outside this village and knows little beyond life with your father and me. I want more for her. Will you take her, Jan? Keep her safe at your side and show her more of the world? Then... before winter, you will both come home to me? Do you agree?"

"Yes," he said without hesitation. "Of course I agree."

Already, he felt a little more like his previous self.

Three days later, Julianna became nearly sick from nerves as she stepped out the main doors of the keep and saw three brightly colored wagons rolling into the courtyard, each one drawn by a pair of enormous horses. The wagons were topped with what appeared to be small houses. Julianna had seen them before—as Nadja's family stopped by each year—but she'd never had a reason to ponder such strange dwellings.

Last year, and the year before that, Nadja and Jan had both journeyed off when the wagons departed, and Julianna had remained behind with Zupan Cadell. This year, the outcome of the Móndyalítko visit would be quite different, as Julianna would be leaving with them.

The thought caused her stomach to tighten.

The wagons stopped, and almost instantly a surprising number of people emerged from small doorways or jumped down from the tops of the makeshift dwellings, bustling about, chattering to each other, and unharnessing the horses.

"Doreena!" a voice cried.

Nadja burst through the keep's doors, her face beaming with a smile as she attempted to hurry forward. Of late, her knees had been troubling her, and she could no longer run.

"Come, Julianna," she said, still walking across the courtyard and not looking back, "My sister is here. I knew she would come today. I felt it as soon as I woke up."

Julianna remained rooted where she stood.

After having made the mistake of letting Nadja dress her this morning, she didn't feel like herself. Had Nadja really known her sister would be arriving? This new red dress was so... red. Julianna also wore the purple sash around her waist and three bracelets dangling from her left wrist. What if she looked so much like one of the Móndyalítko, they would expect her to know their customs and ways?

Yes, she'd agreed to this journey, but now that the prospect was upon her, how was she ever going to climb into one of those wagons and leave Chemestúk behind?

The answer came to her as Jan nearly ran out the front doors of the keep and stopped at the sight of her.

"Oh... Julianna, you look so... you look..."

This was the first time he'd seen her today.

Jan had an almost unbelievable ability to flatter women and make them fall in love with him—or he'd had this ability not too long ago. Him being so uncharacteristically tongue-tied shored up her determination to accompany him, to help him... as Nadja had asked her to do.

"What now?" Julianna asked uncomfortably.

"Now? Come and greet my family. I know you'll love them all."

That remained to be seen, but she followed him toward the wagons. As she drew closer, she couldn't help noting the charm of the small homes built onto the backs of the wagons, with doors and windows and painted shutters.

Nadja was already in the embrace of a dark-haired woman who looked over and saw Jan approaching.

"Darling boy!" she cried, letting go of Nadja and running to Jan.

Julianna had met Aunt Doreena before, briefly. She was larger and more full-bodied than Nadja, dressed in a full yellow skirt and a white low-cut blouse— with a half dozen bracelets on each wrist. She wore her thick black hair in a single braid, with an orange scarf tied around her head. Her nose was broader than Nadja's, but her smile was wide, and her dark eyes expressed every emotion she felt.

"My sweet boy," she said, embracing Jan in a bear hug and pulling him close. "How I have missed your face."

Her overly enthusiastic manner left Julianna off balance, and the moment the bear hug ended, Doreena's attention turned again. "Julianna? Is that you?"

"Yes," Julianna answered quietly.

"You are a woman! A lovely young woman now. Let me see you."

To Julianna's dismay, Doreena strode over and embraced her like a lost daughter, not seeming to notice that Julianna was too stunned to hug her back.

"Rosario!" Doreena shouted. "Leave off with those horses and come here right now."

Both Nadja and Jan appeared not only comfortable but delighted with Doreena's boisterous nature, and the sight of Jan smiling made Julianna feel more disposed toward his rather loud aunt.

A behemoth of a man came striding from around the side of a wagon, seeing Nadja and grinning at her broadly. "How fine it is to see you."

His chest was as wide as two normal men. He wore his black hair short—and sported a thick moustache. He wore loose breeches, a white shirt, and a russet vest. He too was soon hugging Jan and then kissing Nadja's cheek, and afterward, he turned to Julianna in slight puzzlement, as if wondering who she was and why she was here.

Julianna had seen him before on these brief stopovers, but she'd never been introduced.

"This is Julianna," Nadja said quickly, stepping closer. "She will be taking my place this year in the family travels.

At that, even Doreena fell silent for a few breaths, but then she looked more deeply into Nadja's face, perhaps seeing a good deal in an instant, and without blinking, answered, "Of course she will be most welcome. Jan, introduce her to your cousins."

Already feeling overwhelmed, Julianna could hardly refuse when Jan grabbed her hand and led her around the side of the first wagon.

"Rico," he called.

A man unharnessing a horse turned his head. He was a taller, more muscular version of Jan, with an utterly serious expression. Julianna was struck by the impression that he'd never laughed in his life.

"This is Julianna," Jan said as they approached. "She's coming with us this year. Julianna, this is my cousin, Rico. He has almost nothing to say and he's a bit of a bore, but a solid fellow nonetheless."

Julianna's mouth fell open.

Rico didn't appear to even notice the insult and raised one eyebrow at Julianna.

"Coming with us?" he said. "Did you...? Are you...?"

With deep embarrassment, she realized he was wondering she and Jan were a couple, possibly even married.

"No!" she exclaimed.

Jan frowned at her. "Well, you needn't be so emphatic about it." He turned back to Rico. "She's like my *sister*. Mother cannot come this year, and she wants someone to keep an eye on me."

The word "sister" stung a bit, as Julianna and Jan hardly viewed each other as siblings, but they also weren't a couple. What exactly were they? She had no idea.

However, Rico nodded stoically and looked over the top her head. "You'll need to meet Belle."

Who was Belle?

Before she could ask, a young woman, perhaps seventeen, came walking—swaying—toward them, and Jan's face lit up. "Julianna, this is my other cousin, Rico's sister, Belle."

Again, Julianna's mouth fell open.

Belle seemed to both sway and glide at the same time. She was small and slender with an incredible mass of wavy dark hair. Her skin was pale as opposed to Jan's more dusky shade, but her large eyes were black. Her mouth was heart-shaped and tinted red. She wore a deep blue skirt with a white blouse as low-cut as Aunt Doreena's, but as opposed to Doreena's large breasts, Belle's were smaller and perfectly rounded... with the tops clearly exposed at her neckline.

She was the most beautiful girl Julianna had ever seen.

"Belle," Jan said, "Come and meet Julianna. She's coming with me this year."

Belle glanced in Julianna's direction.

"Charmed," she murmured absently and then focused all her attention on Jan. "You get more handsome every year. You're a little thinner, but it suits you."

He took two steps and picked her up in a hug, the two of them chatting away as if no one else existed. Rico turned back to the horses, and Julianna stood at a loss.

Wasn't Belle Jan's *cousin*? His first cousin if Julianna understood things correctly: both Belle and Rico were the children of Doreena and Rosario.

Just then, Zupan Cadell came around the side of the wagon, and he smiled at her a little sadly. She knew he was going to miss her.

"Getting acquainted?" he asked.

Trying, she thought.

At the sound of Cadell's voice, Belle turned from Jan and appeared to forget him instantly. She curtseyed low.

"Why, Uncle, you get more handsome each year."

To Julianna's surprise, Cadell blushed like a boy.

And then... she realized that Belle probably had no more interest in Jan than she did in any other man. She was one of those women who required the full and undivided attention of anything male in the vicinity.

Julianna sighed.

That didn't bode well for the journey—and Nadja should have warned her.

"Rico," Cadell said. "As soon as you've got the horses settled in the stable, have everyone come into the keep. We'll make a feast and drink some ale together."

By way of answer, Rico nodded once.

Julianna could make no guesses, but there was definitely something odd about him. Although physically, he was even more striking than Jan—which was no easy feat—he appeared to possess none of Jan's wit or charm... or even Jan's previous enjoyment of life. Rico struck her as "serious" and nothing more.

And yet, for better or for worse, Julianna had been introduced to the immediate members of this Móndyalítko family, and she hoped she'd have a little time to get to know all the others before she would be expected to remember names.

The rest of that afternoon and then evening soon proved so busy that she barely had time to worry. She, Nadja, Doreena and a few other Móndyalítko women—not Belle—worked in the kitchen of the keep to prepare a feast of roasted vegetables, chicken stew, and apple tarts.

The night was filled with eating and drinking—followed by substantial clean-up efforts—and Julianna did not get to bed until after the mid of night.

The following morning... after a quietly painful good-bye to Nadja and the zupan, she climbed into a wagon with Jan—as she had promised—and rolled out the broken gate of the keep, down the road, leaving everything she knew behind.

A s dusk set in two nights later, Julianna sank down by a campfire, with Jan settling at her side, and her mind spun from all that she'd learned in so short a time. Life on the road with the Móndyalítko had turned out to be nothing as she'd had expected.

For one, she'd assumed it would be disorganized, bordering on chaotic. But that preconception quickly proved false.

The interiors of the wagons were well structured. Julianna and Jan rode with Aunt Doreena's family. Inside, the wagon-house boasted three beds. Two of them were narrow bunks built into the wall that ran parallel with the front side of the wagon, and a third, wider bed was built into the left-side wall. Doreena and Rosario slept in the wider bed.

Julianna had been unsettled at first to be told that she would take Rico's bunk, and he would sleep outside in a tent with Jan.

"No..." she had stammered. "I cannot take his bed and turn him outside."

But Jan assured her this had been the case for many years, and Nadja had always taken Rico's bunk, and the two young men didn't mind sleeping in the tent in the least. In the end, Julianna had to agree. What was the alternative? That *she* sleep in the tent with Jan?

Meals were also well structured, cooked outside over open fires using pots and iron hooks.

In the morning, as the men readied the wagons, the women made tea and boiled eggs and prepared oats with cream—as the family traveled with their own chickens and a milk cow—and in a surprisingly short time, the wagons were rolling down the road with everyone properly fed. Within these first two days, Julianna had followed the routine closely enough to begin pitching in, gathering eggs, milking the cow, searching for firewood, and Doreena complimented her more than once for her efforts.

Belle never lifted a finger and no one expected her to.

The mid-day meal was served quickly, while the horses were given a short rest, consisting of sliced apples and small hunks of cheese.

Then everyone was back on the road.

Julianna had never spent so much time in motion, and the rolling of the wagons sometimes bothered her stomach, but she kept such troubles to herself.

The end of the first day had been a great relief, and tonight, once her stomach settled, she was even prepared to enjoy herself. Evenings were proving to be her favorite time.

The women spent as much time as necessary over the evening meal, making rich stews with wild onions and venison or roasting rabbits. She noticed that Rico vanished as soon as they stopped to make camp, and he brought back game to be prepared and eaten on the following night. Julianna thought he must be a skilled hunter.

But the main reason she looked forward to this evening was that only two days into the journey she could see a drastic change in Jan. He was becoming more and more his old self. The moment Doreena learned that he'd lost his violin—when he'd been conscripted—she'd dug through a chest and produced one for him that was presently in need of an owner. The look on Jan's face was worth any discomfort Julianna had suffered so far.

He'd taken it from Doreena's hands like a drowning man might grab a rope and immediately begun to play in fits and starts, stopping to tune it to his own tastes, forgetting everything and everyone around him.

Julianna didn't mind.

At night, once supper was finished and the dishes were washed and packed away, the group would gather around the fire and entertain each other with music and singing and dancing. Julianna never thought she would enjoy such festivities, but she did.

So, now, Jan sat beside her by the fire waiting for everyone to gather, and he began to better acquaint her with the other Móndyalítko.

"That is Rosario's brother, Heraldo," Jan said softly, pointing to a burly man on the other side of the fire. "He and his family live in the second wagon." Looking around, he gestured to a thin young man perhaps eighteen or nineteen years old. "That's Corbin, Heraldo's adopted son."

Julianna had noticed Corbin before and felt rather sorry for him. She wondered from where he'd been adopted. He had none of Rico's serious strength or Jan's charm. His pinched face reminded her of a rodent, and he tended to jerk nervously a good deal, like a rodent. His hair was thin and unwashed, rather like the rest of him.

However, this didn't stop Belle from flirting with him at any opportunity.

Julianna pushed such petty thoughts from her mind and tried to focus on Jan's words as he continued explaining small things about the rest of the traveling group. There were fifteen people in all, sharing three wagons. In the late spring, summer and early fall, several of the younger members slept outside in tents.

She learned that everyone had at least one skill or talent, from reading palms or telling futures, to performing astonishing card tricks, to playing the violin, to singing... to dancing. It came as no surprise that Belle's talent was dancing, and she knew how to move seductively to the sound of slow music.

As of yet, though, the group had not entertained anyone besides each other.

"How do they earn their living?" Julianna asked.

The light from the fire reflected off one side of Jan's face as he looked at her. "What did Mother tell you?"

"She didn't tell me much."

"We'll begin to set up shows as soon as we reach Serov."

Julianna shook her head, not following.

"Mother didn't even tell you that much?" He turned his entire torso toward her. "We're heading southeast to a town called Serov. The vassal of Serov Castle is a friend of Uncle Rosario, and so the town magistrate allows our family to set up for a whole moon each autumn."

"A whole moon?" Julianna repeated.

"Yes, the people there have come to expect us. Aunt Doreena is a skilled fortune-teller, and Uncle Rosario plans shows for the rest of us to perform. He puts out hats, and people toss in coins. Villagers from leagues away come to see us." He paused, thinking, as if he'd not expected to be explaining this to her. "After we finish up on Serov, we move on to Kéonsk for the Autumn Fair."

Julianna gasped, "Kéonsk?"

This information was coming rather quickly. Kéonsk was the largest city in Droevinka, and soldiers from the House of Väränj zealously guarded it.

Jan held up one hand. "Don't worry. We needn't enter the gates if we don't wish to. Every autumn, Kéonsk hosts an enormous fair in the open area outside the west gates. It's like a temporary marketplace. Farmers and merchants come from all over Droevinka, and so do the Móndyalítko. We are welcomed there as we provide entertainment at no cost to the city." He paused. "It's important that our people only go to places where they have permission or they are invited. Sensible families have a yearly path laid out, and I can assure you, for all their bluster, Aunt Doreena and Uncle Rosario are quite sensible."

Julianna absorbed this information, relieved at the thought that they had a destination where they'd camp for a moon.

"Did you think we'd be traveling the entire time?" he asked.

"I did," she admitted, "or rather, I had no idea what to expect."

He smiled. "You'll like Serov."

"Jan!" Aunt Doreena called. "Belle wants to dance. Play one of your slow tunes for her."

Without being asked twice, Jan jumped to his feet and went to join his beautiful cousin. Belle adjusted her clothing, pulling the neckline of her blouse down slightly. Jan raised his bow, and began to play the slow strains of haunting music. Julianna had almost forgotten how good he was with a violin.

Then... Belle began to dance, and Julianna could see every man around the fire forget that Jan was even there as Belle moved her arms and hips seductively. She was graceful and lovely. Looking around the fire at various faces though, Julianna saw only appreciation and approval in most eyes—as most of these men were related to her, and Belle probably brought in a good deal of money via strangers throwing coins into hats. However, Corbin, the rat-faced young man was leaning forward with his hands on the ground, staring at her like he was starving.

Julianna thought Belle would do well to discourage him, as he was not likely a man she would choose to marry.

Instead, Belle moved closer, dancing right in front of him.

Julianna closed her eyes, trying to forget Belle and only to hear the beautiful song that Jan played.

A few days later, in the mid-afternoon, the group rolled up to the outskirts of Serov, and Jan hopped down from the top of the wagon to an unpleasant surprise: there were already four Móndyalítko wagons parked in the family's camping site.

Rico hopped down beside him, his face equally puzzled, but Uncle Rosario nearly shot off the top of the bench—from where he'd been driving the horses —and strode toward the site.

"Sebastian!" he barked, "You cheating, lying, filthy..."

He trailed off as a short, fat man wearing a felt hat and numerous rings in both ears walked lazily toward him from the other camp.

"Rosario," he said, yawning. "How good to see you."

"Don't you try that," Rosario snapped. "What in the seven hells are you doing here? You know Serov is ours."

Behind Jan, the door to the family wagon opened, and he turned to see Julianna stick her head out. "What's happening?" she asked.

"I'm not sure," Jan answered.

He stopped listening to his uncle and the man called Sebastian arguing, and he moved to help Julianna down. However, she needed no assistance and climbed down before he reached her.

Instead of the new dress and paisley sash his mother had made for her, today, she wore her old red dress, and though the color was not as bright and seams were a bit worn, he had to admit that her hand-me-down garment suited her better. The skirt was a little shorter, barely reaching her ankles, and the sleeves were pushed up, and she moved with much greater ease. All the bracelets were gone, and her silky hair was in a braid down her back. Perhaps she had grown tired of attempting to look like something she was not and decided to just be herself.

He much preferred her as herself.

The voices of Rosario and Sebastian grew louder—and then insults began to fly.

"Rico," Julianna said. "Do you have any idea what's happening?"

Rico's ever-serious face was still puzzled, and before he could answer, Aunt Doreena emerged from the wagon, climbing down to the ground.

"What is all this shouting about? Belle is taking a nap." She stopped at the sight of the four wagons in the camping site, and her eyes moved to Uncle Rosario... and finally settled on the fat man. "Why that slimy, disgusting, slug-ridden..."

Making fists with both hands, she started forward, but Rico stopped her.

"Mother, wait. Father's coming back."

Indeed, a red-faced Rosario was striding back toward them, and before anyone could ask, he spat out, "Sebastian says his group was given leave by the town magistrate to camp here and work Serov along with us."

"For the whole moon?" Doreena gasped. "They can't. They'll take half our livelihood, and Serov is ours in the autumn. That is understood."

"I'm well aware of that, my dear," Rosario answered tightly. "I need to go and see the magistrate and get to the bottom of this. But Sebastian will find himself with a black mark among the Móndyalítko families if he's trying to steal our town."

Jan felt something soft pulling at sleeve, and Julianna whispered in his ear. "What is this talk of stealing?"

He glanced back at her. "I'll tell you later."

Many unspoken rules among his mother's people were complicated, but one rule was held above all. Most of the families had a yearly cycle of travels, well established. No family ever encroached on a town or large village that had long been claimed by another.

This was understood.

If Sebastian was truly attempting to take Serov from Rosario, the act was unprecedented—or as far as Jan knew. He'd never even heard of such a thing. The survival of all the families depended on respecting the set territories of the others.

"Well..." Julianna broke in, stepping forward. "What do we do now?"

Everyone stopped talking and looked at her. The outsider, the girl who knew nothing of their ways was asking the only sensible question in the moment.

Uncle Rosario took a deep breath, perhaps attempting to calm himself, and pointed to a break in the trees about fifty pace away. "Set up camp over there. I'm going into town."

As with so many things so far, Julianna underestimated the process of "setting up." Within a few moments of Uncle Rosario heading off into Serov, she nearly forgot the trouble Jan's family was facing as other, more immediate tasks took precedence.

The horses, milk cow, and chickens required attention first, getting them situated in their new home for the next moon. Small sets of stairs were brought down from the tops of wagons and attached to the backs, making entries and exits between the ground and the doors much easier. Chests were brought down and carried inside various wagons.

Wood was gathered and campfires were built. Bags of lentils and onions appeared from nowhere, and some of the women began cooking lentil stew in large quantities. Julianna followed Doreena's lead and helped where she could. Jan assisted Rico with the horses.

Belle sat on a chair by the fire, brushing her hair.

Dusk was just setting in when Rosario finally came walking back into camp.

Looking over at the other camping site, Julianna could see that everyone there had settled into similar activities, and she could smell smoke drifting over from their campfires.

Jan, Rico, Julianna, Heraldo, and Doreena quickly gathered around Rosario.

"Well?" Doreena demanded with her hands on her hips. "What did Master Braxton say?" She paused and glanced at Julianna. "He's the town magistrate."

In spite of his enormous size, Rosario looked somewhat diminished in defeat. "I don't understand it exactly," he began, "but I suspect Sebastian is holding something over his head. Master Braxton didn't want to see me. That's what has taken me all this time. When I was finally granted a meeting, Braxton appeared... embarrassed. But our talk was short, and he told me he's given Sebastian permission to stay and that the town was large enough for both families, which he must know isn't true. Then I was dismissed." He exhaled through his nose. "I cannot fathom this."

"Could you go to the vassal of the fiefdom?" Julianna asked. "Jan said he was your friend."

Rosario shook his head, "The word 'friend' is overstated. Lord Rueben and I respect each other, and we did him a service once. His wife was in difficulty... giving birth, and Doreena delivered both mother and baby safely. That's how we earned our place here. I fear if I asked him to intercede in a conflict among our own people, he might view it as an over-step."

"We cannot let Sebastian get away with this," Doreena said hotly, making fists with both hands.

"No..." Rosario agreed. "But we'll have to deal with him ourselves."

His brother, Heraldo, was about to say something when the pounding of horses' hooves rang out, and Julianna turned to see five men riding up to the camp, pulling in on their lathered mounts.

Right away, she didn't like the look them. Four of the men wore chain armor and swords. The leader was young, perhaps twenty, and well built, with an overly-round face—though it seemed to suit him. He wore black breeches, high polished boots, and an embroidered tunic of rich burgundy. She would have pegged him as a nobleman, but his men weren't wearing tabards of any of royal houses. Perhaps he was the son of a wealthy merchant?

"Rosario," the young man said in a friendly enough tone as he dismounted. "I've heard you returned, and I came directly." His eyes were not on Rosario. They were on Belle, as she sat by the fire. "Is Belle packed and ready?"

Doreena stepped closer. "Donovan? I hope you father is well," she said carefully, "but I don't take your meaning about Belle. She has no need to pack."

The young man blinked, "Well... of course she does. I've come to claim her, as she promised."

A small knot began growing in Julianna's stomach. She glanced over toward the fire as Belle stood up.

Rosario was in no mood to be dealing with young men laying claims upon his daughter, and he barked. "Claim her? What are you talking about?" He turned his head. "Belle!"

Belle glided over, her face a mask of innocence. "Yes, Father?"

Before Rosario could speak again, the young man he'd called Donovan broke in, his voice a mix of anger and panic.

"Belle, you didn't tell your parents?" he asked.

"Tell us what?" Rosario demanded.

"Last autumn, Belle was only sixteen," Donovan stated, his tone firmer now, "and she promised to be mine as long as I waited one more year, until she turned seventeen. I kept her in money and gowns last year, and she promised to be mine as soon as you arrived this autumn."

Jan, Rico, and Heraldo watched this exchange in tense silence, but Doreena shook her head at Donovan in what appeared to be sympathy.

"Belle cannot be yours," she said. "Your father is the wealthiest wine merchant in this province. You dine at Lord Reuben's table. Surely you must know your father would never allow you to marry one of our people."

"Marry?" Donovan repeated. "No, of course not. But I don't care who I marry. She won't matter. I want Belle. She promised to be my mistress, and I will take care of her. You needn't worry."

Rosario's face turned red, and Julianna suspected he'd had about as much as one man could stand in a single day.

"Mistress!" he exploded. Whirling, he turned to Belle. "Did you make such a promise?"

Belle shook her head. "Of course not, Father. I don't know what he's talking about."

She looked the picture of innocence, but Julianna caught a flash of fear in her eyes—just a hint.

Belle was lying.

Donovan's mouth fell open. "You did! You know you did! You took my money and gifts."

Tossing her head, Belle shrugged. "Can I help it if a man gives me gifts? Lots of men give me gifts. I'm sorry if you took my acceptance for more than was meant."

Donovan's expression flattened in shock, and he appeared to be having trouble breathing. His gaze moved down to her waist, and Julianna saw the same hunger in his eyes that she'd seen in Corbin's pinched, twitching face. Something about Belle seemed to drive certain men to behave like idiots.

"You heard her," Rosario said. "Now, shove off. Give my regards to your father."

The shock on Donovan's face twisted into anger, and he didn't move.

Instead he shouted, "Nash!"

One of the armored men on horseback jumped to the ground, and a breath later, the other four followed.

"I misunderstood *nothing*," Donovan hissed at Rosario. "She swore to me, and I have been waiting... and waiting. I'm not leaving this camp without her."

"Belle," Rico said, his voice cold. "Mother. Julianna. Get in the wagon."

Julianna stood fast and so did Doreena. Belle began backing away.

Rico moved to one side of his father, and Jan moved to the other. Rosario's brother, Heraldo, crossed his thick arms.

"If your men pull those swords," Rosario said to Donovan, "I'll have Lord Rueben arrest you. Only his men have military authority here, and you know it."

"My men don't need swords," Donovan sneered, and with that, he swung hard, catching Rosario across the jaw. The impact was louder than Julianna would have expected and Rosario's head snapped back. Donovan was stronger than he looked.

"Father!" Rico shouted.

All four guards rushed forward and one of them took a swing at Jan. He ducked it easily and punched the man in the stomach—surprising Julianna, as she'd never seen him in a fight before.

Still, at the outbreak of violence, she rushed backward, expecting a complete melee to follow as other men from the camp, including Corbin came running.

But... a melee did not take place. Nothing could have prepared Julianna for what happened next.

With Rosario momentarily stunned by the blow, Donovan drew back to hit him again, and a sound like an enraged snarl—from an animal—filled the air. Julianna almost couldn't tell from where it came, but she looked toward Rico and froze.

He shoved Donovan hard enough to knock the young man onto the ground, but Rico's hands were no longer... hands. Short, black fur was sprouting from his arms, and his hands had become claws. His face was changing, and he dropped to all fours as more fur sprouted from his body.

In the span of a few breaths, Rico was gone, and a black cat, the size a small pony, stood in his place, snarling, exposing white fangs.

His breeches fell away on the ground behind him as he rushed forward. His shirt had ripped during the transformation, but shredded pieces still clung to him. Donovan scrambled backward in terror, and all four guards began shouting. One of them pulled a sword, and quick as a flash, Rico's muscled feline body changed directions, dashing inside the man's reach and pinning him to the ground before he could strike. The sword fell away, and the man screamed. The huge cat roared in his face and drew a heavy claw back.

"Rico, no!" Doreena shouted, running forward.

Somehow, she reached him, and put her hand on his shoulder.

"Stop this, all of you!" she shouted.

Donovan was on his feet now, staring the great cat, and the three guards on their feet were stumbling backward, looking to him for orders.

"Just go," Doreena said to Donovan, trying to pull the cat off the fallen guard. "Rico, let him up!"

Julianna was still frozen, trying to understand what had just happened. Jan, Heraldo, and the other men who had come running from the wagons stood poised but didn't act. Julianna had the feeling none of them wanted any more trouble.

Belle had vanished from sight.

The cat allowed itself to be pulled away, and the guard scrambled to his feet and retrieved his sword.

"Go," Doreena repeated to Donovan.

The young man was panting and staring at the cat. He seemed beyond words—as was Julianna. Running for his horse, Donovan mounted quickly, and with clear relief, his men followed suit.

"I'll be back!" Donovan called, finding his voice.

"With Lord Rueben if need be. Belle made an agreement, and she is mine."

Then all five of them were pounding away.

"Change back," Doreena whispered to Rico. "Jan, bring his breeches."

Before taking a step, Jan turned to Julianna, and his face was tight. "Go inside the wagon."

She was still trying to get her head around what had just happened and couldn't bring herself to respond.

"Now!" he ordered.

In their years together, Jan had never ordered her to do anything. A small part of her knew he must have a reason now, so she turned and hurried to the wagon, taking the stairs quickly, and passing through the door.

Belle was inside, sitting on her bunk... and brushing her hair again.

"Did Rico chase them off?" she asked serenely, as if inquiring about the state of the weather.

Julianna could hardly believe this—even after what she'd seen from Belle over the past days.

"How can you sit there, brushing your hair?" Julianna demanded. "You promised that young hothead you'd be his mistress, didn't you?"

Belle seemed taken aback by the confrontational question, and she frowned. "How would I know what he chose to hear?"

Julianna pointed outside. "You caused all that! Your father's face is badly bruised, and your brother... I don't understand what happened there, but he put himself in danger against armed men to defend you."

Belle's frown turned petulant. "He's my brother. It's his job to defend me. You know nothing of our people or our ways." She picked up a hand mirror. "I am a treasure to them, and I can't help if so many men want me. There's nothing I can do about that." She looked Julianna up and down. "You'd understand if you weren't so tall and plain."

Julianna stood looking at the shallow, selfish creature on the bunk and realized that Belle was more than just an annoyance. She was dangerous.

Not long after sending Julianna to the wagon, Jan climbed the steps and knocked softly on the door, uncertain what he was going to say. Almost instantly, Julianna opened it and looked out him. With her, he tended to fall back on honesty, and the words just came to him, as they did now.

"I'm sorry I shouted at you," he said. "Rico would have been embarrassed to change back with you there. But he's dressed now. Would you come and walk with me?"

Her face was still awash in confusion, and he focused on the light smattering of freckles across her nose. He was well aware she probably hadn't followed much of what he'd just said. But she stepped out, closing the door behind herself, and together, they walked into the trees outside of Serov. He spotted a wide stump and pointed to it.

"Over there."

Sitting down beside him, she opened her mouth as if to ask a question, and then closed it again. Jan was hoping his mother had been right, and that Julianna would be able accept there was more in the world than most people realized.

"He's a shape-shifter," Jan said. "He was born that way."

"Born that way?"

Jan nodded. "Occasionally, one of our people is born with an ability... seers called the Mist-Torn, and shape-shifters like Rico. Not all shifters are cats. We have some who change into wolves or other creatures. It seems normal to me. It always has."

"Is he still... himself when he changes? Does he remember and know who he is?"

"Yes, only his body changes."

"That's why he brings back so much game? He shifts when he hunts?"

She really was taking this quite calmly. Perhaps Nadja had been right.

"Yes, but our shifters rarely change in front of outsiders... and I don't mean you. I mean like those men who came today. He shouldn't have done that. We could have handled Donovan and those guards on our own."

"Donovan hit his father in the face," Julianna countered, "and he reacted. If someone had punched Cadell in the face and you... you could do what Rico does, you wouldn't have been able to stop yourself either."

Jan sighed. "I suppose you're right, but if Donovan reports this to the magistrate or Lord Reuben, there could be trouble for us."

Julianna pushed back a strand of hair that had come loose from her braid. His eyes followed the motion of her hand. "Well, if you want to fend off trouble in the future," she said, "someone should do something about Belle."

"Belle? She doesn't cause any trouble."

Julianna's mouth fell halfway open. "Jan, are you blind? She caused that entire mess this evening. She took money and expensive gifts from that wine merchant's son all last year and promised to become his mistress."

For the first time in his memory, he felt a trickle of real annoyance at Julianna. She wasn't helping here. "Belle didn't cause any of that. Men fall in love with her all the time."

"She's lazy, self-centered, and she *makes* men fall in love with her."

He stiffened. "That sounds like you're describing a female version of me."

"You're nothing like her. Of course you like to charm women, but it's a game to you. You never take it too far, and you make sure you don't hurt anyone. You also never deny what you've done if your mother calls you in and tells you to clean up your own mess... and you do clean up your mess. Belle won't even acknowledge that she's made one."

His mood softened at her opinion of him—which was certainly much higher than he deserved. No one else saw him the way Julianna did. However, she was wrong about Belle. Belle was lovely and worshipped by most people who met her and as a result... yes, she'd become a little spoiled but nothing more.

Besides, he'd not brought Julianna out here to talk about Belle.

"So," he said. "You won't be afraid of Rico now?"

"Afraid? Good gods, no. I'll never be on the receiving end of those claws, and he seems very useful to your family."

Jan smiled. He should have expected such an answer.

T he next day, Julianna helped Jan put together a small yard for the chickens—complete with wooden boxes filled with straw. But, beforehand, she noticed that it took Jan a while to choose what he considered would be the best spot. Apparently, the family had been camping for years in the area where Sebastian's group was now situated, and the change of location was causing a few issues.

However... although no one said anything, she also noticed Doreena, Rosario, and Jan continually glancing in the direction of the town, as if waiting for someone to approach. She realized they were worried that Donovan had made a report about Rico, and they feared someone in authority coming to investigate.

No one came.

Perhaps Donovan had been so embarrassed by Belle's rejection that he'd decided not to tell anyone what happened?

In the late afternoon, she was out gathering firewood when Jan came to find her.

"I'm going into town for supplies," he said. "Would you like to come?"

She hesitated. She wanted to go, but she'd never seen the inside of an actual town.

"Don't worry," he teased, as if reading her mind. "I'll protect you."

That did it.

"I don't need you to protect me," she said, walking toward him.

They went back to camp and stacked the firewood she'd found.

Aunt Doreena approached them and spoke to Jan. "Is Julianna going with you?" She didn't wait for an answer. "Good. She can help you carry. In addition to oats, onions, and cooking oil, don't forget we need at least twelve beeswax candles and six bars of soap. Oh and tea. We're running low on tea. Take as much money as you think you'll need from the box and just put anything back that you don't spend."

"Yes, Aunt," he said, turning toward the wagon.

Confused, Julianna followed him. "What box?"

"I'll show you."

He went up the short set of stairs into his aunt and uncle's wagon. No one was inside. Without hesitating, he went straight to the bunk where Julianna slept every night, and he dropped to his knees, reaching under and lifting a floorboard.

"There's a box down here," he said, "where all our community funds are stored. Aunt Doreena oversees it. If you need coin for anything, just tell her, and she'll give permission. Everyone knows it's here. We share almost everything... so different from the villagers back home. It's one of the things I like best about traveling with my mother's family."

"Does everyone put all the money they earn in that box?"

"Just what we earn performing with the family. Anything we earn on our own, we usually keep for ourselves, but... we mainly perform together."

Although, she'd never say it, Julianna was slightly taken aback by the knowledge that everyone stored money in the same box and everyone knew exactly where it was and no one worried.

"Why is Doreena sending you to the market?" she asked. "I would have thought she'd prefer to make her own purchases."

Pulling a metal box from the hole in the floor, he flashed her a grin. "You've never seen me haggle. It's one of my talents." As he opened the box, his grin faded, and he stared downward.

"What's wrong?" she asked.

He didn't answer. Instead, he jumped to his feet and moved past her, hanging out the door. "Aunt Doreena. Uncle Rosario. Come quick!"

Taking a step forward, Julianna looked down. The box was empty.

A moment later, Doreena and Rosario came through the door, and she had to move deeper inside the wagon to make room for them.

"The box is empty," Jan said in alarm.

"That's impossible," Doreena answered, pushing past him and kneeling down. "Was it open when you pulled it out? The coins must have fallen."

Still, for her brave words, she was pale as she glanced at the empty box and reached into the hole.

"No, it was closed," Jan insisted. "Nothing fell out."

A tickling fear crawled up Julianna's neck. She was the only newcomer here, and the box had been stored directly below her bunk. Though she tried to ignore lingering scars from her youth, she still had bad dreams about being a hungry orphan. She was no thief, but whenever food went missing in Chemestúk, she'd been accused. It was easy to blame the orphan, the outsider.

Rosario was shaking his large head in confusion. "It can't be gone. That was two year's worth of our savings. No one would take it."

"What about someone from Sebastian's group?" Jan asked.

Doreena was growing more distraught. "No... they would never steal from other Móndyalítko, not even one of Sebastian's people."

"They stole our camping site!" Rosario countered angrily. "What's to stop them from stealing our money!"

She shook her head. "I don't believe that, and you can't go over there accusing them without proof." Her mouth pursed. "Something is wrong here. Something I don't understand yet."

So far, Julianna hadn't said a word. She was holding her breath. But no one even glanced her way. Perhaps because Nadja had sent her, they considered her above reproach. That thought was somewhat comforting.

"Two years savings," Rosario whispered. "Except for our expenses, everything we've earned was in that box, and now... we're going to have to split this moon's livelihood between our family and Sebastian's."

Doreena frowned at him. "That kind of talk isn't helping." She stood. "I'll get to the bottom of this. Julianna, dear, would reach into that shelf above your head and hand me the tin tea jar you see."

Looking up, Julianna did as she was asked, though a part of her still feared she'd be accused of theft at any moment.

Doreena opened the tin and removed a small pouch. "I keep this hidden in case the wagon is ever searched and robbed by soldiers. They never seem interested in tea." She handed the pouch to Jan. "We still need supplies, but you'll have to shorten the list. Get only six candles, three bars of soap, and enough oats for a few days. Rico can go hunting tonight, and we'll start performing as soon as tomorrow."

Julianna couldn't help being impressed by Doreena's ability to accept a staggering problem— the loss of all their money—and focus on whatever they could do to help themselves in the moment.

All four of them exited the wagon, and once on the ground outside, Doreena repeated to Rosario, "Don't you worry. I'll get to the bottom of this." Dusk was close, and she glanced at Jan and Julianna. "You two best hurry. The stalls will be closing soon after dark."

Jan nodded and motioned Julianna to follow.

She walked beside him down a path through the trees, and within what seemed like only moments, the path emptied into a road.

Serov lay before them.

Alone with him, she blurted out, "Neither your aunt or uncle even considered accusing me."

"You? Why would they accuse you?"

"Because I'm the only outsider traveling with the group, and I've been sleeping right over the top of that box!"

"Don't be ridiculous. You didn't even know it was there." He seemed to completely dismiss her concerns. "Come on. I'll show you the market."

She continued walking beside him, looking all around. Soon, the terrible theft moved a little further toward the back her mind. The outskirts of this town consisted of more homes than shops. Most of the houses were made of wood, but a few were made from stone. The streets were clean, and so were the people walking past. She noted the fine shutters and fresh paint, as if the townsfolk here took pride in their dwellings. Further in, Jan turned right, and they entered a merchant district with taverns and eateries and various shops. She'd never seen anything like this.

The smells of smoked sausages and perfumed candles followed them, and then a delicious, sweet fragrance wafted into her nostrils.

Jan pointed ahead. "There's the open market." He sniffed the air too and broke into a trot, heading for the first stall. Reaching into his pocket, he drew something out and handed it to the merchant—without haggling.

She followed to find that he'd bought a good-sized handful of almonds covered in sugar and cinnamon. He held out his hands.

"Try them."

She hesitated, and as usual, he read her mind.

"Don't worry," he said. "I didn't use the money Aunt Doreena sent with us. My father gave me some coins before we left, and he told me to buy you a few treats along the way."

The sweetened almonds were the delicious scent she'd smelled in the air, and once she learned they were a gift from Cadell, she didn't need to be invited twice. Taking an almond, she put it in her mouth. The sugar, cinnamon and nutty flavor all seemed to melt together.

"Oh, Jan," she said, still chewing.

"Over there," he said, motioning with his head to a clear spot near the booth.

Together, they took a pause, stayed out of the way, and ate every last almond. Julianna had never tasted anything so good.

"All right then," he said, sounding more businesslike. "Let's get the oats first. With the family's money this tight, I'm going to have to be obnoxious. You just stand behind me like an embarrassed wife."

"What?"

"Just follow my lead. Do you think I'll be able to embarrass you?"

Her jaw clenched. "I've no doubt."

He produced a small, folded burlap bag from inside his shirt as he walked up to an older man in a stall filled with barrels. "Four pounds of oats, please," he said.

The man nodded and picked up a scoop. "Cut or ground?"

"Ground."

The man filled the bag and weighed it on a scale, pouring in a few more. "That'll be two groats."

Jan's expression went stricken. "Two groats?" He put his hand to his chest. "Robber!" he cried. "I'm being robbed!"

The oat merchant took a step back, but Jan staggered forward, leaning dramatically on the counter of the stall.

"Robbed, I say!" he cried.

People began turning to stare.

Julianna didn't need to fake embarrassment. She was mortified. "Jan..." she said quietly. "That's not an unfair price."

"Unfair?" he cried so loudly that his voice broke. "Unfair you say? He's stealing any meat we might buy straight from our children's mouths!"

The poor merchant appeared stunned, and he glanced at Julianna. "One groat then..." he stammered, as if he just wanted them to leave.

"Pay him," Julianna hissed at Jan.

"One groat," Jan said mournfully handing over the coin. "Such robbery."

She grabbed the bag with one hand and Jan's arm with the other, pulling him away. His expression calmed instantly.

"Good enough," he said. "You did well. But see if you can manage to look a bit more put upon next time, as if you know I'm a completely unhinged cad who won't stop." He looked around.

"Next time?"

"Onto the candle maker."

"Oh, Jan, no. I'm not—"

She was cut off by the explosion of an eerie sound that sounded somewhere between a snarl and a scream. She and Jan both whirled.

This was followed by the sound of several townspeople screaming.

"There!" someone shouted. "Run."

A second snarl rang out, as people began to scatter, and to Julianna's shock, through the fading light of day, she saw a huge black cat dash out from behind a market stall, chasing a man. As the cat closed, the man seemed to trip and fall forward, and then the creature was upon him, flipping him onto his back and pinning him to the ground.

As if on instinct, Jan darted in front of Julianna, using one arm to push her behind himself.

Before he could act further, the great cat drew

back one claw and slashed the man it had pinned across the face.

Then, as quickly as it appeared, it dashed away and vanished from sight, heading in the direction of the forest.

Julianna was gasping. It had all happened so fast. Then she and Jan both ran for the injured man—along with a dozen other people. His eyes were closed, and his face was bleeding badly from at least three deep claw marks, but she could see his chest rising and falling.

Still half in shock, she tried to calm her breathing and whispered to Jan. "Why would Rico do this?"

His eyes flew to her face. "That wasn't Rico."

After a restless night, Julianna emerged from the wagon just past dawn to help with the morning campfires, but the mood of the group had changed. No one spoke or laughed, and as Doreena came out to help with breakfast, she continually glanced in the direction of the town.

No one knew what to expect. Word of the attack by the great cat had spread, apparently reaching Sebastian's camp not long after it happened. Jan had told Julianna that Sebastian's people knew about Rico—as having a shifter in the group was a symbol of prestige—though Jan didn't seem to view this as a threat. He swore that none of the Móndyalítko would ever betray such a secret.

But... he'd also sworn they didn't steal territory or money from each other either, and both of those things had happened.

Shortly after the breakfast oats were boiling, Julianna heard light hoof beats and looked up. A tall man with silver hair on a dappled gray horse was riding toward the camp. He didn't look angry or threatening, but rather more... uncomfortable.

Before he'd even dismounted, Jan, Doreena, Rosario, Heraldo, Corbin, Rico, and Belle gathered near the fire, all of them pretending to be about their morning duties. Julianna slipped over behind Jan.

The tall man swung off his horse and walked over.

"Morning, Master Braxton," Doreena said, smiling. "Would you like some oats and cream? Or a mug of tea?"

"No, thank you."

Julianna had already suspected he was the town magistrate. The only other person Doreena had mentioned—who might come with questions—was Lord Rueben, the vassal, and this visitor wasn't dressed like a nobleman. His boots were dusty, and although his cloak was well made, it was of coarse brown wool, as if he had little care for his clothing.

"How can we help you," Rosario asked, stoking the campfire. "I don't suppose you've come to run off Sebastian?"

Braxton didn't smile at the poor jest, and he looked over everyone standing before him. His eyes rested for a moment on Belle, who tilted her head and curtsied to him prettily. Then his gaze fell on Rico.

"I've come because..." he trailed off as if uncertain what to say. "Young Donovan came to me with a story yesterday, that your Rico turned into a large black cat and attacked him and four of his father's men. Donovan didn't have a mark on him, and I waved him off, telling him he'd been sampling too much of his father's wine stock." He paused and Julianna tensed, keeping halfway hidden behind Jan. "But then, we had an... event occur last evening. I've got an injured townsman, and a dozen witnesses tell me they saw a cat, the size of one of the lions that hunt in the hills, attack this man."

To Julianna's astonishment, everyone gathered by the morning campfire continued to look at Braxton expectantly, as waiting for him to make his point.

When he didn't continue, Rosario finally said, "And after knowing us all these years, you've come here to... what? To arrest Rico and accuse him of having transformed into a great cat?"

Braxton dropped his gaze, his discomfort turning to open embarrassment. "No, but the report had been made, and after what happened in town... you understand that I needed to come out and speak with you." He raised his eyes again and focused on Rico. "Can you at least assure me that you were here in camp last night?"

Rico nodded solemnly.

Doreena let out a snort. "I am sorry for the man who was injured in town, but I can most certainly promise you that our Rico did not transform himself into a great cat and go prowling through Serov."

The manner in which she said this made it sound so ridiculous that Braxton merely nodded, perhaps relieved the interview was over.

"All right then. You understand I had to come... and I may be back."

Rosario stepped forward to walk him back to his horse. "Of course. Sometimes those mountain cats will go into populated areas if they get hungry enough. We've seen them once or twice ourselves in our travels."

Braxton nodded and put his foot in the stirrup. "Yes, that was my thinking too. I'll speak with Lord Rueben about appointing some extra guards."

"Good idea."

Julianna was bursting with a question. A part of her wished to keep invisible, but she couldn't help calling out, "Sir?"

Mounting his horse, Braxton turned his head toward her and frowned slightly, probably wondering who she was. "Yes?"

"Does Lord Rueben keep a menagerie?"

Everyone stared at her, but she waited for an answer. Zupan Cadell had told her it was common for higher nobles to keep collections of exotic animals, and it was an equally common practice for them to give other unusual animals as gifts.

Braxton paused, thinking. "I... I think he does."

"You might see if he's missing a great cat."

He studied her a moment longer, then nodded and turned his horse away.

Rosario remained in place as the magistrate rode out of sight, and then he slowly turned and walked back to the campfire.

"So..." he began. "As polite as that was, we are officially under investigation."

"You mean, I'm under investigation," Rico said quietly.

"No one can accuse you of anything," Belle put in.

"Unless Donovan's guards all testified that they saw the same thing." Rosario sighed. "And Braxton didn't mention it and he's just waiting for proof."

Both Heraldo and Corbin remained silent, listening, but Corbin twitched once, as if unable to stop himself. Julianna could see that they disliked having their group as the center of any kind of unpleasant attention.

"Maybe it *was* only a hungry mountain cat that wandered into town," Belle continued. She seemed bent on this coming to nothing. Perhaps she felt guiltier than she'd let on.

"No," Jan answered. "You didn't see it. It wasn't hunting, and it wasn't hungry. It made certain it was seen. It maimed someone, and then it vanished."

"What are you suggesting?" Doreena asked. "That the act was intentional?"

"I'm suggesting that someone is trying to expose Rico as a shifter and have him blamed for this crime."

Everyone turned to stare at Jan, but the same thought had already occurred to Julianna—and she was almost certain she knew who it was.

Really, it wasn't difficult to guess.

By nightfall, Julianna had set a plan into motion. She'd been busy preparing all day, and thankfully, everyone else, especially Jan, had been too preoccupied to notice.

All of her instincts and sense of reason pointed to

Donovan. First, whoever was trying to cast doubt on Rico would need access to not only a great cat—but to one at least partially trained and controllable. Donovan was the son of the wealthiest wine merchant in the province and his family dined with Lord Reuben.

Julianna remembered all the stories with which Cadell had regaled her with while they mutually worked on projects in the village, and one of his favorite topics was the excess of the nobility. On his visits to Enêmûsk, he'd seen first hand collections of exotic animals in places called "menageries" kept by higher nobles. It was a sign of status to at least keep a small menagerie, and from everything Julianna had heard of Lord Rueben, she suspected he might be the type—hence her question to Master Braxton.

Between wealth and position, even though Donovan was not noble, he would certainly have access to Lord Reuben's menagerie... though whether it contained a great cat or not was still in question. For all she knew, it could contain nothing more than an aging bear and a few peacocks.

However... second... Julianna was a good judge of emotions, and she'd seen every passion which had crossed Donovan's face during his short visit to the camp. His obsession with Belle had been clear, but so had his hatred of Rico for thwarting him.

He wanted revenge.

Yes, Julianna's speculation was far-fetched: that Donovan had somehow managed to use a great cat from Lord Rueben's menagerie to try and get Rico arrested, or worse, but was it any more far-fetched than Rico's ability to shape shift?

No matter which way she pondered things, her final conclusion was the only possibility that made any sense.

And she had to pursue it.

So, that afternoon, she'd asked Belle, pretending mere curiosity, and learned the location of Donovan's family storage buildings in Serov. She also learned that he and his father resided part of the year at an upscale inn a few blocks away. Sneaking into the wagon alone—and feeling guilty even though she was acting in Rico's interest—she'd found a quill, ink, and some paper among Doreena's things, and she penned a note.

Master Donovan,
    I travel with Belle and am her friend. She has asked me to speak with you alone, to give you a message about why she acted as she did during your visit.
    She would come and see you herself, but she fears her father and brother, and she cannot be seen leaving camp. I am not so easily watched.
    Please meet me just after dark behind your father's storage sheds, and I will tell you of her feelings.

Looking at the note, she grimaced over the dark light in which it portrayed Rosario and Rico. However, this didn't stop her. She knew after reading this message, Donovan would rush to meet her.

Quickly, she engaged a boy to run the message to Donovan's inn, and once he was gone and the plan was set into motion, she realized she'd need to bring some way to defend herself—should Donovan prove dangerous if he suspected what she was really doing.

Several possibilities occurred to her and after a moment's contemplation, she decided on one, but she couldn't take action to secure this plan until she was almost ready to leave the camp after dark.

Her biggest fear was that the mood of the Móndyalítko was so dour that they might skip their normal evening's practice around the campfire. As things stood, Rosario had decided to put off performing inside Serov until he'd ascertained whether or not Donovan had been spreading rumors about Rico.

But to her relief, that evening after dinner, the families gathered around the fire and Doreena asked Jan to play.

"Only if Rico joins me," Jan said.

Without speaking, Rico picked up a violin.

"Perhaps Belle could dance?" Julianna suggested.

Belle flashed her look of mild surprise and smiled. "Of course."

Julianna stepped out to the edge of the circle, and this time, Jan and Rico began a duet with a fast pace, and Belle's body moved more quickly than her typical dance. Unfortunately, she managed to position herself in front of Corbin and continued to torment him.

He watched her with hungry eyes.

Julianna paid little attention, and she kept stepping backward, away from the group as everyone else focused on Belle. Once Julianna was far enough into the shadows, she turned and hurried to the wagon, climbing the short stairs and entering.

Inside, she donned Doreena's wool cloak, and then she hesitated only an instant before going to the wide bed built into the wall and kneeling down.

Rosario kept a small, hand-held, loaded crossbow beneath the bed.

Julianna took and hid it beneath the heavy cloak. Then she slipped back outside and headed for the path leading into the Serov. She knew Jan would most likely miss her before she got back, and he would be frantic, but her task was necessary and she couldn't take the chance of bringing him into her confidence and having him try to stop her.

Her trip through the streets of the town didn't take long. She simply followed the descriptions she'd been given earlier—from Belle—of the location of the two storage buildings, and they weren't hard to find.

Upon reaching them, without even stopping, she hurried around the back and peered through the darkness.

As she'd anticipated, Donovan was already there, waiting for her. His back was to her, but he whirled at the sound of her footsteps and rushed toward her, stopping a few paces away. Beneath her borrowed cloak, she gripped the crossbow.

Closer, his face looked even rounder than before, but his cheeks were covered in stubble, as if he'd forgotten to shave.

His eyes searched her face wildly.

"Are you Belle's... friend? I don't recognize you," he said. His voice was ragged. This poor young man was a fool if he was making himself ill over Belle.

Julianna nodded, bracing herself, and carefully planning her next words. She needed to catch him utterly unawares so that his reaction would be naked to her.

"Yes, I am her friend. She sent me to tell you how sorry she is."

This was a terrible lie, but it couldn't be helped. Donovan closed his eyes in sheer relief, and his body sagged.

"Then she still loves me?"

Julianna hesitated, knowing she had to time this just right. "She has a question, and she wants an honest answer."

His eyes opened, and puzzlement crossed his features. "Anything. I'll tell her anything."

"Were you the one who set that great cat loose in the market yesterday? Were you trying to get her brother arrested?"

His face went blank with shock, as if he barely understood the question, and she shriveled inside at the sight.

"What?" he gasped. "How would I...? Why would she think that I...?" Shock turned to anger. "And that *was* her brother in the market yesterday."

She shook her head. "It wasn't. He was at the camp all evening."

"No, he slipped away somehow! It was him. It had to be."

His accusations about Rico meant nothing, but Julianna could read even subtle faces—like Belle's—and Donovan was not subtle, and his shock at her question had been genuine.

He wasn't the culprit.

She took a few steps back, reeling in disappointment. If not Donovan, then who?

"Tell me her message," he begged in desperation. "What message did she send with you?"

Julianna lessened her grip on the crossbow. This foolish young man was no danger to her. He was more likely a danger to himself.

"She's asked you to stay away," Julianna said. "She's sorry and she never meant to hurt you, but her parents and brother would never let her become your mistress, some kept woman. You'll only cause her pain if you ask her to go against her family."

"No! She promised."

"If you loved her at all, you would never have asked her such a thing!" Julianna snapped, unable to keep her feelings inside. "Let her be. If you love her half as much you claim, you'll leave her alone."

Turning, she strode away, and he didn't follow.

The disappointment in her mouth was bitter.

In the matter of Rico, she was not only certain of Donovan's innocence, but also his ignorance. He didn't know a thing.

Jan tried to enjoy himself, and to help his cousin enjoy himself. Rico rarely played, but he wasn't bad, and the two of them hopped around the fire after Belle, playing tunes to make her move faster and faster.

The families watching them smiled and laughed and clapped, but it felt forced. Having a shifter among a group was a sign of status—as not all the traveling families had one—and they took pride in Rico. Should another attack by this mysterious cat occur and Donovan's men made a larger fuss about what they'd witnessed in this camp, Master Braxton would be forced to do more than visit.

Even though he only spent the autumns with his mother's people, Jan was well aware that when trouble started anywhere, most eyes turned to the Móndyalítko.

As he and Rico finished their fourth song, Belle fell backward into a chair by the fire, laughing and gasping. She alone appeared light-hearted and unworried about Rico.

"Enough!" she cried, still laughing. "I'm done for." Looking around, she said, "Father, come and tell us a story."

Rosario was a storyteller. Jan could see his uncle was not in the mood—and he looked a bit older than his years tonight—but he nodded to his daughter and walked in beside the campfire.

"Tell something light," Rico said. "Nothing dark."

Jan wondered what tale his uncle would choose.

He never found out.

Carrying his bow and violin, he moved toward the outskirts of the group, looking around for Julianna... and not finding her.

"Aunt?" he said, seeing Doreena a few paces away. "Did you send Julianna to the wagon for something?"

"Did I what?" she glanced around, her brow wrinkling. "No. I haven't seen her." She turned toward their wagon. "Julianna! Are you there?"

"I'll go look," Jan said. "Maybe she's tired and went to lay down."

He found that unlikely, but could think of no other reason for her to leave the fire without saying anything. Even those of the group going off into the trees to answer the call of nature told someone. This was only safe.

Walking swiftly, he reached the wagon, leaped up to the door, and looked inside. It was empty... but he noticed Doreena's cloak was missing, and she hadn't been wearing it.

Mild anxiety turned to alarm, and he set his violin on a bunk.

Not bothering with the stairs, he jumped off the back of the wagon and jogged into the trees.

"Julianna!"

"I saw her," a small voice said.

He turned quickly to see a girl about fifteen, with long black braids, standing behind him. She was Macie, Heraldo's youngest. In autumns past, she'd followed Jan around like a puppy.

"Where did you see her, Macie?" he asked.

She pointed to the path leading toward Serov. "There. I saw her go there."

"Toward town?"

She nodded. "Wearing Auntie's cloak, and she was carrying something inside it."

Without even thanking her, Jan bolted for the path. What could Julianna be doing, going into Serov alone at night?

He tore down the path and skidded to a stop at the edge of town, uncertain which direction to take. Where could she have gone?

His panic and his question both became moot as he looked up and saw her coming toward him. She saw him in the same instant and stopped.

He jogged over, unable to contain his anger. "What are you doing? I've been looking for you."

Her mouth tightened, as if he was the one in the wrong, but he didn't care. His mother had placed Julianna into his protection on this journey.

"Answer me!"

"I had an errand," she said finally, but she sounded defeated, almost bitter.

He realized she was holding the front of her cloak closed and without warning, he snatched it open... exposing a loaded, hand-held crossbow.

"Julianna?"

Her expression crumpled inward. "I thought it was Donovan trying to get Rico blamed and arrested, and I went to be certain of his guilt."

"What?"

"It isn't him. When I asked, he was stunned and there was no guilt in his face." Her voice lowered. "It's someone else, and now I have no idea who."

For a moment, Jan absorbed all this, unable to speak, and then he managed to ask, "And what if it had been him? What if he'd realized what you doing?"

She held up the crossbow. "But he wouldn't have realized what I was doing. I lured him out by telling I had a message from Belle, and I just wanted to see his reaction when I accused him. Had he been guilty, he'd still have denied it... but I'd have seen the truth in his face. I'd have pretended to believe him. I'd have delivered my false message to him, and then I'd have gone straight back to camp and told you, Rosario, and Rico what I'd learned."

He couldn't believe this. Julianna was not capable of deception. "You lured him out by..."

Grabbing her free hand, he began pulling her back toward camp. She didn't jerk away or scold him. Instead, she let him pull her along.

"Jan, if it's not Donovan, who could it be? Who would benefit from hurting Rico?"

She sounded so disappointed by her apparent failure that he stopped and turned to face her.

"I don't know, but I promise I'll find out if you make a promise to me."

Her jaw tightened, and a bit of the old Julianna returned. "What promise?"

"That you won't try anything like this without telling me first. Do you swear?"

She silent for a moment and then nodded. "I swear."

The following afternoon, Rosario informed Jan that he'd decided to take a small group into the marketplace and set up a show. He mainly wanted to get a feel for how they would be received, and to learn if there were any rumors flying about.

Also, Sebastian's people had been performing in the merchant district, which was the most lucrative area. Rosario wanted to lay claim to the market place, which was the second more lucrative.

Jan understood. "Who's going today?" he asked.

"Rico should stay here. We'll just bring a small core of the best performers. Heraldo can do magic and card tricks. Doreena can read palms. You can play for Belle and Macie, and they can both dance. I'll alternate with you and tell stories."

"Can Julianna come watch?"

"Of course she can come. If you have her put on that bright red dress and give her a tambourine, she can help you. She's pretty enough."

Jan went to find Julianna, uncertain of how she might respond to his request. But after an instant of initial surprise, she agreed. He probably should have expected that. She was always ready to pitch in and help.

So, after a bit of preparation, not long past mid-day, the small group headed over into the market-place. Heraldo carried a box with his cards and tricks. Rosario carried a table, and Doreena carried two light chairs.

Jan was amused to see Julianna glowing with a kind of excitement as she gripped her tambourine.

He couldn't help smiling at her as they walked. "I thought you weren't comfortable in that dress?"

"I wasn't... but now it feels more like a costume," she said. "I feel like one of the Móndyalítko going out to earn my living."

Still smiling, he shook his head. She did make quite a picture, with her colorful sash and bracelets. Though her hair was normally straight, she'd been wearing it in a braid, and now that she'd taken it out, it fell in waves down her back.

Upon reaching the marketplace, Jan turned his attention to their reception, but several of the sellers in their stalls called out cheerful welcomes.

"Rosario! Doreena! How good to see you."

Jan relaxed. It appeared no one was blaming them for the attack, and he knew their group brought more people to the marketplace—who then often spent money at the stalls.

Doreena waved back and stopped to chat with a few townsfolk while Rosario chose a spot where they would be visible but out of the way. He soon set up Doreena at the table with the chairs, and people came hurrying over to have their palms read. Doreena was good at palm reading, not so much because she could tell the future, but because she had a gift for listening and telling people what they needed to hear.

Later, Heraldo would borrow the table for his show.

Rosario took Jan, Belle, Macie, and Julianna about twenty paces away to an open area, and he set out three hats at various intervals. Then he nodded to Jan.

"What do I do?' Julianna whispered.

"Just stay with me and hit the tambourine in time to the music I play."

A look of panic crossed her face, as if she had no idea what he meant, but she nodded.

Lifting his bow, he hit his first note, and the rest of the world faded. He played lively tunes at first, vaguely aware of Belle and Macie, dancing swiftly to the sounds coming from his instrument. Then he heard Julianna's tambourine as she quickly picked up on the melody, and she never missed a beat.

As the first song ended, a crowd had gathered and exploded with applause, but all eyes were on Belle, who smiled and bowed and soaked in the worship. She loved to perform more than anything else.

Jan took no issue with this, and he was glad when the townspeople began tossing coins into the hats. Aunt Doreena needed the money for their community box. Turning, he looked at Julianna and saw she was still glowing... and that she was enjoying herself. He realized this was the first time she'd ever experienced the joy of performing and the sound of applause. Normally, she preferred to work behind the scenes, in kitchens or hen houses or out gathering firewood, so it pleased and surprised him that she was having a good time out here on display in the marketplace.

"Ready?" he asked her.

She nodded, and he began the next song.

The afternoon passed quickly, with Uncle Rosario and Heraldo spelling the musical numbers about every third or fourth song. At one point, only Jan and Belle performed, so he could play something haunting and mournful, and she could do one of her slow, seductive dances that kept the audience mesmerized.

Aunt Doreena read palms and told fortunes, and Jan anticipated that tomorrow, Uncle Rosario would bring a larger group into town. This was a relief. Perhaps they had all been worried over nothing regarding Rico.

However... the worry over Sebastian's invading family was still very real. Normally, Rosario would start in the merchant district and move to various locations through the town. If Sebastian's people had played out the better areas, there would be little coin available for another family of Móndyalítko coming in and performing the same types of shows.

Something had to be done. Jan simply didn't know what yet.

As dusk set in, Rosario called a halt. He bid any remaining audience members a good night and promised to return tomorrow.

Jan was just walking over to help Heraldo pack up when the first eerie cry rang out, and he whirled around, going instantly cold.

"No," he whispered.

Townspeople in the market began screaming as a great black cat dashed past a candle-seller's stall and went after a woman carrying a child.

Jan dropped his violin and bolted forward, with no idea of what he might do, but driven by the need to do something.

He was too late.

As with the previous attack, as the cat reached the woman, she appeared to stumble and then fell. The child rolled free, but the cat was atop the woman, slashing twice this time, catching her across the face and shoulder.

As Jan reached them, the cat darted away, dashing the way it had come, leaving the injured, bleeding woman writhing on the ground.

Glancing back, Jan saw that Julianna had run after him, and she was holding the child, gripping it tightly to her chest. He fell on his knees beside the woman. Three jagged claw marks marred her face, and her shoulder was bleeding badly.

"Someone help!" he called. "The cat is gone! Go and fetch a healer!"

Rushed footsteps sounded behind him, and he looked back again to see both Master Braxton and Rosario running up.

Braxton dropped down beside Jan.

"I've sent for a healer," he said. "What happened?"

Jan hesitated. "Same as before. A great cat appearing... slashing... and then vanishing again."

Braxton looked down at the woman and then up at Rosario. "Where is your son?"

No arrest was made, but the mood at the camp that night was tense and fearful. The group did not wish to lose Rico, and Jan even heard whispered suggestions that they should all pack up and leave in the night.

Jan knew that Doreena and Rosario would most likely never agree to that, or at least not yet. They'd worked too hard to create a yearly cycle of places where they were welcome to stay and work—and they would be hard pressed to give up Serov.

And yet... the fear of the other family members caused him to ponder something Julianna had said last night.

If it's not Donovan, who could it be? Who would benefit from hurting Rico?

Just the possibility of Rico being arrested, of being taken away, already had half of the family ready to pack up and leave.

If that happened, who would most benefit?

Only one name came to mind: Sebastian.

As the women prepared dinner, Jan looked over to see his aunt and Julianna both busy at the fire. Neither one noticed him looking. He knew Rico and Rosario were both tending to the horses.

Quickly, Jan went up the steps of the wagon, and he quietly opened the door. Belle was the only person inside, and she was asleep on her bunk. Ignoring her, he went to his aunt's shelf of herbal remedies, and he randomly chose a tiny stoppered vial, which he dropped into his pocket. Then he found a clay pitcher and went back outside.

Belle never even stirred.

Once outside, he slipped beneath the wagon, knelt beside a small cask, and filled the pitcher with dark, red wine. He always kept a dagger inside a sheath in his right boot, but he didn't think he'd need it.

After glancing again at his aunt and Julianna, he headed across the way, entering Sebastian's camp. Similar activities took place over here. Women cooking. Children playing. Men tending to horses.

A girl about sixteen who was leaning over a pot, stood up as he approached. He gave her his most charming smile and raised the pitcher.

"I've come for a drink with Sebastian," he said. "Can you point me to his wagon?"

In addition to being overly handsome, he looked like one of the "world's little children," and his smile did the rest.

Without word, she pointed to the largest wagon. It was the one he would have guessed, but he couldn't have been certain.

Sweeping back with one leg, he bowed. "My thanks."

She didn't speak but continued watching him as he walked toward the wagon. Taking the steps swiftly, he decided on a light knock.

"Come in," a gruff voice called.

Jan opened the door but didn't enter.

The rotund man sitting behind a desk looked up at him and blinked in surprise. Inside, the wagon was cluttered with rolled papers and clothes and bottles and saddles and boxes. It smelled of stale dust, and Jan wondered when it had last been cleaned. A single bunk was visible at the front, built into the wall, and the only other furniture was the desk where Sebastian sat.

Blinking his heavily folded eyes, Sebastian said, "You're... you're...?"

"Rosario's nephew." Jan held up the pitcher. "My father is the vassal of Chemestúk and its surrounding fiefs, and my uncle has been giving me more authority in the family. We performed in the marketplace today, and I know your people were in the merchant district. I thought you and I might have a drink and work out some... boundaries for dividing the town between us."

He'd worded his statement carefully, first stressing that his own father was in a position of authority for the House of Äntes—no small feat—and then that his uncle was favoring him with more authority—which wasn't remotely true—and finally that Rosario may have softened and was willing to divide Serov without resistance after all.

Sebastian's eyes glinted. This was probably more than he'd hoped for so soon. "I won't promise agreement," he said casually, "but pour us some drinks and we can talk." He stood, his girth filling half the width of the wagon, andhe reached to a shelf above his head, bringing down two clay goblets. "What did you bring?"

"Dark burgundy from Kéonsk."

Sebastian suddenly smiled, exposing stained teeth. "Well, that bodes well. You've got the good sense not to offer the cheap stuff."

Jan poured the wine, set down the pitcher, and handed a goblet to Sebastian.

"To a meeting of mutual benefit?" Jan asked, raising his goblet.

Sebastian's smile broadened. "Why not?"

Again, this must be far easier than he expected given the fact that he'd broken with long established Móndyalítko agreements. Jan waited as Sebastian took a large swallow, downing half the contents of his goblet. Then Jan raised his own goblet to his mouth and set it down on the desk.

"Giving up the marketplace would be hard for us," Sebastian began, shuffling papers aside on his desk, "so I hope you won't you suggest that. Perhaps we could alternate?"

Jan remained silent until the rotund man looked up from the desk.

"I have a better suggestion," Jan said coldly. "You tell me whatever it is you're holding over Master Braxton or you'll be dead within a few moments. I've just poisoned you."

Sebastian stared at him and then glanced down at the goblet. "What did you... what did you...?"

"I put a special mix of my aunt's into the wine," Jan explained, taking the tiny vial from his pocket. "I normally prefer not to be murderer, unless I can't help it, so this is the antidote. Tell me what you're holding over Braxton, and I'll hand you this vial. Easy enough."

Turning red, Sebastian looked down at Jan's goblet. "Then you poisoned yourself as well."

"I did not. My goblet's full. I didn't take a sip."

Sebastian's eyes widened, tinted with fear.

"Right about now," Jan went on, "your throat is beginning to close up and your tongue is beginning to swell. Within a few breaths, you won't be able to swallow at all."

"You wouldn't do this! You're Móndyalítko! We don't kill our own."

"I'm only half Móndyalítko. My father serves the

Äntes." He leaned forward, placing one hand on the desk and holding up the vial with the other. "Tell me! What do you have on Braxton?"

Sebastian put one hand to his throat and focused his gaze on the vial. "He stole some taxes! Last spring, he married a girl half his age, and she wanted a finer house, so he started to build her one. He couldn't finish paying for work and materials, and when he delivered Serov's quarterly taxes, he held some back and made an excuse to Lord Rueben. One of Braxton's servants found out and I... I acquired the information and threatened to go to Lord Rueben unless we were allowed to stay."

Jan took a step back, letting anger flow into his voice, "And then you somehow got hold of a great cat that you set loose in the marketplace to ensure Rico would be blamed and we'd have to leave."

"What? No!" Sebastian shook his head adamantly. "I had nothing to do with that. I may be trying to earn a little extra coin, but I'd not expose one of my own people's shifters."

Jan studied his face. He was being truthful.

Whoever had set that cat loose in the market... it wasn't Sebastian.

"Give me the vial!" Sebastian cried.

"Why?" Jan slipped the vial back into his pocket. "You don't need it. I didn't put anything in the wine."

Sebastian stared at him, panting. "But... my throat... my tongue."

"You believed me, and your body reacted." Jan leaned forward again, this time putting both hands on the desk. "Here's what's going to happen. Tomorrow morning, you will pack up your family and leave. I want you gone before the midday meal. And if you don't, I will go into Serov and begin spreading word about Master Braxton stealing those taxes, and I'll make sure everyone knows the information came from you. I'll make certain Master Braxton believes that you've been spreading his dirty secret. I believe he has some pull with the magistrates of a number of towns and villages in this area. Even if he falls from power over this, you will have made quite an enemy."

Sebastian went pale. "You would do that? You'd let my entire family suffer, keep them from finding a welcome and a place to perform?"

Jan turned away and headed for the door. "Be gone before mid-day."

D inner was going to be served late tonight, but no one seemed to mind. Julianna was helping Doreena reheat some chicken and lentil stew from the night before. No one here ever minded eating the same thing two nights in a row either.

Belle came out of the wagon, yawning from a nap, and she sat down in her usual spot. Rico was crouched by the campfire, staring into it, and offering no hint of his feelings.

Doreena leaned over the large cast pot—hanging on a hook over the low flames—and stirred it. "I'm not sure we have enough for everyone. Julianna, I bought some tomatoes at the market today. Would you run to the wagon and fetch them? We can cut them up and add them."

Fresh tomatoes in the stew sounded promising.

"Of course. Be right back."

Julianna hurried off, went to the wagon, and found a box of tomatoes on the floor. She wasn't certain how many Doreena wanted, so she hefted the entire box, intending to go right back to the fire.

However... as she descended the steps, movement caught her eye, and she looked over to see Corbin coming out of the wagon he shared with the rest of Heraldo's family. The sight of the twitchy young man exiting his own wagon was nothing out of the ordinary, but something about the way he moved, something furtive, caused Julianna to stop and observe him.

He crept down the steps as if he feared being heard or seen, and he carried something in his arms. Darkness had fallen, but the moon was full, and Julianna squinted to try and see what it was he carried.

Instead of heading toward the campfire, he turned and slipped away through the trees, vanishing into the forest.

After only an instant of hesitation, Julianna set down the box of tomatoes and went after him, passing through the exact same spot in the trees and trying to listen for his footsteps. She heard nothing but continued onward until she reached a clearing, and then she stopped at the edge of the brush, peering through the leaves.

Corbin stood inside the clearing, bathed in moonlight.

As he adjusted the bundle in his arms, one of his hands became more visible, and she realized he was carrying two separate items. The bundle was black and appeared to be a large piece of folded cloth, and the other object was a small, hand-held rake... with three sharp, metal prongs.

She stood frozen, realizing she was on edge of witnessing something important, but as yet, she had no idea what.

Still gripping the three-pronged hand rake, Corbin shook loose the folded cloth. It was beautiful, black and sheer, and it glimmered in the moonlight like no cloth Julianna had ever seen.

With one hand, Corbin swung the cloth over his shoulders, and the world around him shimmered briefly. Julianna stifled a gasped. Instantly, Corbin was gone and a great black cat had taken his place. The sight was nothing like what she'd observed when Rico had transformed. There was no alteration of features or fur sprouting or claws growing.

In a blink, Corbin had vanished and the cat had appeared.

Although Julianna had no idea exactly how this was being done... she now knew *who* was doing it, and he should be ashamed of himself.

Unable to keep still a moment longer, she stepped into clearing.

"Corbin! Take that cloth off right now!"

She was not about to let him go into Serov and maim some poor townsperson. She wasn't afraid of him. She was traveling with his family and was therefore considered "one of the people."

His head swung toward her, and his glowing yellow eyes fixed on her.

A hint of uncertainty passed through her, but she stood her ground. "Corbin, this has to stop," she said, surprised at the calm in her voice. "You must know that."

His lips drew up, exposing fangs, and he snarled.

Then he charged.

Julianna whirled, running back toward the camp. "Jan!"

J an strode back from Sebastian's camp, not terribly proud of what he'd just done, but satisfied that these interlopers would be gone in the morning.

He realized he was hungry and sniffed the air as he approached the campfire of his own camp, smelling simmering chicken. Aunt Doreena was stirring the pot, and he glanced around.

"Where's Julianna?" he asked.

Doreena looked up. "I sent her to fetch some tomatoes, but she should have come back by now."

Frowning, he took a single step toward the wagon when a cry rang of the forest.

"Jan!"

He bolted, running so fast his feet nearly flew over the ground, not slowing down when he reached the trees but crashing through the brush.

"Julianna!"

He couldn't see her, and he shouted her name again.

Then he heard the sounds of something in the trees ahead, and he darted forward, breaking between two aspens to the sight of Julianna running toward him.

His relief was short lived as she appeared to be shoved forward and she fell. His heart nearly stopped as a great black cat appeared behind her, leaping on top of her.

Without thinking, Jan ran forward and kicked the cat in its side. He expected to feel heavy resistance and was surprised when the cat flew off of Julianna and rolled. Dropping to one knee, Jan jerked the dagger from his boot, not sure how much good it would be, but it was his only available weapon.

True to form, Julianna scrambled to one side and grabbed a heavy branch, whirling back to defend herself. Good. If she could bash the cat just once on the head, he might be able to finish it with his dagger.

But neither of them got the chance to act further.

A black form streaked past them, snarling, and it crashed into the cat on the ground, raising one claw to slash. Jan drew back, trying to get in front of Julianna, as the two great black cats were locked in battle.

"Rico, no!" Julianna cried. "Don't hurt him. It's Corbin."

The cat on top, with its paw still in the air, looked over at Julianna, and she dashed past Jan, running forward. Dropping beside both cats, she reached out for the one pinned on the ground, appeared to grab its fur, and she jerked. A black cloth came away in her hands.

The world shimmered.

The cat on the ground vanished, and a terrified Corbin cowered in its place.

N ot long after, Jan was standing by the campfire with the entire family, and he was still trying to make sense of what he'd just witnessed.

Rico had dragged Corbin back into camp, and Jan had followed, bringing Julianna to an empty chair by the fire and telling her to sit down. She normally didn't like being fussed over, but he could tell she must be shaken because she didn't argue. He stood behind her with his hands on the back of her chair. Some of the family members whispered among themselves.

Aunt Doreena was now holding the black cloth, but she seemed beyond words.

With everyone looking on, both Rosario and Heraldo faced Corbin, who stood staring at the ground.

"Why?" Heraldo asked in pained confusion. "Why would you do this?"

Corbin's face twitched, but he didn't look up.

"Answer him!" Rosario ordered.

Jan had never seen his uncle so angry.

Corbin was silent a moment longer and then whispered, "For Belle."

A hush fell over the group. Belle was sitting by the fire, near Julianna, but she didn't react in any way to Corbin's words.

"For Belle?" Rosario asked.

"So she would turn to me!" Corbin suddenly cried, looking up. "She loves me. She's told me so, but Rico protects your family, and so she doesn't need me. If he... if he was gone, she would need me, and if she needed me, she could be with me."

Rosario and Heraldo both seemed so stunned that neither could respond, but Doreena stepped forward, holding out the glimmering cloth. "So you what... you stole an enchanted cloth that allows you to shift your shape?"

"I didn't steal it!" Corbin shouted at her. "And it doesn't change my shape. There is no cloth that could make me into a shifter. It's a glamour... nothing more. When I wear the cloth, people see and hear a great cat." He pointed to the metal hand-rake on the ground. "I used that for my claws."

Rico was tightly poised outside the circle, glaring inward, and as Jan glanced over, he hoped his tall cousin would stay out of this and leave it to Aunt Doreena and Uncle Rosario and Heraldo.

The two older men still appeared speechless, trying to absorb a betrayal they probably thought far, far beyond one of their own.

"You bought the cloth?" Doreena asked Corbin. "From whom?"

"A kettle witch, when we stayed in Enêmûsk over the summer. I learned he was skilled with glamours, and I asked him to make it for me."

Jan tensed as the story grew more bizarre. The term "kettle witch" was used by the Móndyalítko to describe someone without natural powers like the Mist-Torn or the shifters but who had created power for him or herself via the study of spell components. Most of the Móndyalítko avoided them when possible.

"But Corbin..." Doreena went on, her voice softer now. She held up the cloth again. "Glamour or not, this cloth is no trifle. Just the components would cost dearly. You could not possibly have purchased this with any side money that you earned from..."

She stopped. An instant later, Rosario's eyes widened.

"The box?" he asked hoarsely.

Julianna reached up and gripped the back of Jan's hand, and the implication became clear to him. Corbin had stolen the money from the group's community box. That would mean that Aunt Doreena hadn't checked it since leaving Enêmûsk, but why would she? Serov was the first place where they'd needed to purchase supplies.

"Two years, Corbin," Doreena said. "Two years of saving."

After that, everyone remained quiet for a few moments, and then from his position outside the circle, Rico asked, "What are we going to do? We cannot turn him over to Braxton."

"Why not?" Jan countered. "Maybe we should just turn him over and let him pay for maiming two townspeople."

Corbin began breathing faster.

"And tell Braxton what?" Rosario asked raggedly, finding his voice. "That Corbin was trying to discredit my son, who is a shifter, to get Rico arrested? And that in order to do so, he purchased a cloth to make himself appear as a great cat? Is that what we tell Braxton?"

Jan looked away, feeling foolish. "No... no of course not."

"I'll handle this," Heraldo said, his eyes bleak. "He is my responsibility, and I was blind." He glanced over at Belle. "About many things."

Grabbing Corbin's arm, he led the young man away, but Jan knew nothing would ever be quite the same among the family again. One of their own had betrayed them. Rosario put his arm around Doreena gently, and the two of them walked off, speaking quietly to each other. Other people headed for their own wagons as if wishing to be away from the scene they'd just witnessed.

Rico turned and stalked toward the forest. "I'm going hunting."

Jan didn't blame him for wanting to be alone.

Finally, only Belle, Jan, and Julianna remained by the fire.

Julianna was uncharacteristically quiet. It left him unsettled, and he remembered what she'd told him a few days before... about someone needing to do something about Belle.

"Isn't anyone going to eat dinner?" Belle asked.

Jan stared at her. "You'll need to apologize to Heraldo for your part in this, and try to make amends."

"Me? Make amends for what?"

He could barely believe her answer. "I've seen you leading Corbin on, teasing him, dancing for him. But I'd no idea how far it had gone. He said you told him that you loved him. Have you?"

"Of course I have!" Her eyes flashed. "I love all my family. Men fall in love with me all the time, Jan, and you know it! It's no fault of mine." She turned away angrily, putting the back of one hand to her eye, as if she were the injured party. "I can't help what men feel."

Shaking slightly, Jan realized that more words were futile, and he drew Julianna up to her feet.

"Let's go to the wagon."

Julianna walked beside him. Doreena and Rosario had wandered off, and Jan and Julianna had the inside to themselves. She sank on her bunk, and he sat beside her.

"Are you all right?" he asked.

"Yes. Do you think Rico will be all right?"

"I think so." Jan paused. "No one can prove anything against him, and the attacks will stop now."

He studied her profile and thought on how she'd uncovered the truth tonight. He remembered the sight of her scrambling around and grabbing the branch to defend herself. Also, she'd seen the danger Belle posed when no one else had. Long suppressed feelings rose up inside him, and he struggled to keep from reaching out and grasping her hand.

"I'm... I'm so glad you came with me on this trip," he said quietly.

She turned to him in surprise. He didn't often express such sentiments.

"I'm glad too," she whispered.

They were both quiet for a little while, and he wondered how she'd react if he did take her hand, touch her fingers with his.

"So, what happens tomorrow?" she asked, breaking the moment.

"Tomorrow? I expect we'll go into town and set up a show. Do you want to come with me and bring your tambourine?"

She smiled. "I do." ■

THE
SLEEPING CURSE

Julianna sat atop the roof of a small house built onto the bed of a rolling wagon, and she breathed in the damp, fresh afternoon air of mid-autumn. Having lived her entire life to date in the small, dark village of Chemestúk, this was her first journey—and she was still surprised by how much she enjoyed it.

Two similar wagons rolled along behind them.

"There's Kéonsk up ahead," Jan said excitedly, rising up onto his knees beside her.

She glanced at his face. Her relationship to him was complicated and confusing at best. She'd been orphaned as a girl, and his parents had taken her in. He and she had spent years living in a situation as siblings, but they had certainly never, ever viewed one another as brother and sister.

His uncle Rosario and his Aunt Doreena were down on the front bench of the wagon, and Rosario drove the team of horses.

Indeed... the high walls of Kéonsk had come into view. Though she couldn't see much on the other side of the wall, the top of the castle loomed above, seemingly positioned near the city's center.

In spite of Julianna's enjoyment only a moment ago, she couldn't help a wave of anxiety. Kéonsk was the largest city in Droevinka, and she'd never even visited a small city. Until recently, she'd never seen a town.

"Don't worry," Jan said, looking at her. "You'll love the fair. I promise."

She tried to smile, taking in the sight of his eager expression and not wishing to spoil his pleasure. She'd only come on this journey for his sake, to try and help him recover from an ugly experience he'd undergone... to try and help him regain his former light-hearted self. And he *was* recovering—though they never spoke of this.

The two of them had a tendency to avoid speaking of things that truly mattered, and she sometimes wondered if this was because they were so different from each other.

She was tall, nearly as tall as him, and gangly with long, light brown hair and a smattering of freckles across her narrow nose. She was hard working and liked to view herself as quite sensible.

When standing next to him, she often felt invisible.

Jan was probably the most handsome man she'd ever seen. At the age of twenty-five, five years older than herself, he was slender, with even features and coal-black hair that hung to his shoulders in a wild, unruly mass.

He was charming and vain and skilled at only a few things, such as playing the violin or making women fall in love with him. As a result, Julianna was cautious... caring for him while not allowing herself to feel too much.

However, they'd now been thrown into a journey together and were almost constantly side-by-side.

Jan's mother was of the Móndyalítko people, "the world's little children." Since he was a boy, his mother, Nadja, had taken him to travel with her sister's family for several moons in the early autumn. This year, Nadja had not felt well enough to leave home, and so Julianna had come instead.

She'd fully expected to have a dreadful time, but that hadn't proven the case—or at least not yet.

"There's the Vudrask River," Jan said, pointing. "Can you see the mules and barges?"

She got up on her knees too, but the river was still somewhat distant. Jan crawled forward to the front of the roof of the little house, and he looked down.

"Uncle Rosario, could you take the side road by the river so Julianna can see the barges?"

"Of course," a deep male voice answered.

Julianna crawled up beside Jan and looked down as well. Two middle-aged people sat on the wagon bench below.

Jan's Aunt Doreena was a large and full-bodied woman, dressed in a yellow skirt and a white low-cut blouse—with a half dozen bracelets on each wrist. She wore her thick black hair in a single braid, with an orange scarf tied around her head. Her nose was broad, her smile was wide, and her dark eyes expressed every emotion she felt. She often used phrases like "darling girl" when speaking to Julianna and had a tendency towards spontaneous hugs and kisses. At first, Julianna had found Doreena's open manner somewhat off-putting, but now, she'd developed a deep affection for the woman.

Doreena's husband, Rosario, was so large that he dwarfed his respectably sized wife. His chest was wide as two normal men. He wore his black hair short—and sported a thick moustache. Today, he was dressed in loose trousers, a white shirt, and a russet vest. Julianna had grown fond of him as well.

"There," Jan said, still pointing. "Now you can see better."

He seemed to enjoy showing her new things.

But she drew in a quick breath at the sight of the wide, flowing river, and several barges being pulled upstream by mules. Men on board used long poles to keep the vessels from bumping into the bank.

Other barges were in dock, being loaded or unloaded. She had never seen anything like this.

As Rosario drove the wagon, Julianna's attention soon turned to an unbelievable sight out in front of the city's west gate. Jan had explained to her that every autumn, large numbers of farmers, merchants, and Móndyalítko converged upon the city of Kéonsk for a fair, far too many to be allowed inside the already crowded city, so the fair took place outside the walls.

Wagons, tents, and market stalls were now set up in a vast open area. People and animals milled around in an overwhelming mass.

Just looking at it all... Julianna suddenly found it hard to breath. Where they really going to roll the wagons into the middle of *that*?

However, Rosario pulled up at the edge of the mass of activity and set the brake. Both the other wagons—drawn by various members of the extended family—pulled up as well.

"Why are we stopping?" Julianna asked.

Jan crawled to the side of the wagon. "We need our assignment first." He motioned her toward him. "Come on."

Assignment? What did that mean?

But she followed. He dropped off the side and landed lightly on the ground. She preferred to climb down, as it was an easy climb for her. She wore an old dress that stretched and moved comfortably with her body. The skirt barely reached her ankles, so she never tripped.

Before she could ask Jan further about their "assignment," the back door of the wagon-house opened, and two other members of their traveling companions emerged from inside: Jan's cousins, Rico and Belle.

Six people shared this one wagon, but Jan and Rico both slept outside at nights in a small tent.

Rico came out first. He was a taller, more muscular version of Jan, with an utterly serious expression. Julianna wasn't certain whether he'd ever laughed in his life. She often thought he'd be handsome if his expression weren't always so hard, but he was a strange man... a Móndyalítko "shifter." At will, he could turn himself into a great black cat, and he was the family's hunter and their main protection.

His sister, Belle, came out next. She yawned and stretched as if she'd been sleeping in her bunk—which she probably had. At the age of seventeen, Belle had already learned how to walk in a manner where she seemed to both sway and glide at the same time. She was small and slender with an incredible mass of wavy dark hair. Her skin was pale as opposed to Jan's more dusky shade, but her eyes were nearly black, looking even darker in contrast to her skin. She wore a deep blue skirt with a white blouse as low-cut as Aunt Doreena's, but as opposed to Doreena's large breasts, Belle's were smaller and perfectly rounded... with the tops clearly exposed at her neckline.

She was beautiful.

Unfortunately, she was also conceited, lazy, and incapable of thinking about anyone except herself. While Julianna respected Rico, she found it very, very difficult not to actively dislike Belle.

"Do we have our assignment yet?" Rico asked, walking over.

"Not yet," Jan answered.

There was that comment about an assignment again. Julianna glanced at Jan in puzzlement.

"Oh," he said, perhaps having forgotten this was her first visit here. He motioned with his hand toward the vast array of wagons and stalls out front of Kéonsk. "This is all overseen by a city administrator named Master Deandre. He's lord of the fair, and he assigns where we'll be allowed to set up. Places are assigned based on the entertainment value of the Móndyalítko group or family."

"Entertainment value?"

He nodded. "Our group has no Mist-Torn seers, but Aunt Doreena is a good palm reader, and Belle can draw a crowd with her dancing. The more people we draw to a show, the more of them stay to spend money at the stalls—and the city takes a portion of all sales. Any Móndyalítko groups who draw smaller crowds tend to end up all the way at the back."

"We're normally given a good spot," Belle put in, pulling her blouse down a little lower. "People love to come and see me dance."

Julianna nodded politely and tried not to roll her eyes.

Just then, Doreena and Rosario climbed down from the wagon's bench as a small man with a thin moustache and a quick step came trotting toward them. Even in a hurry, he had a business-like manner about him, and yet he held out both arms to embrace Doreena.

"My dear," he said. "So good to see you."

"Master Deandre," she said, embracing him back. "You never age a day!"

To Julianna's surprise, the small man turned and embraced Rosario next as if they were all old friends —which they probably were.

"And Rosario," Master Deandre said, "You have your usual place in the north market sector. It's empty and waiting for you. Roll right on in."

"Don't let him fool you," Jan whispered in Julianna's ear. "If we stopped drawing an audience, he'd have us half a league away putting on shows for the chickens."

"Is our assigned spot a good one?" she whispered back.

"It's not among the three best, but it's good enough to be envied by the other families. We're in a sector where a lot of food and wine and ale are sold. People who enjoy our shows tend to be free with the coins they toss into Rosario's hat."

With his task done, Master Deandre strode off as quickly as he'd arrived, and Rosario and Doreena climbed back onto the wagon bench. Julianna put her hands to her back and stifled a groan. The last thing she wanted to do was climb back onto that wagon.

"Uncle, I think we'll walk," Jan called. "We need to stretch our legs."

Julianna sighed in relief, silently thanking him.

"Well, I'm not going to walk," Belle said, going through the door at the back of the wagon and closing it behind herself.

The teams of horses started forward, heading into the fair, and Julianna, Jan, and Rico strolled behind.

About sixty paces outside the gates, they passed another family of Móndyalítko. This group had four brightly painted wagons, and the people looked as if they'd been settled for a few days. A middle-aged sinewy man with a yellow scarf tied around his dark hair smiled as Jan's family rolled by.

"Rosario!" he called up. "Good to see you. Come and visit us once you're settled. I bought some of that tobacco you like from the Yegor province. We'll share a pipe."

"My thanks," Rosario called back, though Julianna couldn't see him from where she walked. "We'll bring spiced tea from Enêmûsk."

"The families here all know each other," Rico told Julianna as he strolled beside her. "It is good to have friends."

Julianna certainly agreed with that.

However... upon passing the west gate, Julianna looked over and saw a number of armored men in red tabards guarding the city entrance: Väränj soldiers. She stopped and stiffened. So did Jan.

Rico glanced over. "What is it?"

"Are the Väränj still allowed to guard the city?" she asked in disbelief.

"Of course... why would you ask?" He seemed confused by her question.

Jan's mouth was tight, but he didn't speak.

At present, the House of Äntes was in power over the nation, with their prince serving as elected grand prince of Droevinka. No matter which house was in power, the grand prince always came to Kéonsk and lived at the castle here. The unlanded house of Väränj was not allowed to have their own prince serve in this position; so instead, they had the honor of guarding the royal city.

However... several moons ago, the house of Väränj had declared war upon the Äntes—due to what they considered a slight upon their honor—and the two houses had been embroiled in a violent dispute ever since... which had spilled over into great suffering for anyone unlucky enough to be in their path.

Julianna and Jan's home had fallen in their path.

The Äntes had come through Chemestúk first, conscripting all the able-bodied men, including Jan, and taking them away. Then... the Väränj had come through and burned Chemestúk to the ground as if by way of retribution.

And now, here were the Väränj, shamelessly guarding the gates of Kéonsk as if nothing had happened.

There was something very wrong here, but clearly Rico had no answers, and Jan didn't appear to want to discuss it.

"Here we are," Jan said quickly, still slightly shaken. "Over there beside those stacked casks of ale."

Looking ahead, Julianna saw a cleared spot, just large enough for the three wagons.

"We'll be cozy," she said, trying to lighten his mood even though she herself could not stop thinking on the memory of Chemestúk being burned.

Within moments, all three wagons were in position, and it was time to get to work setting up. There would be horses to attend, a campfire to build, food to be cooked, and wagons to be readied for a stay of an entire moon.

Other family members dropped down from the rooftops or emerged from doorways, and nearly everyone went to work right away.

Julianna helped Doreena with the fire and the cooking, and soon, they had a large pot of lentil and onion stew bubbling over the flames. Jan helped Rico with the horses. Belle, however, did not emerge from the wagon.

Just as Julianna was about to ask what she might do next, she saw Master Deandre coming toward them again at his brisk, steady trot.

"All is well?" he asked. "You have enough space?"

"More than enough," Doreena answered with her broad smile. "We'll be fine. Can we get you some tea?"

"No. I just came to check on you. I have more farmers and merchants arriving, and at least a hundred duties to attend."

He turned to leave, but Jan appeared from the around the side of the wagon and stopped him.

"Sir," he asked, sounding unusually hesitant. "I couldn't help noticing... are the Väränj guarding the city with the blessing of Prince Rodêk?"

Master Deandre blinked. "Yes, of course." He paused. "You haven't heard then? The dispute between the Äntes and the Väränj is over."

"Over?"

"Yes. The Väränj threatened to lay siege to Enêmûsk, and the other noble houses would never tolerate that. If the Väränj could lay siege to the home of one grand prince, they could lay siege to another. The other houses sent men to aid the Äntes, and the dispute was ended."

Julianna stepped closer. "How?"

"It was a tricky business. The other houses need the Väränj to guard Kéonsk, regardless which grand prince is in power. Thank the gods Prince Rodêk was wise enough to see that. Instead of executing their leaders, he called for a council, and the Väränj were also wise to see how vastly they were outnumbered. Prince Rodêk apologized for any 'misinterpreted' slight upon their honor, and an uncomfortable peace was agreed upon."

Taking this in, Julianna wasn't sure how she felt. She'd heard that other villages besides Chemestúk had been burned. People were dead, men had been ripped away from their homes, and now the nobles behaved as if nothing had happened? That didn't seem right.

"Was Enêmûsk ever attacked?" Jan asked.

"No."

He glanced at Julianna, and she was thinking the same thing. Perhaps the men conscripted from Chemestúk were on their way home. Jan had escaped on his own, but he'd not been able to rescue anyone else.

Deandre clicked his heels. "Forgive me. I must get on with my duties."

Julianna nodded. "Of course."

He was already walking away.

Unbidden memories nearly overwhelmed her... of the horrors that had occurred in Chemestúk, which were now probably forgotten by both the Väränj and the Äntes.

Turning from the fire and heading for the wagon, she said, "I'll go and unpack your tent."

Her mind wouldn't stop churning. What if some slight upon the honor of one house or another could launch another such blood bath. Again... it wasn't right. She simply had no idea what could be done to stop it.

Suddenly, Jan was beside her. "Are you all right?"

"Of course." At the moment, she didn't want to talk to anyone, not even him, and she walked faster, leaving him behind.

"We can't control the world, Julianna," he called after her. "I finally realized that. All we can do is fight to protect ourselves from whatever comes and in the meantime, try to be happy with what we have now."

Stopping, she looked back at him. He always read her better then anyone she'd ever known... and right now, he was probably right.

The following morning, Julianna woke up feeling better. Perhaps Jan's words had slowly been absorbed into her thoughts during sleep, but something about them brought her comfort—that at present, she had nothing to fight and a good deal to be happy about.

Pushing back her covers, she stretched her arms. Inside, the small wagon-house boasted three beds. Two of them were narrow bunks built into the wall that ran parallel with the front side of the wagon, and a third, wider bed had been built into the left-side wall. Doreena and Rosario had taken the wider bed while Belle and Julianna slept in the bunks.

Julianna had given Rico's bunk, and he slept outside in a tent with Jan. Before winter, she and Jan would go back to Chemestúk, and then Rico would sleep inside again.

The others inside the wagon were beginning to stir, and Julianna suddenly wondered how she should dress.

"Doreena," she said quietly, as she tended to speak quietly in the mornings while the family was waking, "Will Rosario have us performing today or will we still be settling in?"

Climbing out of bed in her white shift, Doreena rubbed her eyes. "We'll start after the mid-day meal. Best wear your good gown and sash."

"All right."

Before Julianna had left Chemestúk, Jan's mother had kindly provided clothing to help her fit in, starting with a gown of rich scarlet—as Julianna loved the color red. The dress laced up the front with a v-neckline. The sleeves were long and slender and hemmed without cuffs. The waistline was cut perfectly for Julianna's slight figure and the skirt was full, but not so full as to be cumbersome. She'd also been given a purple paisley sash to tie around her waist, and a number of dangling bracelets.

To earn their living, the family put on shows for the public. Everyone had at least one skill or talent, from reading palms or telling futures, to performing astonishing card tricks, to playing the violin, to singing... to dancing. Belle was a dancer and knew exactly how to draw an audience by moving seductively to the sound of music. Jan played the violin while Belle danced, and even Julianna took part in the shows.

To her astonishment, the family had asked her to play the tambourine while following Jan. Doreena had insisted that she was "quite pretty" in her scarlet dress and would be able to add sound and color to Jan's performance. The prospect had been terrifying at first—and Julianna hardly viewed herself as pretty—but she soon realized that what they asked was not difficult... and she'd come to enjoy it.

"Belle," Rosario said, "time to get up."

"In a moment," Belle murmured, rolling over.

No one suggested for a second time that she get her bottom out of bed, and Julianna sighed. Belle never helped with meals anyway.

Julianna dressed carefully, making certain her sash was properly tied. She decided to wait on the bracelets.

Shortly after, she stepped outside to find the camp already abuzz with activity. A fire was lit and water was boiling for tea.

Looking all around, she couldn't help being a bit overwhelmed by having the wagons parked here within this enormous market. Stalls were being opened for business and early customers were arriving. Goats bleated and chickens clucked and the smells from everything between roasted sausages to perfumed candles wafted on the air.

Jan was up and about, tuning his violin.

"Morning," he said, smiling. "I see you're dressed for business."

She smiled back, wondering how her life would have played out had she never met him—as he'd been the one who'd sent her to his mother. Without him, where would she be now? Certainly not traveling the country in a beautiful red gown with a family of Móndyalítko performers. That was certain.

After breakfast, the morning passed quickly, and as everyone prepared to perform, Jan filled her in on what would be expected.

"The shows here work a little differently than they did in Serov," he began.

The town of Serov had been their last stop.

"We won't be moving around between sectors like we did there," he continued. "Master Deandre insists that everyone perform only in their assigned locations." He gestured back toward the wagon. "So Aunt Doreena will be reading palms inside all afternoon... which means the wagon's off limits. Get anything that you're going to need for the rest of the day out of there now."

"I will."

He pointed to a small, circular area not far from the campfire. "The rest of us will be performing there. Uncle Rosario plans one full show for just past mid-day and another one for late afternoon. Our job with these two shows is to provide lively entertainment that will draw an audience who then stay and spend money at the stalls of farmers and merchants selling food, drink, and wares."

Julianna nodded. "Only two shows a day?"

"No, the final show takes place after the sun is down and the stalls are closed, and that one is for us, staged just to earn money for us. It's a little darker, a little more seductive, a little more... Móndyalítko."

She raised an eyebrow, uncertain what the last part might mean, but she supposed she'd need to wait and find out. She knew from experience that asking Jan to explain would do no good. He'd only smile and try to make the whole event sound even more mysterious.

Just past mid-day, the family was ready, and Rosario took his place in the performance area—standing up on a tall stool with three legs stout enough to support his weight. Belle came to stand on the ground beside him.

"Come and gather!" his deep voice boomed. "For the finest show in the land! Learn your fortune from the great Doreena!" His arm swept back toward the wagon where Doreena stood in the doorway, covered in bangles, and she bowed dramatically.

"See the magnificent Belle dance the dance of the three veils!" he bellowed. Belle offered a blinding smile and curtseyed low as he continued. "Witness feats of magic and hear stories to amaze you!"

Julianna found him quite a sight up there, with his broad chest and thick moustache, and his voice that seemed to carry forever.

Within moments a crowd had gathered, and both Jan and Rico jogged into the performance ring, holding their violins and bows up over their heads. They ran around the circle a few times, and Rosario jumped down and grabbed his stool, leaving Belle where she stood, holding three sheer handkerchiefs in her hands

Julianna knew to wait until Jan hit his first note.

When he did, she ran out beside him. Then he hit a long second note... and Rico joined in and the violins made music in perfect sync... and Belle began to move, swirling the sheer cloths around herself.

People fell silent, watching her.

Julianna had to admit that for all Belle's faults, she was mesmerizing when she danced. Jan and Rico began playing faster, simultaneously moving about Belle. Julianna stayed with Jan, letting her dress swirl and hitting her tambourine in time to the song he played.

The music kept growing faster, and Belle danced faster... and people stared.

Finally, when the song ended, it ended on one sharp dramatic note, and Belle dropped to her knees.

The gathered audience burst into shouts and applause. Rosario had placed a hat at the edge of the circle, and people began to toss in coins. Julianna had previously found this a bizarre way for a family to earn a living, but now she was used to it, and it felt quite normal.

Julianna and Rico sat out the next song.

This time, as he played his violin, Jan sang comic

stanzas about a young man in love who was continuously spurned by the object of his affection, and as Belle danced, she acted out the part of the girl spurning the young man in more and more outrageous ways.

The audience laughed loudly, and Julianna began to understand what Jan had meant by the daytime performances being lively and entertaining. Looking through the crowd, she noted Master Deandre was out there, watching. He met Rosario's eye and nodded in approval. Then he walked away.

When the song ended, Rosario's brother, Heraldo, carried out a small table and began his magic show.

Jan jogged over to Julianna, panting, and she handed him a mug of water, which he gulped down. "Soon as he's finished, we're up again for two more songs, and then Uncle Rosario will get up on his stool and tell a story."

She nodded. While merely telling a story didn't sound all that exciting, Rosario could hold an audience spellbound.

"After that," Jan went on, "a few of the younger girls will dance, and then Heraldo will perform his card tricks. Then Belle's up again. Rosario and I planned the rotation carefully."

Looking at Jan, she couldn't help a swell of admiration. The people back home viewed him as beautiful, amusing, and useless... because he was not skilled at anything valued in Chemestúk such as growing crops or thatching roofs.

But he was more than skilled at helping to run this show. He absolutely shone.

"What?" he asked as she studied him.

"Nothing... I just. I wish your father could see you here."

"My father? He wouldn't find much value in this."

"Well... I do."

Then she flooded with embarrassment. What was wrong with her? Wasn't he already vain enough without her contributing?

Instead of preening or making a joke at her compliment, he glanced away, at a loss, and motioned
with his chin toward Heraldo. "Two more magic
tricks, and he's done. Get ready."

Even with everyone spelling each other, they were
all exhausted by the time the first show had ended,
but Rosario was pleased with the money they'd
earned and announced that he was going to go out
and buy more grain for the horses.

Everyone else rested until it was time for the next
show—which went as smoothly as the first.

That evening, as Julianna helped Doreena prepare
dinner, for the first time, she didn't resent Belle for
going straight to the wagon and taking a nap.

Belle had worked hard that day.

"I can't believe everyone is going to perform again
tonight," Julianna said, looking down into the large
kettle where she was stewing two chickens.

Doreena smiled broadly. "Yes, but the nights are
different, a little slower and a little more... for us."

Again, Julianna wondered what this meant. She
and Doreena boiled the chickens until the meat fell
off the bones, and then they picked out the bones
and added diced potatoes, carrots, parsley, and a little flour for thickening.

Jan took some of the money they'd earned that day
and bought a small cask of red wine to be shared.
Julianna had only tasted wine a few times in her life,
and she wasn't sure she liked it. It only seemed to
make her more thirsty.

But Rosario was pleased, and he laughed and
toasted to the day as Julianna began to serve dinner.

Later, when the sun was down, and the dishes were
put away, people began arriving for the evening performance without Rosario doing a calling or saying a
word. Instead, he built up the campfire. For the
evening performance, it seemed they would perform
in a more intimate setting.

He stepped up near the fire, and began by telling
a story... a dark tale of an angry ghost taking

vengeance upon his murderer... and Julianna began to understand what Jan and Doreena had meant earlier. Rosario's stories at the first two performances had been light and comic and suitable for the ears of children. This one involved blood and hatred and revenge.

Like everyone else, she listened, captivated until the end.

"Who's next?" Rosario asked, once his tale was finished.

Then Julianna realized there was no set rotation—or any planning at all. The family would perform as they wished.

Jan stepped forward, playing a slow, haunting tune, and Belle joined him, dancing just as slowly, sultry and seductive.

Somewhat tired after a long day, Julianna almost hoped Jan wouldn't need her to join him. She rather felt more like watching than performing herself, so she carefully moved outside the crowd gathered around the fire and tried to be invisible.

It was then that she looked over and spotted Rico speaking to an unfamiliar young woman.

The girl was lovely, perhaps eighteen years old, with long, silky hair a shade of deep brown and large brown eyes to match. She was short with a small waist and generous figure—dressed as one of the Móndyalítko in an emerald green dress with an orange sash. Normally, a pretty girl speaking to one of the men in Jan's family would not have caught Julianna's attention, but this was Rico. In the time that she'd known him, he'd never once shown real interest in anything besides hunting. Even the violin didn't particularly interest him. He played it because he was expected to.

Now, as he looked down into the girl's face, he appeared blind to anything else around him. Slowly, she reached out to touch his hand with hers, and Julianna could almost see his sharp intake of breath.

He grasped the girl's hand and drew her to the outside of the circle, keeping her close to him and speaking to her softly.

For some reason, the sight of this troubled Julianna, and she had no idea why.

The following day followed a similar pattern. Rosario and Jan varied the two afternoon shows only by the songs performed or the stories that were told. Doreena was busy inside the wagon reading palms, and once again, by the time evening had settled in and Julianna found herself helping with dinner, she could see Rosario was pleased again with the money they'd earned.

After leaning over the fire to see what she was cooking in the cast iron pot, he straightened and took a long swallow of wine. He was so large that she felt unusually small beside him. She was accustomed to looking most men in the eyes.

"You did well today, girl," he told her. "Soon we'll have you dancing with Bell."

That was never going to happen.

"I'd rather play the tambourine for Jan," she answered and then changed the subject. "Even I can see that we're earning a good deal more money than we did in Serov. Will the whole moon be like this?"

Rosario nodded and took another swallow. "We earn more in this moon of autumn than the rest of the year combined. That's why I'm so glad to have Jan back with us. He and Belle are magic together when they perform, and he knows how to help me run a show. So long as we can maintain our assigned place here, we always have a nice nest egg for the rest of the year."

Listening to him, Julianna realized how important this fair was to the family's livelihood.

"Are you hungry," she asked him, reaching for an empty bowl to fill.

He smiled. "And I'm glad you're with us too. I think Doreena would keep you if she could."

After spending years in her youth as orphan, his words touched Julianna. She couldn't help wanting to be wanted. But Jan's mother needed her too, and as much as she was enjoying this adventure with Jan, a part of her had never stopped missing their home.

After handing Rosario a bowl of boiled mutton with herbs and onions, she called everyone else to dinner, and the evening passed quickly.

Then... once the dishes were washed and put away, again, Rosario built up the flames just as people began to arrive.

As before, he started off the fireside entertainment, only tonight, he told a tale of a young bride forced to marry a wealthy stranger who took her to his isolated castle and refused to let her go outside. He gave her a ring of keys that opened every door in the castle save one, and he forbid her to touch that door. Then one day, when he was out, she found the key in the pocket of a cloak he'd left behind, and she opened the door to find six dead women—all in their wedding clothes—hanging from hooks. All were in various states of decay.

Knowing that she would be next, the young bride tied a message onto the leg of a bird and sent it to her brother, who cared for her. Time passed, and just as she feared her husband was about to murder her as he had the other women, her brother arrived and cut off the husband's head.

When Rosario finished the story, nothing could be heard except the flames cracking in the night, and Julianna almost wished she'd not remained to listen. His description of the bodies of the hanging women had been far too vivid.

The dark story cast a mood upon the rest of the performance, and Jan stepped out to play an even more haunting song than he had the night before. Again, Julianna slipped to the outside of the small crowd, not wishing to be noticed, but... then she looked over by the wagon and saw Rico with the same lovely, brown-haired girl from the night before.

He was staring into her face with longing, and she was gripping his hand.

After a moment, the girl began to step away, drawing her with him, and he followed as if being separated from her was unthinkable. They vanished around the back of the wagon into the darkness.

Julianna hesitated, well aware it would be wrong to follow them, and yet... there was something odd about Rico's behavior.

Awash with shame, she silently walked over to where they'd slipped behind the wagon and she peeked around the corner.

They were only a few paces away. Neither one noticed her in the dark.

"Please," the girl was begging. "No one can do this except you. You are the only one who could get past the guards and back out again. My family needs this. We could lift ourselves from poverty."

Still gripping her hand, Rico shook his head, and his voice filled with pain. "I cannot. I would do almost anything for you, but what your grandmother asks of me is a death sentence, and I have my family to protect."

The girl began to weep quietly, and he pulled her close, "Lydia," he whispered. "Don't ask this of me. I cannot do it."

Whatever she was asking, his refusal was firm, though it clearly tortured him to tell her no.

Beyond ashamed of herself for having witnessed so private a moment, Julianna drew back and walked away—yet she could not help wondering what the girl had asked that Rico believed would result in a "death sentence."

She considered telling Jan what she'd heard... but that would mean admitting she'd been spying on Rico—which she had no wish to do. Anyway, whatever the girl had asked, Rico had refused.

Julianna decided to keep silent for now.

J an was happy. The next few days followed a similar routine, but he never found himself bored or restless. He loved helping his uncle to plan and rotate the shows—and he loved performing. Even more, he found himself pleasantly surprised by Julianna having acknowledged his skills and hard work. It had never occurred to him that it would be satisfying to have someone he cared for admire his work ethic, but he did. To him, this life with his aunt and uncle felt more like "work with no work." Julianna appeared to view things differently.

He was also surprised by how much he relished her presence and companionship on this year's travels. Always before, he'd viewed the autumn travels as a time for him and his mother, Nadja, to share a special closeness and to leave the rest of the world behind. Now... Julianna's company had become even more important to him.

And he didn't know why.

He only knew that each day, he grew more and more grateful that she was the one who'd accompanied him this year. During performances, he was proud to have her swirling beside him in her red dress, striking her tambourine in time to his music. Her light brown hair and blue eyes and narrow face —with its charming smatter of freckles—were exotic among the family of Móndyalítko, and he liked that so many people assumed she was *with* him.

Five evenings after their arrival at the fair, once the dishes were put away and the small crowd began to gather around the fire for the nighttime show, Uncle Rosario stepped over beside the flames, and Jan wondered what sort of story he would tell tonight. It never ceased to amaze Jan how many stories his uncle had memorized, and he rarely told the same tale twice.

However, just as Jan was turning his attention toward the campfire to listen, he noticed a familiar sight outside the circle... that was beginning to concern him.

Each night since their arrival, a pretty young woman with silky hair and a generous figure had slipped into their group unseen and gone straight to Rico. She was clearly Móndyalítko, but Jan had never seen her before this year, and he didn't have a clue to which family she belonged. There was nothing outwardly unsettling about her arriving every night and clinging to Rico. Members of one family formed romantic attachments to members of another all the time.

It was Rico's reaction that caught Jan's attention. Rico was a year older, and Jan had known him since childhood. In all his life to date, Jan had never seen his cousin show an ounce of interest in anything besides hunting and offering his family protection.

A few days ago, Jan had asked Rico the girl's name and been stunned by the vehemence with which his cousin had told him to "mind his own business."

And now, Rico looked like a moonstruck fawn, holding the girl's hand and staring into her eyes like a man who'd found something he never knew he'd lost.

This behavior was... unusual at best.

Jan forgot all about his uncle's story, and instead, he stood watching Rico and the girl.

Tonight, she'd brought a small pitcher and a goblet. She poured a dark liquid—probably red wine—into the goblet and handed it to Rico with a smile. Rico never smiled, so he didn't smile back, but his eyes were warm as he took the goblet and drank deeply.

He didn't seem aware that anyone else in the world existed.

Unable to stay rooted and content himself to watch any longer, Jan pressed through the small crowd and headed toward his cousin. As he approached, the girl saw him coming, and she turned and vanished into the darkness. Rico started after her.

"Lydia!" he called.

"Cousin?" Jan ventured.

Turning quickly, Rico saw Jan, and his eyes narrowed. "Why did you do that?"

"Do what?"

"Chase her off like that."

"I didn't chase anyone off," Jan stated flatly, finding the situation growing ever more strange. "She ran. Who is she? And *don't* tell me it's none of my business."

Rico was silent for a moment and then finally answered, "Lydia. Her name is Lydia."

His voice was filled with such longing that Jan couldn't help feeling that perhaps he had intruded and chased the girl away, and he decided not to press the matter.

"Your father's almost finished with his tale," Jan said, "Fetch your violin and come play a song with me. We can perform a dark duel."

In their world, it would have been considered beyond bad manners for Rico to refuse this request, but for an instant, Jan thought he might. Then, his cousin nodded unhappily.

The violins were in their cases on the back steps of the wagon, and by the time Rosario completed his story, both younger men had their bows and instruments in hand. Jan led the way toward the campfire with Rico following.

They'd almost reached it when Jan heard the sound of stumbling behind him. Turning, he watched Rico swaying uncertainly on feet, as if dizzy.

"Jan?" Rico said, putting his bow hand to his forehead. "I feel..."

He never finished the sentence and fell forward, landing face first on the ground.

"Rico!"

Jan dropped down beside his cousin as Julianna and Aunt Doreena ran up.

Julianna knelt down as well, touching the side of Rico's throat. "He's breathing."

"What happened?" Doreena asked in alarm.

"I don't know," Jan answered in panic. "He just fell."

A small crowd was gathering. After putting his violin aside, Jan reached out and rolled Rico over onto his back as Uncle Rosario came rushing up. Rico's eyes were closed, and he appeared unconscious.

"Someone fetch some cold water from the well!" Doreena ordered.

Thankful for something—anything—to do, Jan got to his feet.

"I'll get it."

There was a community well only a few stalls away, and he nearly flew across the ground to reach it, filling a bucket and taking the communal pail without a second thought. He couldn't exactly run on the way back without spilling his burden, but he did his best to hurry.

He could see the first of the family's wagons just ahead when someone stepped from the shadows beside the wagon into view.

Jan stopped.

It was the young woman: Lydia.

Suddenly, he remembered the sight her pouring dark liquid into a goblet, and anger flooded though him, replacing the fear he'd felt for his cousin.

"What did you feed him?" Jan demanded angrily.

Lydia didn't flinch or back up. Instead she raised one hand. "There is nothing I can do now, and I acted only as I was told. If you wish to save him, you need to speak with the Nana in my family. No one else can help."

His first instinct was to drop the bucket, grab Lydia's arm, drag her into camp and let Aunt Doreena have a try at getting some answers.

Almost as if reading his thoughts, Lydia said quietly, "That won't help. No one can help him except our Nana... and she wants to see only you. You must come."

Jan didn't like this. His second instinct was to walk back into camp, tell Rosario about this odd request, and see if his uncle knew the identity of this "Nana" among the Móndyalítko, but he rejected this notion just as quickly. If he said a word, Rosario might not allow him to go... and he believed Lydia when she said that no one else could help.

Gritting his teeth, he nearly snarled. "You stay right here. I'll be back in a few moments."

Hurrying onward, he jogged back into the outskirts of the crowd near the campfire, and he tried to catch Julianna's eye as she knelt beside Rico. Finally, she looked up, and he motioned with his head. Frowning in confusion, she got up and came to him. Everyone else seemed focused on Rico, who had not been moved yet and still lay unconscious on the ground.

"What are you doing?" Julianna asked the instant she reached him. "Doreena is waiting for that water."

Handing her the bucket, he said, "I have to go. Help Rico as best you can and cover for me."

"Cover for you?" Her mouth fell open. "What do you mean you have to go? Can't you see your cousin is—"

"That girl," he interrupted. "That strange girl who keeps coming to him. I know you've seen her. She handed him a goblet of something tonight not long before he fell. I need to go and find out what it was."

Julianna froze. "All by yourself?"

"Yes!" He was growing angry again now. "I'll be fine, but you have to cover for me. Promise?"

With reluctance, she nodded.

After Jan vanished into the darkness, Julianna carried the bucket to Doreena, who used her own waist sash as a kerchief, dipping it into the water and using to sponge Rico's face. He lay on the ground where he'd fallen.

"The cold water might bring him round," Doreena said, dipping the sash again.

Everyone watched expectantly, hopefully, but Rico didn't twitch. His eyelids didn't flutter.

"We should get him inside into one of the bunks," Julianna suggested.

With his face gone pale, Rosario nodded and glanced around. "Where's Jan?"

Swallowing hard, Julianna answered, "He handed me the bucket and said he was going for help."

"Help from who?"

"I'm not sure." Julianna shook her head. "Maybe Master Deandre or a healer."

This was a weak response, but Rosario appeared too worried about Rico to press the matter. Instead, he called upon his brother, Heraldo, and between the two of them, they lifted Rico and carried him toward the wagon.

Julianna ran ahead to get the door.

"Lay him in the bunk where I've been sleeping," she called back, wishing she could do more.

Rico's body hung from their grip like he was dead, and Julianna felt a knot growing in her stomach as she wondered where Jan had gone.

U ncertain whether he should be more enraged or more nervous, Jan followed Lydia through the fair all the way to the very back where the poorer Móndyalítko were normally placed. He expected her to stop at one of the wagons, but she passed the few shabby wagons and led him through the tree line and into the forest.

"Where are we going?" he demanded.

"I told you. To see Nana."

This was no answer, but he had little choice except to continue following her. She pressed on through the trees with familiar ease and emerged in a clearing. Jan paused and took in the sight before him.

In the darkness, he had to make it out by the flames of two campfires: one large and one small.

There were two rickety wagons, badly in need of repair and fresh paint, along with four horses and five skinny chickens. Seven people turned to stare at him: four women, one little girl, a youth about fourteen, and an old man with a pipe. They were all Móndyalítko, but he'd never met nor seen any of them before.

Right away, his full attention turned to one of the women—who was standing next to a cauldron on a hook over the largest of the campfires.

"I've brought him, Nana," Lydia said.

Jan studied the woman. "Nana" was often used as a term of endearment for a grandmother, so he'd expected a crone. The woman by the fire was in her mid-forties with long dark hair only now streaked with a few strands of gray. She was slender, wearing a faded blue gown that fit her well, and her narrow face showed signs that she'd once been beautiful.

Jan didn't care.

"What did you do to Rico?"

By way of answer, the woman glanced at Lydia, who nodded and said, "Yes, it's done. He drank the wine."

Then the woman smiled at Jan. "Please call me Nana. Everyone does."

"What did you feed him?"

Nana held up one hand. "Nothing that can't be undone." She tilted her head. "But I have need of something... something I dare not get myself. Lydia tried to engage Rico's help, but she failed, so I began to watch your family, and I noticed you were clever. Rico might be a shifter, but I think now that perhaps you being clever is a greater strength."

All nervousness fading, Jan strode toward her. "Whatever you fed him, you give me the antidote right now, or I'll go straight to Master Deandre and accuse you of poisoning."

"By all means, do so. That won't save your cousin, and from what I've observed, the rest of your family finds him... valuable."

Jan froze. "Are you saying there's no antidote?"

"Not in the sense that you mean. There is no herb or potion you can pour down his throat. He's not been poisoned. He's been cursed." She gestured to the cauldron hanging near the fire. "I spent much of life studying spell craft, attempting the creation of my own spells, but they got me nowhere, earned my family almost nothing. Perhaps I had no gift. Not long ago, I discovered the value of taking the spells of others and learning to use them. For *this*, I do have a gift."

Jan glanced at Lydia, who was listening with an unreadable expression, but his anger faded as his anxiety returned. He didn't like where this conversation was going. Nana was clearly what the Móndyalítko referred to as a kettle witch: someone without natural powers like the Mist-Torn or the shifters but who had created power for him or herself via the study of spell components. Most of the Móndyalítko avoided them when possible.

"I used such a spell on your cousin," Nana continued. "A sleeping curse. The wine itself was cursed, not your cousin, but he took it from Lydia's hand and drank it willingly. The components alone were quite costly, and I expect a good return."

Jan stared at her without speaking, breathing through his teeth.

"Waking him is simple," she said. "You only need to complete a task I set for you, and he will awaken. Fail or refuse, and he will remain asleep. In three or four days, he'll die from a lack of water."

"You would kill him?" he asked raggedly. "One of the Móndyalítko? That goes against all the beliefs of our people. You'll be an outcast."

Holding both palms up, she said, "Ah, but I wouldn't be killing him. You would. It is fair game for me to cast a spell that presents a challenge to another family. That is allowed."

Still breathing in through his teeth, he wondered if she was telling the truth regarding what was "allowed." There were many elements of his mother's people that he didn't fully understand.

"What is it you want?" he blurted out.

He felt trapped and helpless... and he hated nothing more than being helpless.

She smiled again. "A scroll. That is all. Just a scroll. I can even tell you its location. You simply need to get it and bring it to me, and the curse will be broken and your cousin will awaken."

Dropping to one knee, Jan pulled dagger he kept in his right boot and stood up again. "I'm not full-blooded Móndyalítko. My father serves the Äntes. What if I cut your throat? Would that break the curse?"

To his surprise, none of the other family members moved to try and stop him, not even Lydia. They all stood watching.

Nana shook her head calmly. "It would not."

Lowering the dagger, Jan ran a hand through his hair. He didn't know what to believe, but he couldn't let Rico die.

Gritting his teeth, he asked. "Where is this scroll?"

B ack in the wagon, Julianna sat on the floor, near the door, feeling useless as she watched Doreena and Rosario try to wake Rico.

Doreena got down a bottle of strong smelling salts, opened it, and placed it under his nose. He didn't twitch.

Rosario resorted to slapping him lightly, trying to bring him around.

"Rico," he said. "Wake up!"

Nothing happened.

Belle stood deeper inside the wagon, on the other side of her parents, wringing her hands, appearing genuinely distraught, and the walls felt close with so many people inside—hence Julianna sitting on the floor near the door.

Movement outside in the darkness caught her eye, and she peered out to see Jan waving her toward him.

Everyone else was too focused on Rico to notice Jan outside, and so she backed toward the doorway. "I'll give you all more space."

No one answered.

After slipping outside, Julianna quietly pulled the door closed behind herself and then went down the steps. At the bottom, she was surprised when Jan grabbed her arm and pulled her around the side of the wagon. She couldn't break his grip and was somewhat taken aback by the strength in his hand.

"What are you doing?" she whispered as he stopped and let her go.

"I have to go into Kéonsk," he whispered back, sounding slightly manic, "inside the castle... to find a scroll."

If he'd told her the sun was going to rise in the west tomorrow morning, she wouldn't have been more confused.

"What?"

In fits and starts, he began to recount what had happened to him since he'd left her here a short while ago, and her incredulity only grew.

"A curse? She cursed the wine? How is that possible?"

"She said she'd stopped studying and begun stealing the spells of other casters. She probably stole the one she used on Rico."

"And this scroll she wants you to fetch. What is it used for?"

He shook his head as if the question were unimportant. "I don't care. She said it came into Kéonsk years ago along with some papers removed from an ancient Knaanic monastery."

Julianna had no idea what that meant... but how exactly would this Nana person have any idea what was stored inside the castle?

"She seems very well informed for a Móndyalítko from a family so poor they are not even allowed a minor assignment at the fair."

Again, he seemed to view this as unimportant and

waved her off. "Well, I think she's trying to remedy that and is putting every penny into spell components for now, but I don't care! I need to go. She told me the scroll she wants is in the cellars on the north side of the castle, in the second alcove on the right of the first passage."

Julianna grabbed his sleeve. "And yet she won't even try to get it herself! Jan, Väränj soldiers guard that castle. You'll never get inside, and even if you do, you'll never get back out again. You'll be caught and killed and then the family will have lost both you and Rico!"

To her further surprise, he pulled away briefly and grasped her hand. "Trust me. I have to try. Cover for me again, just until I have time to get inside the city gates. If Uncle Rosario knows where I'm going, he'll try to stop me."

She stared at him, realizing that no words from her would change his mind. He was set on this mad course.

Well... if she couldn't stop him, another idea occurred to her.

Nodding, she said, "All right. I'll cover for you."

He studied her face with sudden suspicion, as if doubting her sudden agreement, but then he glanced around. "Where's my violin?"

"Here," she answered, pointing towards the back steps of the wagon. "Belle put it back into its case."

"Thank you." He took up the case but continued casting his gaze around. "Where's Uncle Rosario's hat?"

"There." She pointed to the ground near the campfire. Jan hurried over and picked it up.

Turning away, he said, "I'll be back before sunrise. I swear."

He hurried off into the darkness toward the west gate of the city, and Julianna remained in place, watching him go.

·　　·　　·

Although Jan had no idea how he was going to get himself inside the castle, he anticipated no trouble with getting inside the city itself.

Once he was outside the temporary autumn market, he crossed the main road in front of the city. A short path led straight forward to the huge arch and rounded wooden gates of Kéonsk's west entrance. Guards in varied light armor manned the entrance, but they all wore the bright red tabards of the Väränj, marked with the black silhouette of a rearing stallion. In truth, though, the men posted on the outer gates were more of a formality, and they seldom denied anyone.

No one else was attempting to enter at this late hour, and Jan walked up to one of three guards currently on duty.

He smiled, holding up his violin and the hat. "Thought I'd go in after the market closed out here and try to earn a little coin on my own."

This was not uncommon, and the guard began stepping aside to let him pass.

"Jan!" a familiar voice called from behind. "Wait."

Incredulous, he turned to see Julianna running toward him. Wearing her red dress, paisley sash, dangling bracelets—and carrying her tambourine—with her long hair flying, she looked every inch a young Móndyalítko woman ready to perform.

"You got ahead of me," she panted at him and smiled at the guard, who smiled back. Her eyes turned to Jan. "Did you forget I was to accompany you?"

With his jaw clenched, he glared at her. "I thought to go in alone tonight. You should go back to the camp. Now."

"I can't. Your *uncle* asked me to come and perform with you. Should I go back and tell him you sent me away?"

The muscles in his jaw tightened further as he heard her implied threat: that either he allow her to come along or she would go back and tell Rosario everything.

"No, of course not," he answered, resuming his own smile.

The guard finished stepping aside, allowing them both through the gates and inside the city, but as soon as they were out of earshot, Jan turned.

"What do you think you're doing?"

"Helping you," she answered. "You don't know how to get inside a castle."

"And you do?"

"Not yet."

The answer infuriated him. "You find some place to hide and wait here for me! I mean it, Julianna."

"Nope." She walked forward. "And if you try to leave me behind, I really will go and fetch Rosario. I'm not letting you get yourself killed."

With his mouth hanging open, he watched her walking away. She was serious, and he could not have his uncle interfering. Rosario was not subtle—and this was going to require subtly. Jan also felt guilty, almost responsible. He should have spotted Lydia for trouble two or three nights ago and looked into her more carefully.

But one thing was clear. Julianna was not going to hide or leave.

With a harsh sigh, he jogged after her, catching up quickly.

They passed through the open cobblestone area that made up the year-round city market area. It was quiet and still now, with canvas tarps covering scores of booths and carts that would come alive at dawn with hawkers selling goods to the city's population.

After that, they entered a district of inns and taverns where the night was not so quiet. Bargemen, prostitutes, and gamblers kept late hours. A slender young woman in a doorway caught Jan's eye. She smiled and held up a hand, rubbing fingers and thumb together to indicate that coin was required for her company.

He looked away quickly, before Julianna noticed the silent exchange.

By far, the most common inhabitants moving in the night streets were soldiers. Most were small patrols of Väränj, but there were occasional groups wearing the light yellow tabards of the Äntes.

Both sides ignored each other as if they'd not recently been engaged in near civil war. Jan found this almost unfathomable.

He led the way directly toward the city center and the gates of the castle.

But as soon as those gates were in sight, he and Julianna stopped and kept to the shadows. A half dozen Väränj soldiers in red tabards guarded the courtyard's entryway, and more patrolled the ramparts and walls.

By the dim light of a streetlamp a half block away, Jan raised an eyebrow at Julianna.

"And now what do you suggest?" he asked sarcastically, not expecting an answer. They certainly couldn't attempt to scale the wall.

But her gaze was on the front gate guards. "I think we need to get closer, close enough that we can hear any exchanges between those soldiers and anyone they actually let inside."

He blinked. That wasn't a bad idea.

Then he shook his head to clear it as he studied Julianna's profile. She was a survivor, and he well knew it. They were both here to save Rico, and instead of resenting her for following him, he realized he should stop playing the fool and accept her offered help.

"All right," he breathed, peering forward to a dark shop closest to the gates. "If we head one street over and come in the south side, we should be able to slip up and peer around the corner of that shop, and I think we'll be close enough to hear."

Nodding, she motioned him forward, and he led the way. Within moments, they were one street over, and he hurried up the block and then turned south until they approached the correct shop and crept up to peer around the corner—with Jan standing and Julianna crouching below him. The front gate guards were even closer than Jan had expected.

"You wanna play dice later, once we're off duty?" one of them asked another.

"Naw," the other answered. "I'm out of coin until the end of the moon."

After the two men had spoken, Jan glanced down at Julianna as she looked up. They could hear the exchange perfectly. As of yet, Jan had no idea how this might be useful, but at least the first thing they'd tried had proven a success.

And so... they both hunkered down to wait and to see if they could gain some idea of who the guards might be letting in and out of the castle.

Time passed.

Almost nothing happened.

A few Väränj soldiers went in or came out with little more than a polite nod or greeting to the guards, but no one else even attempted to enter.

Finally, Jan whispered, "Maybe I could catch one of them alone, knock him out, and steal his uniform?"

Julianna frowned up at him thoughtfully. "I'm not sure you could pass for a Väränj. Your hair is so long... and your skin is dusky."

He paused. She had a point. A few of the soldiers wore helmets, but even if he managed to procure a helmet and hide his hair, there wasn't much they could do about his skin tone.

Still... he couldn't think of anything else to try, and he wanted this done tonight. He wanted Rico awake and drinking water.

Just then, female laughter sounded near the gates, and he peered around the corner again. Five young women with painted faces and brightly colored gowns walked right up to the guards.

A middle-aged guard with a beard, and wearing a helmet, stepped out to greet them, his expression a mix of annoyance and relief.

"You're late, Mira," he said to the woman leading the small group. "Commander Rupert expected you right after supper. The officers are all waiting." He glanced over the others, and his eyes stopped on two women at the back. "I don't know them."

Mira couldn't have been much over twenty years old. Her red-gold hair hung loose around her oval face as she tilted her head. "Don't be so suspicious, Sergeant Greer," she answered. "They're new recruits, but you know Madam Clarissa only sends her best here." She pursed her mouth in a pout. "And we're late because our cook served some bad fish last night. Half the house is sick."

The sergeant nodded, and then he glanced over the group again. "Wait... where's Lorenzo?"

Mira shrugged. "Sorry. He ate the fish."

Sergeant Greer's expression shifted to a new combination, somewhere between alarm and embarrassment. "Lorenzo's not... he isn't coming?"

"Sorry." Mira repeated, and her small nose wrinkled. "But trust me, Commander Rupert would *not* want his company tonight."

The alarm on the sergeant's face increased, but he motioned her forward. "Well, you five had better hurry inside. Like I said... the officers are waiting." He turned to a much younger guard. "Take the girls into the main hall and don't try to explain Lorenzo's absence to the commander. Let Mira handle it. If there's any fallout, I'll deal with it myself."

The young guard nodded once and ushered the women into the courtyard.

As Jan was taking all this in, Julianna stood up beside him in the darkness. He wondered if she had a clue what was transpiring, that a small group of prostitutes had been hired to entertain some of the officers... and one of the commanders preferred men —or at least preferred a man called Lorenzo.

When Jan turned to try and whisper a brief explanation, he found Julianna studying his face, and judging by the look in her eyes, her mind appeared to be working quickly.

"We need to act fast," she whispered. "Leave the hat and bring your violin."

"What do you think we're going to...?"

Her eyes left his face and moved down his body, and a shocking realization hit him. She understood *exactly* what had just transpired.

"No!" he hissed.

"Why not? You're slender and handsome enough to be called pretty. I don't see any other way... and we have to hurry."

"Julianna?"

"Come on."

With her scarlet dress flying around her feet and her tambourine in hand, she ran for the gate, and after only an instant of further shock, he grabbed his violin and followed. Slowing as she reached the sergeant, Julianna continued panting as if she'd been running.

Though her face wasn't painted, her long hair was loose. Her purple sash and dangling bracelets certainly set her apart from a normal townswoman. Jan stopped just behind her, stunned that she was taking the lead here. After all... he was the trickster, not her. But on little more than instinct, he let her continue.

She smiled. "Are you Sergeant Greer? I'm sorry we're late. Mira thought it best to take the other girls and go on ahead." She motioned to Jan. "Madam Clarissa was still trying to find a replacement for Lorenzo." She leaned forward and added quietly. "This is Renaldo. He does not care for fish."

By the light of the braziers on the both sides of the gate, Greer looked out at Jan, taking in the sight of his face, slender form, and longish dark hair. Jan seethed inside. The man's assessment was beyond insulting. Jan was clearly a ladies man and not some male strumpet. This was never going to work.

Julianna must be mad, and now she'd brought them both out in the open.

Then, Sergeant Greer nodded in what appeared to be open relief, and he stepped aside. "Mira's already gone in, but if you hurry, you might catch her before she reaches the hall."

Jan fought to keep his mouth from falling open. The guard believed Julianna's story? He took Jan and Julianna both for... prostitutes?

Julianna, however, suffered from no such surprise. "We'll hurry."

Greer turned to a large guard in his early thirties. "Take them in."

Before Jan had time to seethe any further, he found himself ushered forward through the gates, and then he realized they were inside the courtyard walking toward the main doors of the castle.

Julianna had managed—through some very quick thinking—to get them inside. Pushing down his injured pride, he focused on the moment at hand, knowing that he'd soon be required to do some quick thinking of his own.

A few guards, all in red tabards, inside the courtyard glanced their way, but as they were under escort, no one spoke to them. Jan strode behind their escort, with Julianna trotting beside him, he couldn't help wondering how in the world she'd understood the situation so rapidly. Before this journey, Julianna had spent her entire life in the small village of Chemestúk —where there were most certainly no brothels or madams... or fancy male strumpets named Lorenzo.

As they reached the main doors to the castle, they'd not yet caught up to Mira and the other women, which was a good thing. Their escort paused long enough to open one of the doors and motion them through.

Jan and Julianna stepped into an entryway with a long passage running north, a long passage running south, and a wide one running straight ahead.

More importantly, as Jan looked around, there was no one else in sight. For the moment, the three of them were alone.

"Where is everyone?" Jan asked before thinking, but the guard didn't appear to find his question strange.

"As the prince is not in residence, few servants are

needed. Most of the officers will be in the main hall at this hour," the guard said.

"Which way is the main hall?" Jan asked. "I've not been inside before."

The guard stepped past him toward the wide passage. "I'll take you. Just follow me."

As he neared the corner of the stone passage, Jan moved in a flash, dashing forward, grabbing the man by the back of his neck and slamming his head into the wall. A crack resounded, but Jan jerked the guard's head back and slammed it again. Never having trained as a fighter, he'd learned to rely on the element of surprise.

"Stop!" Julianna gasped softly.

What had she expected him to do?

Jan dropped the guard, who fell to the ground, his eyes closed, bleeding from his forehead.

"Did you kill him?" Julianna asked, dropping to the floor and touching the side of the man's throat.

In truth, Jan had no idea. He hadn't really thought about it. His only goal was to remove the guard, so that he and Julianna would be free to head down the north passage unencumbered.

"He's breathing," Julianna said. "But we need to get him out of sight. Everyone in the courtyard saw him escorting us."

Yes, of course she was right.

"Grab his leg," Jan told her.

Without a question, she stood up and did as he asked, and he grabbed the other leg.

"Down the north corridor," he added, remembering what Nana had told him.

The scroll is in the cellars on the north side of the castle, in the second alcove on the right of the first passage.

He knew it still troubled Julianna that this woman had somehow known exactly where the scroll was hidden, but Jan still didn't care how she'd known or what was in the scroll itself. He couldn't think beyond saving Rico.

Dragging the unconscious guard, they headed north.

Jan tried to not pull faster than Julianna was able.

"We need to find a stairwell... quickly," he said. There was no telling how soon someone might come along and see them here in the main floor.

She glanced over at him in annoyance. "Yes, that had occurred to me."

Chastised, he fell silent and continued dragging the guard, keeping an eye out for anywhere to stow an unconscious body. Unfortunately, the few doorways they passed were open arches—with no actual doors.

Julianna was beginning to pant with effort when she suddenly stopped and pointed to the archway of a small antechamber in the passage. "Let's just pull him in out of sight and lean him up against the wall. No one will find him for a while."

While Jan found this suggestion risky, they did need to free themselves for easier movement, so he nodded. "Take my violin and give me his other foot."

Using both hands, Jan dragged the guard into the antechamber, out of sight, and hoped for the best.

"All right," he whispered, coming back out. "Let's find a stairwell down."

Wordlessly, Julianna walked along beside him down the passage. Near the end, just before the passage made a turn, they came upon a narrow, open archway with a burning torch on each of the side-walls.

Lifting one of the torches, Jan led the way down a dark set of stairs, going lower and lower until they stepped out into another passage.

"Do you think we've reached the cellars?" Julianna asked. "Or could there be another level?"

"I don't know."

But he made his way to the second alcove on the right side of the passage and breathed deeply in relief. Inside, there were shelves lining the walls... and the shelves were filled with texts and scrolls.

"This is it... or this is what Nana described to me."

Julianna looked around by the light of his torch. Her face seemed pale. "Yes... but look at them all. How will we know which one she wants?"

"Which one? Oh, we'll know. She said it's in a blue painted scroll case with a silver stopper."

Turning to him, Julianna shook her head. "Jan... are you telling me that she not only knows its exact location, but what the scroll case looks like?" She paused. "I mean, I understand her not wanting to risk coming down here to steal it herself, but how does she know so many details?"

"I don't care," he said again, and he didn't. "Let's find it."

Her concerned expression had not relaxed, but she set his violin case on the floor and moved to help him. As most of the scrolls were in tan-colored cases, they were able to scan the shelves quickly, and Jan found himself beginning to panic by the time he'd completed his third shelf and found nothing re-motely close to what Nana had described to him.

"Jan, come here. This book is a fake."

At the sound of Julianna's voice, he turned to see her examining a fat text, lying flat on a shelf, that appeared to have thick pages, but as he walked over and looked more closely, he could see the lines of the pages were an illusion.

Reaching out, he lifted the top cover, which was made from wood, and he peered inside. The interior was velvet lined and encased a blue scroll with an etched silver stopper.

"This is it. You found it!"

Her expression was still troubled as she looked him in the eyes. "Are you sure you want to do this, give this to someone capable of killing Rico without a thought? Jan, we don't even know what it is."

"We know it'll save Rico. That's all that matters." Taking out the scroll case, he slipped it inside his shirt. "Now, we have to get ourselves out of here. Any ideas?"

Julianna was silent for a moment, staring at his chest where he'd hidden the scroll, and then she answered. "If you can get us back to the front gates, I think I can get Sergeant Greer to let us through."

That meant attempting to walk out of the castle and through the courtyard with no escort, but Jan had nothing better to suggest. So, they made their way to the stairwell and up the stairs with Julianna carrying her tambourine and Jan carrying his violin case and the torch.

"Wait," he whispered at the top.

Peering around the corner of the narrow arch, he saw the passage was empty, so he stepped out and placed the torch in its bracket. After that, they hurried down the north side passage to the entryway, and again, he paused before the main doors. They'd made it this far with relatively little violence —just once unconscious guard—but Jan had no idea if visiting "entertainment" was escorted out as well as in.

As if reading his face, Julianna shrugged.

"We don't have much choice," she whispered. "Just walk out as if you know what you're doing, and if possible, try to look offended."

"Offended?"

"Just do it."

He wasn't sure he liked the sound of that, and with a puzzled frown, he opened one door and they stepped out into the courtyard, walking at a steady pace for the front gates. A few guards looked their way, and Julianna smiled coyly as she walked. No one tried to stop them—suggesting that people leaving the castle required less security than anyone trying to come in.

As they reached the open front gates, Sergeant Greer turned and saw them coming. His expression shifted to discomfort, and yet at the same time, he didn't seem surprised.

"Now," Julianna whispered. "Try to look put out or offended."

Still puzzled, Jan did his best, and she went straight up to Greer.

"Commander Rupert was not best pleased with Renaldo," she began and then leaned closer. "He said Renaldo was too... *old*."

Jan stiffened. That was her plan? So, he was not only playing the part of a male strumpet, but he was now a rejected male strumpet?

Again, Sergeant Greer shifted uncomfortably, though it appeared he might have been expecting this. Apparently, he knew this Commander Rupert fairly well.

However, then the sergeant became more businesslike and asked Julianna, "Why were you sent away?"

"I wasn't, but Renaldo is new, and I thought to walk him back to the... house and explain to Madam Clarissa. He didn't do anything wrong. Your commander is just overly particular."

Ignoring the last comment, Greer looked toward the doors of the castle. "Where's your escort? Why didn't Guardsman Avery come back with you?"

Jan tensed, preparing to take a hard swing with his violin case and yell to Julianna to make a run for it.

But she made a sympathetic face. "He's still inside... explaining to the commander why Lorenzo isn't here. I thought it best to leave." She tilted her head. "I'll take Renaldo home and come right back. The festivities inside are just beginning. Perhaps you can join us once you're off duty?"

The sergeant blinked. "Um... yes, perhaps."

Jan went cold in near disbelief. This was certainly a side of Julianna he had never seen before. Again, he was the performer—the actor—whenever they needed to distract or fool someone else, but she had taken over here... and was doing quite well.

Without asking permission, she stepped past the sergeant and other guards, walked through the gates and out into the city.

Jan followed.

"I told you you'd need me," she whispered.

He couldn't bring himself to answer.

He did need her.

Reaching up with his free hand, he touched the scroll inside his shirt. For now though, he needed to save Rico.

A short while later, Jan walked back into the shabby camp of Nana and her family. He'd come alone after sending Julianna back to his aunt and uncle. She'd argued at first, but he'd engaged her with the task of explaining what had happened. In truth, he didn't want her anywhere near this middle-aged kettle witch.

Both Nana and Lydia were standing by the fire, and Lydia's eyes flickered in surprise—and possibly pain. He didn't have time to wonder at that and walked up to Nana, who stared at him expectantly... eagerly as if he was bringing her a treasure.

"You have it?" she breathed.

Reaching inside his shirt, he withdrew the scroll case, but held it in his grip. "And now Rico will wake? He will be safe?"

Looking as if she was struggling to keep from snatching at the scroll, she said quickly, "Yes, yes. That is part of the spell to create the curse... the challenge. Once the challenge is met, the victim will awaken." Her voice filled with greed. "Put the scroll in my hand!"

With no choice that he could see, Jan reached out and placed the scroll in her long-fingered hand. She clutched it her breast and closing her eyes.

"At last," she breathed.

Lydia had gone pale, staring at the scene as it played out, and a flicker of discomfort, of uncertainty, passed through him.

"Rico is awake now?" he asked.

"Yes, yes." Nana waved him away. "Go now."

She walked swiftly toward her wagon, and Jan stood in place for an instant, before he turned and broke into a jog for the tree line. He was desperate to find out if all this effort, all this risk had been worth it—if indeed, Rico had been saved.

As he reached outskirts of the vast market and was just about to enter, a voice spoke from behind.

"Wait."

His body jerked to a stop, and he whirled.

Lydia was standing about ten paces away. Though her expression was calm, tears flowed down her face. She looked small standing there in her green dress, almost like a child with large brown eyes.

"You just gave it to her," she said, "without a question or a thought."

She sounded too much like Julianna, and he strode back, closing the distance between them.

"What did you expect me to do?" he asked. "You *poisoned* my cousin. You won his love, and then you fed him cursed wine! Your Nana gave me the only way to save him."

She winced, and he fell silent. She might only be a puppet in all this too, and he didn't want to hurt her.

"There is a spell inside that scroll case," she whispered. "Don't you want to know what it does?"

His uncertainty, and his unwanted sense of guilt, was increasing. The problem was... he didn't want to know. He wanted no responsibility in any of this beyond saving Rico.

But she looked so stricken he couldn't help asking, "What does it do?"

"It will remove a person's will and replace it with the will of the caster. For now, Nana means to use it on Master Deandre... so he will give us the prime location at the fair. The family has a few skilled performers left to earn money for her."

Lydia paused and stared at the ground before continuing. "After that, I don't know what she will do. But she will stop at nothing to gain what she wants. We have lived in poverty for so long while she hunts her spells and uses every penny we earn for her components. This was *the* spell she has been seeking, the one for which she has forced us to sacrifice so much."

He wondered about the "sacrifice," but her presence here confused him more.

"Why are you telling me all this?"

She raised her eyes, and they struck him as haunted. "Did you note a lack of men in our family?" she asked. "Only my aged Uncle Grigory and young Emanuel remain. The rest are all dead... at her bidding, as she ordered them one by one to do what you did tonight, to steal her some spell or scroll." Her voice filled with bitterness. "My brother went first. She'd heard rumors of a scrying spell created by a male kettle witch near the southern border of Stravina, and she sent my brother after it. He brought her the spell, but to get it, he took a knife wound in the back, and he died the following day."

"A scrying spell?"

"When she learns of anything new that she might seek, she casts the scrying spell and puts herself into a trance. When she wakes, she knows exactly where the next scroll or spell is located. Once she possessed this ability, she would stop at nothing, and no one in my family had the strength to fight her. She is our leader by right, and we all just obeyed." The tears on her face flowed more freely. "I loved my brother. He was my friend."

Without knowing the right thing to say, Jan repeated, "Why are you telling me all this?"

"Because I never thought you'd succeed. I never thought you'd place that scroll in her hand. You've given her to power to remove someone else's will and replace it with her own." Lydia turned away. "I cannot imagine what she will do with such power. I wanted you to know what you've done."

She began to walk away, and he realized this wasn't over. He couldn't allow it be over.

"Lydia," he called.

She stopped with her back to him.

"Where does Nana keep all her stolen spells?"

The girl was silent for a long moment, and then: "Our wagon. She keeps them in our wagon."

Without another word, she vanished into the trees.

Jan stood there for a while, uncertain how long, and then continued to the outskirts of the market, to the unkempt Móndyalítko wagons at the back. The first person he saw was an aged woman stoking a fire, and he walked up to her.

Digging into his pocket, he removed a small silver coin his father had sent with him.

"Old mother," he said politely, using a common greeting of the Móndyalítko. "My family has run low on oil. Might I trade this coin for a flask?"

The coin he offered her would purchase a barrel of oil, and her eyes lifted to his face.

"I need it," he said softly. "Will you trade me?"

"Of course, my son," she answered, going to a wooden box of supplies and taking out a flask. "But you offer too much."

"This is for your kindness and trouble." He handed her the silver coin and looked to a candle lantern hanging off the back of her wagon. "And may I borrow that? I promise to return it soon."

One of her bushy gray eyebrows rose in an unspoken question, but she clutched the coin in her hand and nodded to him.

"I'll bring it back," he told her, lifting it down.

She watched him as he closed the shutter on the lantern and headed back into the tree line, back toward Nana's camp.

What he was about to do troubled him, but after what Lydia had told him, he couldn't simply return to his family. As much as he hated feeling responsible for a heartless woman having obtained a tool of great power, he *was* responsible, and he could not leave things as they were.

As he reached the clearing, he stopped behind a spruce tree, peering out. Lydia and Nana were not in sight, but the other three women, the little girl, the youth called Emanuel, and the aging man, Grigory, were all at their own campfire near the second wagon. A few small tents had been set up, and Jan wondered if perhaps everyone except Nana and Lydia lived out of the second wagon.

Nana's dwelling was much closer to him, just a few paces away, with its own larger campfire—along with the cauldron and iron hook. In the darkness, he slipped up behind the wagon.

Through an open window, he heard voices.

"I'm going to need mandrake root," Nana said. "Can you get it for me?"

"Yes, Nana," Lydia answered in an emotionless voice.

Both women were inside.

Carefully and quietly, Jan open the flask of oil and began dousing the back of the wagon. When the flask was empty, he crouched down out of sight of anyone across the camp, and he opened the shutter on the lantern to remove the lit candle inside.

Then he ignited the oil.

Flame began to spread rapidly, and when he was certain the fire would become a blaze, he ran out around the side of the wagon and shouted.

"Fire!"

Gasps and a panicked cry sounded from inside, following by shuffling and something being knocked over. Lydia came running out first, nearly flying through the door. Nana came out next, but she clutched the blue scroll case and several pieces of rolled parchment.

Jan struck in a flash, before she even saw him coming. He grabbed everything in her hands and threw it all onto her campfire.

"No!" she screamed when she saw what he'd done, and she ran toward the campfire.

Instantly, he caught her from behind, pinning her arms and lifting her off the ground. She screamed and fought him, struggling uselessly to break free as the scroll and parchments burned. Behind them, he could hear the blaze of the flames engulfing the back half of the wagon.

Lydia stood a short distance away, just watching him. She said nothing, nor did she move to try and help her grandmother. Across the camp, the other family members were on their feet, watching in silence as well. No one interfered.

When the scroll and parchments were burned black, he let Nana go and stepped away, loath to touch her any longer than necessary.

She whirled to see her wagon ablaze, but her eyes were wild, mad, and before he realized what was happening, she ran for the wagon door.

"My spells!" she cried. "All the rest!"

She was through the door before he even thought to move, and then he bolted to go after her. The wagon was burning on three sides, and the night wind fed the flames.

"No!" Lydia cried, running between him and the door. "She is not worth your death!"

Jan stopped. The doorway was on fire, and wagon was completely engulfed. Over the roar he thought he heard a scream.

"She's not worth anyone's death," Lydia said.

He'd not meant to kill tonight, but had he? Had he killed Nana or had she killed herself? He wasn't sure.

The other family members came over, and in silence everyone watched the rest of the wagon burn.

Jan had left them without a leader, and with only one dwelling for seven people. When Nana's wagon was nothing but smoldering blackened remnants, he turned to Lydia.

"I'll bring food, supplies, and blankets from our own camp," he said. "This is my doing."

Her gaze was on the remains of her home. "I don't blame you. You only did what the rest of us could not."

She was a strange, composed young woman. Perhaps she had been through so much in the past few years that little affected her anymore.

He was about to draw her away when shouting and footsteps sounded from the trees.

"There!" a familiar voice shouted. "I smell smoke over there!"

A moment later, Rico burst through the tree line with wild eyes. Uncle Rosario, Aunt Doreena, and Julianna came running behind.

Rico was awake.

Before Jan could even feel relief, Rico spotted Lydia and ran to her, grabbing her hands and looking at her fingers.

"Are you hurt? Are you burned?"

"No," she whispered, shaking her head.

"What in the seven hells did you think you were doing?" Rosario shouted, closing on Jan. "Taking something like this upon yourself? You fool! Suppose you'd been killed? How would I ever face your mother again? Did you think of that? Did you?"

Behind, Julianna watched helplessly and gave Jan a pleading look that seemed to say, *I couldn't stop them.*

He nodded as Aunt Doreena joined her husband in a shouting rant, threatening Jan with violence should he ever try something so stupid again.

"Auntie," he interrupted quietly, motioning to the small, silent group behind himself. "These people need our help."

She looked over at the little girl and the underfed women. "Oh... oh." Then she was off, bustling over to see what could be done.

Jan turned his eyes back to Julianna as she stared at him. Without her, he was well aware that he'd never have bluffed himself inside that castle, he'd never have stolen the scroll, and Rico would have died of thirst in his sleep... under a curse.

And she was the only one who saw him exactly as he wished to be seen.

There was no one in the world like Julianna, and it was time he admitted to himself that he couldn't live without her. He could never live without her.

It was time he ensured that he'd never have to.

L ate that night, Julianna lay awake in her bunk, unable to sleep. Her mind was too busy with all that happened.

Rosario had decided that the few remaining members of Lydia's family would be unable to safely travel alone or to earn enough to support themselves, and so he'd offered to let them travel with Jan's family at the end of the autumn fair. Lydia had readily—and thankfully—agreed.

Julianna was glad. No one blamed Lydia for what happened, most certainly not Rico, and it seemed that perhaps the risks and fears and tragedies of this night might have all been for the best in the end.

Still, Julianna couldn't sleep.

She couldn't stop going over the adventure she'd embarked on with Jan, deceiving her way into that castle, and now feeling embarrassed by how much she'd... well, how much she'd enjoyed it.

She also couldn't stop think of Jan himself.

She couldn't stop thinking of the handsome lines of his face, and how other women responded to his smile, to his wiles, to the beautiful music that came from his violin. These thoughts brought her pain. He thrived on female attention and admiration, and what she could give him would never be enough.

With a soft sigh, she climbed from her bunk and wrapped a blanket around her shoulders. Quietly, she slipped outside and walked over to the long dead campfire with some chairs still placed around it.

Then she froze.

Someone was sitting in one of the chairs. She could see the back of his head, his long legs and boots.

Jan turned his head. "Julianna?"

"I couldn't sleep."

"Me either."

Walking over slowly, she thought to sit down when he suddenly stood up.

"Before everyone went to bed, I'd wanted to ask you something," he said, "and there was no chance, and I didn't want to wait until tomorrow so I've been just... sitting out here wondering what to do."

He seemed almost distraught, and she wasn't sure she wanted to hear whatever it was he had to say.

But she steeled herself and asked, "What is it?"

Turning to face her, with absolutely no warning, he blurted out, "Marry me?"

Julianna's stomach lurched in sheer surprise.

"I know what you think of me," he rushed on, "but I swear no one else will ever come between us. I'll change. And when we get back home to Chemestúk, I'll work harder at home to help my father. I will strive to be more worthy of you."

How could he think that? How could he sell himself so short? Unbidden, tears leaked from her eyes.

"You already are worthy. You are worthy of anyone. Can't you see that?"

He froze, his locked on her face. "Then you will?"

She didn't need to think about her answer. "Of course I will."

As if he still didn't believe her, he stressed, "You'll marry me?"

"Yes, but I want to wait until we get home, so your mother and I can arrange a proper wedding."

His body was tense, and then finally, he nodded. "Anything you want, as long as you keep saying yes."

At that, she fell into silence. He loved her. He feared being without her. The realization made her determined never to use that power against him.

"I won't stop saying yes. I promise."

Slowly, he leaned forward and touched her mouth with his. The kiss was soft, and she wished it would go on, but instead, he pressed his forehead gently against hers and breathed outward.

She grasped his hand as the following past few

moments truly sank in. Never, in her most far flung thoughts would she have expected this when she first left Chemestúk with Jan.

When they arrived back home, there would be a wedding...

SILENT BELLS

U pstairs in her bedroom at Chemestúk Keep, Julianna stood in front of a mirror looking at herself in her wedding gown.

"What do you think?" she asked.

Nadja, her future mother-in-law, was in the room as well, making a fuss over lacing the gown "just so" and pulling at the sleeves and skirt. Julianna didn't mind.

"You are beautiful, my girl," Nadja said.

For the first time in her life, Julianna found herself almost believing those words. She and her betrothed, Jan, had recently returned home after a nearly three-moon journey traveling with several members of his mother's side of the family. Though a number of memorable events had happened along the way, the most important was their decision to marry. Within moments of their return home, Jan had informed his parents, who'd rejoiced at the news, and by that evening, preparations for a wedding had begun... starting with the creation of the cream-colored, muslin gown Julianna now wore.

Stepping closer to the mirror, she could see the fine stitch work Nadja had put into the square neckline.

Julianna was tall, with persistently straight hair a shade somewhere between dark blond and light brown. Her face was narrow and pale with a light smattering of freckles across her nose. She'd never liked her height or what she considered her "gangly" build or her smattering of freckles, but in this fine cream gown with her hair pinned up—and only a few strands dangling to frame her face—she almost felt pretty.

"The color suits you so well," Nadja said, standing at her shoulder.

"I should take it off before I brush against something and soil it. I want it perfect for tomorrow."

Nodding, Nadja stepped behind to unlace the back. "I'll help you out of it."

In her mid forties, Nadja could still be called lovely. With shimmering dark hair and a dusky, smooth complexion. Once she had been light of foot and agile, but this past year, she had slowed a little and often had to catch her breath after crossing a large room.

Julianna worried about her, for Nadja was much more than a future mother-in-law.

When Julianna had been orphaned as a girl, Nadja and her husband, Cadell, had taken her in and treated her as a daughter. Perhaps it should seem strange that Julianna was now marrying their son, but so far, no one had appeared to find it strange it all.

No one had even seemed surprised.

Still looking into the mirror, she shook her head. "I almost can't believe Jan and I will be married tomorrow."

Nadja stopped unlacing the gown. "You love him very much, don't you?"

"More than I can say. I only wish I'd realized it sooner."

Leaning forward, Nadja hugged her briefly from behind. "My girl."

⋅   ⋅   ⋅

Out in the courtyard of the keep, Jan was engaged in a much more communal task with at least ten other men. His mother's side of the family was from a people who called themselves the Móndyalítko—"the world's little children"—and they traveled in wagons a good deal of the year. Jan normally traveled with them during the autumn, and this year, he'd brought Julianna along, never realizing how the journey would end.

He was in love, real love, for the first time in his life.

And now, his family was preparing for a wedding.

Four Móndyalítko wagons—that also functioned as homes—were parked in the courtyard, and this small group of men had placed two of them parallel, about thirty paces apart. Jan's father had produced a flattened piece of canvas from what had once been an enormous tent, and now their task was to string the canvas between the paired wagons' rooftops to create a covered space.

Everyone would gather under there tomorrow.

In spite of late autumn weather, Julianna had requested the ceremony take place outside in the courtyard beneath the keep—her one home—and yet among the wagons of the Móndyalítko—which she now considered her other home. She also wanted anyone from the village below to feel welcome to come take part in both watching the ceremony and the feast to follow, and so extra tables had been set up in the keep's main hall, which meant there was no room in there for a ceremony.

Jan was determined to make all this work in any manner she wished. He didn't care where or how they got married, so long as she married him.

"Do you think the space between the two wagons is wide enough?" he asked.

"Yes, it's just right," his father answered.

The mix of men out here almost struck Jan as amusing. His stoic hardworking father was a contrast to the Móndyalítko, who were in turn a contrast to a few keep guards also doing their best to help. Most of the guards wore simple clothing: chain armor over light padding with rough wool tunics on the outside. None of them bothered with helmets and only wore swords while on duty.

Jan's father, Cadell, was the Zupan of five fiefdoms and the current vassal of Chemestúk Keep. He was a barrel of a man in his late-fifties with pale skin, fading freckles, and cropped red hair flecked by gray. He always wore brown trousers and a brown shirt. His fingernails were forever stained dark from hard work.

Jan looked nothing like his father but rather had inherited his appearance from his mother's side. He normally wore high boots and loose brightly colored shirts.

Many of the other Móndyalítko men were dressed in a similar fashion.

His Uncle Rosario came striding over. "Jan, you'll need to climb up onto a wagon rooftop to secure one side of the canvas."

"Yes, Uncle."

Rosario was not brightly dressed in his black pants, white shirt, and russet vest, but he definitely stood out. A giant of a man, his chest was wide as two normal men. He wore his dark hair short—and sported a thick moustache.

Before scaling the side of the wagon, Jan paused and looked back to his father. "We'll need small tables on each side of this covered area. Julianna told me some of the women will bring fresh flowers tomorrow morning."

His father nodded and for once he appeared... pleased. "Good. I knew Julianna would want flowers. She's not a frivolous girl, but she's always liked flowers."

Jan's father adored Julianna and had spared no expense for this wedding. The feast for tomorrow afternoon alone must have cost a small fortune: two roasted pigs, a venison haunch, casks of wine and ale, six vegetable dishes, honey cakes, and countless apple tarts—not to mention extra hired kitchen help.

However, Cadell's expression then darkened slightly. "I was glad when you told me of this marriage. You are beyond fortunate to have won her hand, but you do mean to honor her, don't you? Not to fall back on any of your..." he trailed off as if uncertain how to finish.

Normally, Jan kept his guard up around his father and didn't allow himself to be blind-sided, but he fought hard not to wince. Unfortunately, this time his father wasn't entirely unjustified. Jan had a well-earned reputation for breaking hearts. In the past, to amuse himself, he'd often played at making women fall in love with him—because it was so easy. Between his looks, his charm, and his gift for flattery, young women tended to swoon at his feet, and not too long ago, he had found this most diverting.

Justified or not though, it hurt that his father would throw the past into his face the day before his wedding.

Summoning up all the inner strength he could muster, Jan answered, "I don't need to be reminded of how fortunate I am. I will honor Julianna all the days of my life. No one else will ever come between us."

His father blinked at the blunt answer and nodded. "All right then, get up the side of that wagon and let's string this canvas. We have a wedding tomorrow."

That evening, in the main hall of the keep, Julianna could scarcely remember having been so happy. This "night before the nuptials" supper had somehow turned into a celebration of its own.

In addition to Jan, Julianna, Nadja and Cadell, all the Móndyalítko from Jan's mother's side of the family had joined them, and Cadell had opened a cask of good ale. The women had baked fresh bread and put together a savory chicken stew, and now everyone was eating and drinking and visiting in anticipation of tomorrow's festivities.

Julianna sat with Jan and looked across the table at some of the Móndyalítko who had become dear to her in the past few moons in which she'd traveled with them. Her gaze paused on enormous Uncle Rosario, and he raised his mug to her. She then looked to Aunt Doreena, a larger and much more boisterous version of her sister, Nadja. And sitting beside Doreena was their son, Rico.

He was a taller, more muscular copy of Jan, with black hair, dusky skin, but unlike Jan, he always wore an utterly serious expression. He never laughed or smiled. Julianna often thought he'd be handsome if his expression weren't always so hard. Rico was also a Móndyalítko "shifter." At will, he could turn himself into a great black cat, and he was the family's hunter and their main protection.

Yet, in the past moon, he had changed—softened— a bit, and a pretty young woman named Lydia sat quietly beside him as he fed her from his own plate. Lydia was a new addition to their traveling family, and Julianna suspected it wouldn't be long before another wedding was announced.

Turning her head, she took in the sight of Jan's profile. "I'm so glad Doreena and Rosario decided to stay for a while and help us celebrate. Tomorrow wouldn't be the same without them."

"Agreed," he said, offering her a sip from his cup. "But I'd marry you if there was no one to help celebrate except a few skinny chickens."

She felt her cheeks flush and glanced away. A part of her had mixed feelings over him turning his gift for flattery in her direction. In their lives to date, he'd not often tried his wiles on her before, and this was one of the reasons his relationship with her had been different from his relationship with any other woman. With her, he'd always been honest, always been himself.

Of course she enjoyed his attention, but she didn't want their method of interacting to change. She needed no flattery to be sure of his love.

Still trying to think of a response, something else across the hall caught her eye. "Oh... Jan, I think Belle has her hooks into poor Klayton. You might want to go call her off."

Jan looked to where she gestured and sighed audibly.

His other cousin, Belle, was leaning forward and smiling seductively at one of the keep's guards. At the age of seventeen, she was small-waisted and fragile in appearance—with an incredible mass of wavy dark hair. Her skin was pale as opposed to Jan's more dusky shade, but her eyes were nearly black, looking even darker in contrast to her skin. She wore a deep blue skirt with a white low-cut blouse. Her breasts were perfectly rounded... with the tops clearly exposed at her neckline.

She was quite beautiful.

Unfortunately, she was also conceited, lazy, and incapable of thinking about anyone except herself, and her favorite past time was seeking the attention of men.

Jan stood up. "I'll go rescue Klayton. He's been through enough without having to recover from Belle's... charms."

As he walked away, Julianna thought on his words regarding the guardsman. Last spring, two noble factions—the Äntes and the Väränj—had launched into a civil war. The Äntes had come through Chemestúk and conscripted every able-bodied man in the village and the keep, including Jan and the few hired guards here. These men had been given no choice and were ripped away from their homes. Any of them who had tried to escape along the road had been executed.

Before the conflict was officially over, Jan had managed to escape. Julianna still wasn't sure how, as he never talked about it, but he'd not been able to free anyone else. The other men had been forced to remain in service to the Äntes until peace was declared. Soon afterward though, they'd been released... to walk all the way home.

Thankfully, most of them had come home, but several bore scars—inside and out—of an experience in which they'd been powerless to help themselves. When Jan had first returned alone, he too had shown signs emotional trauma, but three moons on the road with Móndyalítko seemed to have healed him.

Julianna watched as he reached the hapless Guardsman Klayton, who stared at Belle in awe. Jan took Belle's hand and quickly steered her in another direction as he whispered in her ear.

She frowned, as if he'd spoiled her fun.

Guardsman Klayton followed them with his eyes, as if Jan had taken away some beloved treasure.

Julianna shook her head in disgust. The foolish man probably didn't realize he'd just been rescued.

Uncle Rosario stood up from the table. "Let's have some music!" he called in his booming voice. "Jan, fetch your violin."

Jan flashed a smile from across the hall, and Julianna fought to keep her expression still. A part of her was embarrassed by how much she loved him... and by the joy in her heart at the prospect of marrying him. As he headed for the hearth to retrieve his violin case, one of the hired servants from the village came hurrying into the hall.

Julianna knew her. Her named was Sari, and she was normally a composed woman, but now she appeared distressed as she looked around until spotting someone else. Sari then rushed to Nadja, leaning down to whisper something. Fearing that something had gone amiss with the food being prepared for tomorrow, Julianna stood up and hurried over.

"What is it?" she asked upon reaching the bench where Nadja sat.

Sari looked up. "There's a... visitor, a lady in the entryway, but she's—"

"A lady?" Julianna interrupted in confusion. "Don't you mean a woman?"

Sari winced and opened her mouth to speak again. Whatever was about to come out never emerged as the sound of gasping and running feet caused everyone in the hall to turn and look to the open arch leading out into the main passage to the keep's front door. A slender young woman ran in and looked about wildly.

Her manic eyes matched the pale blue of her fine silk gown, but the gown's hem was torn and filthy. With flawless ivory skin, her red-gold hair hung to the small of her back but was tangled and uncombed. The cloak thrown back over her narrow shoulders was muddy all the way to the top, as if she'd been sleeping on the ground.

Her gaze stopped on Jan near the hearth, and she sobbed once.

"Jan!" she cried as if her heart would break.

Jan froze, his eyes wide.

Julianna watched in stunned silence as the woman ran stumbling across the hall, threw her arms around him, and began weeping like a lost child who'd been found.

"Jan, Jan," she kept saying over and over. "I've found you."

Julianna's feet felt stuck to the floor, no one else in the hall moved, and Jan's dusky skin paled.

"Gisele... I...?" he said, not touching the clinging woman, but not trying to remove her either.

Julianna's mouth dropped open. He knew her. He knew her name.

"You couldn't believe I would give up after he sent you away," Gisele babbled, still clutching him. "But I had to wait... wait until he'd gone away. I couldn't take anything with me. I had to slip away, but you must have known I wouldn't stop trying. I walked all the way. I've found you, found you, and now we can be together."

Her half-mad words were beginning to slur, and

she seemed to be clinging to Jan partially to keep from falling.

Nadja rose to her feet, staring at her son in horror.

Julianna was numb. This Gisele wasn't some peasant girl with whom Jan had flirted. Her dress was silk, and she had left her home and walked a good distance... believing Jan to be in love with her.

Nadja appeared beyond speech, and in her place, Julianna fought to force one of her own feet to move. It did. The other foot followed.

Walking silently across the room, she kept her eyes on Jan as he watched her coming. He looked as if he was about to be sick, but he still did not push Gisele away. Instead, he was holding her up now.

Shaking his head, Jan whispered, "Julianna, don't think... please don't think—"

"Doreena," Julianna interrupted, keeping her voice impassive. "This lady is weary and ill. Could you and Belle take her upstairs to a bed and bring her broth and tea?"

Her words broke the spell in the hall.

Doreena came bustling over. "Yes, yes, of course. Belle, come and help me! Sari, you fetch the broth and tea." Reaching out, she took Gisele's small shoulders in her hands. "Come, my dear. You need to lie down."

For just an instant, Gisele allowed herself to be drawn away, and then she pulled free and clutched at Jan again. "No! I won't be parted again!"

With his face nearly white, Jan suddenly picked her up as if she weighed no more than a kitten and started for the stairwell leading up. "Aunt Doreena, come with me," he said over his shoulder. "Julianna... go up to my parents' room. I'll join you shortly."

Then he was up the stairs and out of sight.

Julianna stared after him in silence, unable to think, unable to feel until something touched her shoulder. Turning, she found Zupan Cadell standing beside her with bleak eyes.

"Come, my girl, upstairs with Nadja and me... and Jan will join us shortly.

Somehow, again, Julianna put one foot in front of the other.

J an was desperate after settling Gisele in his own bed, as he wasn't about to put her in Julianna's. He left her in his aunt's care and went straight to his parents' bedroom, knowing Julianna would be waiting there for him.

As of yet, he had no idea what he was going to say. If he'd ever been able to explain what he'd once done to Gisele, he'd have done it a long time ago.

Opening the door to his parents' room, he was caught off guard at the sight of not only Julianna, but his mother and father as well. His father's face was like a thundercloud, and his mother stared at him there in the doorway as if she didn't know him.

"Jan," she whispered.

Julianna didn't look at him.

"Who is this woman?" his father demanded.

Jan wanted to back out, run, and hide until the right words came to him.

But he didn't step out. With slow breath, he entered and closed the door.

"Gisele is the wife of Lieutenant Braeden, an Äntes nobleman who conscripted me," he began quietly. "I couldn't see a way out... couldn't see a way to free myself... until we stopped for the night at his family manor. I talked my way in by promising to provide entertainment... music... card tricks... and then saw his wife was young and how badly he treated her. I knew I'd be able to use her."

"Use her?" his mother whispered, coming closer. "What do you mean?"

Jan closed his eyes. He'd never wanted anyone to know about this, about what he'd done. But the rest of his life was on the line now, and he had to try to explain.

"I made her believe I loved her and convinced her run away with me. When she went upstairs to pack, I told her husband what she was doing and, that unless he set me free, I'd make sure everyone in the house, including the other officers, knew that his wife had agreed to run away with a half Móndyalítko peasant." Jan stared at a spot on the wall. "He's a proud man. I knew he could never allow that to happen... so he let me go."

"And you just abandoned the girl," Cadell asked. "You left her to face her husband?"

"I had to," Jan stated flatly, still not looking at anyone. "I had to get home... to all of you."

"How did she know where you live?" Julianna asked.

"I told her that my father was the vassal of the keep here. I needed to convince her that I could take care of her."

The words coming out of his own mouth were making him ill, but these three people, the people who he loved most had not been *there*. They could not possibly understand what he'd faced and that he would have done anything to escape.

Anything.

"So now she's run away from her husband and come to find you," his mother asked, "thinking that you'd been sent away against your will and that you indeed still love her?"

"I don't know what she..." he snapped, and then realized there was no avoiding this. "Yes," he bit off.

"We'll have to cancel the wedding tomorrow," Julianna said.

"What?" His head jerked toward her as anger flooded through him. "No! I won't have you use this as an excuse to punish both of us!"

"Do you wish for that young woman to have arrived here," she asked, "believing you're deeply in love with her... after leaving her husband and her home, only to witness your wedding?"

Her voice was so small and hurt that his anger gave way to fear.

"I didn't have a choice, Julianna. It was the only way I could see to escape."

When she didn't answer, he ran a hand over his face, and silence hung too long in the room.

"Maybe you're right... about the timing," he said. "The ceremony should be postponed."

"Yes," Julianna whispered. "Postponed."

The following morning, out in the courtyard of the keep, Julianna walked slowly beneath a piece of canvas stretched between two Móndyalítko wagons. A number of small tables had been set along each side of the space, just as she had requested. As only a few people yet knew that the wedding would be cancelled, there were vases of autumn wildflowers on every table, along with various little bells that had come from the Móndyalítko themselves.

Julianna had learned it was a Móndyalítko custom after a wedding for people to ring the bells in celebration.

Now... those bells would stay silent.

She still didn't know what to think or how to feel, although she had learned a few things between last night and this morning.

Doreena had related that when she undressed Gisele, she'd found numerous bruises and other injuries on the young woman. Someone had been beating her where it would not show. Gisele had escaped by waiting until her husband left for an overnight trip to Enêmûsk. She'd convinced a few of the house guards to take her into the local village for errands. After entering a shop alone, she'd managed to slip out the back and run for the forest with nothing but the clothes on her back. She had walked for days—and nights—to reach Chemestúk.

This must have taken courage.

Julianna felt no anger or hatred or blame toward Gisele, but that didn't alter the fact that everything was different now. Perhaps it wouldn't be if she'd pressed Jan much sooner about how he had managed to free himself. Her mind slipped back to the day he'd returned—after having been conscripted.

She'd run down the road to meet him.

Did you... did anyone else escape with you? She had asked.

No. I was only able to... and I had to do something... awful... to get free.

She should have pressed him right then, but she feared that maybe he'd killed someone and didn't wish to ever tell her. She should have realized he would have been forced to fall back on his real strengths.

Of course she could forgive him for using one of the few skills he possessed: making women fall in love with him. From everything Gisele had told Aunt Doreena, the young woman was not a fool if she'd managed to escape her own guards, and yet Gisele believed without a shadow of doubt that Jan loved her deeply. In the span of a single evening, he'd convinced her so completely that she'd risked leaving everything behind out of faith in him.

Was it possible that Julianna had fallen for the same lie?

No, Jan loved her... didn't he?

She wanted to weep. Why had Gisele come last night of all nights?

Julianna looked back toward the keep, wondering if she should go inside. She knew she'd need to make a formal announcement that the ceremony had been cancelled. Maybe Zupan Cadell would do it? She hadn't seen Jan since she'd left him the night before and gone to her room to cry herself to sleep.

"Julianna!"

She turned to look toward the courtyard's gate. One of the village boys, Gideon ran toward her. He was about twelve and quite skinny, with crooked teeth and hair that stood up in the front, but Julianna had always found him quick witted.

"Get everyone inside," he shouted as he neared. "Soldiers in yellow tabards are in the village, but now they're coming up here now!"

Whirling, Julianna ran to the nearest wagon and pounded on the door. "Wake up! Everyone, get inside the keep! There are soldiers coming!" Looking over her shoulder, she ordered, "Gideon, run and tell the guards in the barracks."

J an walked down the stairs to the main hall of the keep, uncertain he was up to facing anyone but knowing he couldn't hide all morning. With Gisele in his bed, he'd slept on the floor of what had been once been a room for servants.

He'd not slept well.

Upon entering the hall, the first person he saw was his father staring back at him with disappointed eyes. Well aware that he'd never win his father's approval, he found that it really didn't matter; but he had to fix this.

Jan looked away and around the hall for Julianna, for only she mattered.

As of yet, he had no idea what he was going to do about Gisele, but he'd think about that later today. Right now, he needed to know Julianna still loved and trusted him. As long he knew that, he could deal with anything.

Finishing his scan, he realized she wasn't here. Only his parents and Aunt Doreena were present, along with a few hired servants from the village who were laying out breakfast.

Could Julianna still be in her room? That wasn't like her. She was an early riser by nature, but this was hardly a typical morning.

He was about to cross the hall to speak to his mother when a loud banging echoed from the open archway leading in from the passage to the front doors. Numerous voices and running feet came next, and then Julianna and Gideon dashed through the archway, followed by Rico, Uncle Rosario, the keep's six hired guards, and the rest of the Móndyalítko.

"Soldiers..." Julianna panted, "in yellow tabards... riding up from the village."

Jan went cold. The Äntes wore yellow tabards.

"Jan! Rico! Bar the front doors," his father ordered. "Rosario come with me up to the tower. Everyone else get below into the cellars."

Startled into action, Jan raced for the front doors with Rico on his heels. Over the summer, his father had made some improvements to the keep. With the outer wall crumbling, there was no point to fixing the broken gate, and the cost of fixing the wall was far outside of their yearly stipend. Instead, Cadell had installed two sets of iron brackets on each side of main doors, and he'd had two beams made from solid oak.

Skidding to a stop in the main entryway, Jan pointed left. "Rico, grab that side."

Together, they hefted the first beam into the top pair of brackets and then the second beam into the lower ones. Then they heard pounding hoof beats outside in the courtyard.

Panting, Rico looked to Jan. "Now what?"

Jan glanced up the passage before answering. "Up to the tower to join our fathers. I want to see what's happening."

With a knot growing in his stomach, he had a terrible feeling he already knew, though he hoped he was wrong. This could be a coincidence. Anything was possible. Running up the passage ahead, he led the way through an interior narrow arch into a stairwell that went up several stories. They both came out onto the turret of the keep's single tower to find their fathers already peering down over the keep's front.

Cadell and Uncle Rosario leaned out between the stone "teeth" or merlons of the turret. Then Jan saw the men weren't alone. Julianna had disobeyed the order to go below, and she looked back to Jan.

"How many?" he asked instantly.

"I count ten," she answered in a hush. "One is about to try the doors."

Jan crept toward her with Rico following, and he leaned out between two merlons just far enough to look downward. The tower stretched up three stories in height above the two-level keep, but that still left Jan with a clear view of the courtyard and everyone in it.

There nine men on horseback near the front doors. A tenth horse stood without a rider, and Jan heard pounding on the doors, which he couldn't see from above.

"Open up!" a voice ordered. "In the name of Prince Rodêk!"

Jan's father leaned out a little too far and called down in a booming voice, "I serve Prince Rodêk, and I don't know you!"

Booted footsteps sounded as the leader of the contingent below stepped away from the doors and came into view as he looked up.

Jan quickly jerked backward out of sight as his breath caught in his chest. One glimpse of the tall man with sandy colored hair and a clean-shaven face was all he needed to confirm his initial fear.

He'd have recognized Lieutenant Braeden, Gisele's husband, anywhere.

As Jan dropped low behind a merlon, he found Julianna watching him.

"Who are you?" Braeden shouted up.

"The prince's appointed vassal of this keep," Cadell shouted back. "Who in the seven hell's are you?"

Jan's father was not easily intimidated. Unfortunately, neither was Lieutenant Braeden. He was probably the most arrogant man Jan had ever met.

"If you're the vassal, then I'm here to arrest your son," Braeden called.

"On what grounds?"

"Desertion."

"Ridiculous! The Äntes and the Väränj have declared peace."

"You will turn over my wife... and your son, or I will take action."

The knot in Jan's stomach grew. Apparently, Braeden had no intention of arguing the point, and he would have known right where to ride to find Gisele.

Uncle Rosario leaned out an opening between two of the merlons. "Jan's not here," he called down. "He was conscripted last spring and never returned, the gods rot you! And we've never seen your wife, so if you've lost her, that's your affair."

Braeden was silent for a moment and then spoke in a voice that carried. "You are a liar. I've already questioned your villagers. A young woman with red-gold hair arrived last night, and she would have only come here for that half-blood deserter. Bring them both out immediately or you will regret it."

Jan went cold as he looked to Julianna. He—and she—knew what "questioned" meant. Braeden had been torturing people in the village... because of Jan.

When Jan looked up, his father was speechless. Uncle Rosario scowled. Both likely reasoned what had happened in the village.

"What's he doing now?" Rosario whispered, looking down again.

When Jan's father didn't answer immediately, he couldn't help rising and trying to peer down without being seen from below. Two soldiers had dismounted and were using flints to light torches as Braeden pointed to the four Móndyalítko wagons.

"Bring out my wife and the deserter or I'll burn those wagons. Then I'll start on your stables."

Julianna gasped, and Jan found breathing difficult. The wagons were the only homes his Móndyalítko mother's family possessed... and their horses were in the stable. Braeden was about to destroy everything they owned.

"Touch those wagons, and I'll have you brought up on charges!" Cadell shouted. "They belong to guests of the keep, and this keep and its holdings are the property of Prince Rodêk."

But even from this height, Jan could see a sheen of fury on Braeden's face. The lieutenant was beyond reason, beyond fear for himself, and he pointed to the largest of the wagons—Rosario and Doreena's.

"Burn that one," he ordered his men with the torches before looking up again. "When the stables are gone, I'll start on the village."

The village.

"Stop!" Jan called, leaning out so he could be seen. "I'm here! I'm coming down! Just get your men away from the wagons."

"No!" Julianna cried. "Jan, you can't."

He ignored her, watching Braeden. The tall lieutenant hadn't called off his men, and he once more faced the wagons, as if his lust for revenge, for destruction had reached a boiling point, and he didn't want to stop.

"Burn those wagons," Jan shouted, "and I'll stay in here with Gisele until the end of time!"

"Halt," Braeden ordered his men, and finally, he looked up at Jan.

The hate in his eyes was clear.

For Julianna, what followed was like something out of a nightmare from which she couldn't awaken. Jan ran down the stairs and the rest of them followed, and then Rico *helped* him unbar the front doors.

All Julianna could do was watch.

The instant the front doors were unbarred, two Äntes soldiers shoved them open and grabbed Jan to drag him outside and tie his hands. They searched him for weapons, removed a dagger from his right boot, and he didn't even struggle. Worse, she couldn't understand why Zupan Cadell, Rosario, and Rico were allowing all this to happen.

Why hadn't they called up the rest of the men? The keep had six of its own guards in the cellars below. Why weren't they fighting? Why didn't Rico turn

himself into a great cat and attack those two soldiers gripping Jan?

"Where is my wife?" Lieutenant Braeden bit off as
if the words were difficult to say.

"She's inside," Cadell answered. "Upstairs in bed.
I'll have her brought down."

Before anyone could move, Braeden swept an arm
forward and two more of his men pushed in past
Cadell and down the passage.

"Please," Julianna begged, unable to keep silent.
"The lady is ill. Let me get her. Let me tell her
what's happening."

But the lieutenant ignored her and both his men
strode down the passage.

"What will happen to Jan?" she demanded.

Now that she'd spoken, she couldn't seem to stop.

This time, Braeden glanced at her and then Cadell
before answering. "He'll be taken to Enêmûsk and
hanged... as a lesson for any would-be deserters."

"Hanged," Julianna gasped. "But the war is over!"

Braeden appeared to enjoy this. "The war wasn't
over when he deserted, and he embarrassed the captain in charge of our contingent. As soon as Captain
Oakes learns I have the deserter in my custody and I
remind him of what happened, I will have no trouble
getting a death warrant signed."

Jan offered no reaction at all, and neither did
Cadell. Julianna didn't understand any of this.

Two saddled horses were led out of the stable, and
then Julianna heard an anguished cry echo up the
front passage. She turned to see the two soldiers
who'd entered the keep now dragging Gisele toward
the front doors... wearing nothing but a borrowed
nightgown.

"No! No!" Gisele was screaming, struggling wildly
to break free.

When the men pulled her outside and she saw Jan
in custody and being led toward the two extra saddled horses, she stopped fighting and her face lost
all expression.

"No," she whispered one last time.

The lieutenant glared at her with a hatred that bordered on madness as the sheen on his face glistened in the morning light.

"Sir, please," Julianna begged again, hoping he might listen. "At least let me fetch the lady a cloak. Enêmûsk is days away, and you'll be sleeping outdoors. Please, just wait for me to get her a cloak!"

He behaved as she hadn't spoken, and one of the soldiers lifted Gisele onto a horse.

Jan climbed up into a saddle and took the reins with his bound hands. He looked over at Julianna, and she clenched her own hands in frustration. Braeden barked an order to pull out, and all twelve horses broke into a trot, passing through the gate and down the road.

Julianna stood there sucking in harsh breaths, unable to believe what had just happened.

Jan was gone.

Zupan Cadell watched the contingent riding away for a few long moments.

Behind him, Rosario asked, "How long do we wait?"

"Midday," Cadell answered. "Give them a good head start, and we'll make sure they're well away from our fiefdoms. No one will connect them to us if they vanish."

Julianna blinked, uncertain what she was hearing.

Cadell turned around and looked at Rico. "You can track them?"

Rico nodded. "I can track them."

S hortly before mid-day, Julianna walked out the main doors of the keep and headed straight for the stable. For the first time in her life, she was about to make a demand of Zupan Cadell... and she wasn't taking no for an answer.

Her preparations had been simple and quick. She'd cut away the bottom of an old wool dress so that it only reached her knees, and then she'd donned a pair of boy's pants, boots, and a well-worn cloak.

Upon reaching the door to the stable, she took a deep breath and entered—with a fairly good idea what she'd find inside.

Six horses had been saddled and six men moved about inside preparing for a journey. The size of the group made sense—large enough to get Jan back while small enough to travel swiftly.

Zupan Cadell, Rosario, and Rico were packing supplies into saddlebags. Rosario appeared enormous inside the stable, and she hoped his horse would be able to carry him. Guardsman Klayton and two of the keep's other hired men, Logan and Sawyer, were discussing weapons. The three of them wore swords, but they seemed to be choosing options for the others.

"Get Zupan Cadell a crossbow and a dagger," Klayton said. "He's never used a sword."

As Julianna stepped in, Cadell glanced at her, looked around at the others, and then looked back with a frown at the sight of her pants and boots.

"What do you think you're—?"

"I'm coming," she answered before he could finish asking.

At that, both Rosario and Rico looked over at her. She couldn't tell what either one was thinking.

Cadell's face went red, and he sputtered, "No, you are not! You're staying right here with Nadja. Jan's already been taken, and I'll not have her losing the both of you."

"I'm coming," she said quietly. "I want a horse and a small crossbow."

His face still red, Cadell strode straight at her, but she didn't flinch and she didn't budge.

"If you try to leave without me," she added, "I'll wait until you're gone and come after you."

He stopped in his tracks.

"Father," she said. She'd never called him that before, even though he'd been a father to her. "It's Jan. I'm coming."

"Let her come," Rico put in.

Before the zupan could say anything more, Julianna turned to Guardsman Klayton and repeated, "I want a crossbow."

J an rode behind Gisele all day, heading west toward Enêmûsk. By nightfall, she was swaying atop her horse to the point that he feared she would fall.

Finally, Braeden called a halt and ordered his men off the road so they could make camp.

Jan's thoughts hadn't stopped churning all day, but as of yet, he hadn't come up with a plan to save himself or Gisele.

Back at the keep, his only goal had been to stop Braeden's men from burning the wagons and the stable and then likely the village. He'd not thought a moment beyond that. Now, he couldn't stop seeing Julianna's stunned face as she'd watched him mount up in the courtyard with his wrists bound.

This should have been the happiest of days for her, and he'd made it one of the worst.

It also embarrassed him that he'd been relieved when she'd shouted "No!" upon his decision to turn himself over. She'd have watched Braeden burn the wagons instead. That meant she still loved him. But he couldn't have let the wagons be burned. Once she'd had a moment to think rationally, she would have realized this.

"Günter! Terome!" Braeden called. "Get a fire going. Jacon, see to the horses. Sergeant Cullen, you guard the prisoner."

He continued giving orders as camp was set up, but he neither mentioned nor looked at Gisele, who still sat shivering on her horse, wearing nothing but a nightgown as she clutched her mount's mane to keep from falling.

Jan wondered what would happen if he dismounted and tried to help her.

The problem was solved for him as a late-middle aged soldier with a graying, close-trimmed beard walked swiftly over to her and reached up with both hands.

"My lady," he said. "Try to put your hands on my shoulders, but otherwise don't assist me. Let me lift you down."

The mix of pain and pity in his voice startled Jan.

"Cullen," Gisele whispered.

The man was old enough to be her father, and his expression held a fatherly countenance as he lifted her down and carried her to tree stump a few paces away.

"Sit here, my lady. I'll have the fire built close by."

Once she was seated, he stripped off his cloak and wrapped it around her.

"Can you hold the front closed?" he asked.

Her exhausted eyes seemed to clear, and she looked up at him. "What about you? Won't you be cold without your cloak?"

"I'll be fine, my lady. Old soldiers like me don't get cold."

Still mounted, Jan wondered what to do—what he would be allowed to do. Slowly, he swung his leg over and dismounted, standing beside the horse.

Another soldier, this one younger with a pock-marked face, walked by Cullen and Gisele, and his lips curled back into a sneer. "I wouldn't waste my cloak on a faithless strumpet, Sergeant, and the lieutenant won't thank you for it."

Cullen turned quickly and his eyes narrowed. Just as fast, a third soldier—this one tall with broad shoulders and dark hair—strode at the one who'd spoken.

"Close your mouth, Günter," he snapped, "or I'll break it! And get away from her."

The pockmarked one opened his mouth but thought better of any retort and walked away.

The dark-haired soldier leaned down. "Forgive me, my lady. I'll not let you hear such words again."

Gisele met his gaze. "Thank you, Corporal Rowan,

but do not trouble yourself. I have no wish for you displease my husband. Cullen already risks himself enough."

Rowan straightened, glowered in Braden's direction, and then walked off to help gather firewood.

Suddenly... Jan realized there was a dissention in the ranks here. Some of the men were loyal to Lady Gisele and angry at the treatment she was receiving. It took him a moment to absorb this, but it made some sense. As a lieutenant for Prince Rodêk during the civil dispute, Braeden had probably been away from home a good deal, and Gisele had shown herself to be kind. Some of these men had to have been guarding Braeden's family manor and probably dealt more with her in recent years than with him. She was their "lady"—theirs to protect.

There were also soldiers here like that Günter, who walked by and cast Gisele looks of contempt and disgust. They had likely been afield with their lieutenant and, like him, considered her a "faithless strumpet" for having run off.

Jan's thoughts began racing again as he stored all of this away until he could think of a way to use it. Could he play one side against the other? As of yet, he didn't see how, but he couldn't continue to simply stand here, and he caught Sergeant Cullen's eye.

"May I sit?" he asked, motioning to the stump.

Cullen frowned, and Jan couldn't help noticing how well trimmed the man kept his graying beard. He was particular about appearances. Finally, Cullen nodded and pointed to the far side of the stump.

"Over here. Well away from my lady."

"Could you get me a drink of water?" Gisele asked him.

Cullen glanced once at Jan but appeared to decide there was nowhere to run—or at least not to get far. "Of course. I'll be right back." He headed toward the horses.

With a sigh, Jan walked over to the stump and sat down.

"Thank you," he told Gisele. He had a feeling that she'd sent Cullen off on purpose.

Gisele didn't answer, and Jan sighed again.

"I'm sorry about this," he said. "You must believe me. I'd never have turned you back over to... him, but he was threatening... my people, my family."

Still, she didn't speak. Perhaps she was wondering why he made apologies and spoke of his family. Did she still believe he was mad with love for her? The thought filled him with guilt. Then again, why would she think anything else? He hadn't told her the truth.

"I *know*," she whispered, her head tilted forward so that her red-gold hair covered half her face.

"You know?" he repeated, confused.

"Your aunt told me today was to be your wedding day... to that girl, the tall one."

Jan said nothing. What could he say?

"So it's true?" she asked, "What my husband told me? You played me for a fool, tricked me into agreeing to go with you, only so could you threaten to humiliate him? To make him let you go?"

"I was desperate. I never would have hurt you."

"You let him hurt me instead... and still I didn't care. I thought someone loved me, wanted me."

His stomach clenched, and a part of him wanted to walk away. He had no wish to sit here and listen to an account of his sins. Somehow, he stayed. She deserved that much.

"I'd have done something else, anything else, if I could have," he said.

She didn't respond.

"In my case, it was all for nothing anyway," he added. "Your husband plans to hang me. I don't think he'll go that far with you."

"With me?" She looked up and her hair fell back so he could see her face. "No, he wants to hide that this ever happened. No one besides these nine soldiers will ever know where he went or why. He wants his *lady* to grace his table and play hostess to his guests. I won't be hanged or quietly strangled in some back room. He won't release me with death. He'll punish me in his own good time."

When no answer worth speaking came to Jan, he leaned over and put his face in his hands.

J ulianna rode directly behind Zupan Cadell all afternoon with the others in their group behind her. They passed through several villages but didn't slow once. By nightfall, Julianna expected to make camp. Instead, Cadell slowed his mount and looked over his shoulder.

"Rico, you take the lead."

Julianna pulled up her horse—a good-natured bay gelding—while Rico rode past and to the front, and they continued west. Strangely, she wasn't even tired, and now that they were going after Jan, she didn't want to stop. She just wanted him back.

Soon, she lost track of time as the night grew darker and darker.

Without warning, Rico held up one hand as he pulled in his mount. His body was rigid as he stared straight ahead.

"Off the road," he said.

All seven of them steered their horses into the trees on the road's north side, and Julianna waited to see what would happen next. Everyone began to dismount, so she did too, realizing how stiff her body had become only after her feet touched the ground.

Rico pulled off his shirt and handed it to his father. "I'll find their camp. I won't be long."

Without another word, he vanished into the forest.

Julianna knew why he'd removed his shirt and suspected that he'd waited to transform due to her presence. Once he was alone, he'd finish undressing and shift into a great cat with a much stronger sense of smell and hearing—and greater speed.

Guardsman Klayton asked, "What now?"

"Set up camp," Cadell answered. "Rico will locate their position, but we won't take action tonight. We're still too close to Chemestúk."

"How long is the journey to Enêmûsk?" Julianna asked.

Cadell patted her arm once. "At least three days. Don't worry. We have time."

Disappointed, she nodded. She'd thought they would have Jan back by tonight, but the wiser part of her knew Cadell was right. Saving Jan was going to involve shedding Äntes blood, and any bodies found later could not be connected to the vassal of Chemestúk Keep. Cadell was responsible for the welfare of five fiefdoms, and before his appointment, many peasants had suffered from neglect and from having no one to speak for them.

Cadell was too essential to lose.

Ever skilled at accepting the situation at hand, Julianna turned to helping with camp. While Klayton and Guardsman Sawyer saw to the horses, Guardsman Logan began collecting firewood. She and Rosario dug through the packs to try and put together some dinner. They hadn't even finished when Rico reappeared from trees, slipping into camp wearing his pants and carrying his boots. He pointed west.

"They've made camp on the other side of the road. Most are asleep with only two on watch."

Cadell nodded. "Good. They'll probably do the same tomorrow night."

"What if they stay in a village instead?" Julianna asked.

"They won't. Braeden wants to keep all of this a secret, at least the part concerning Gisele. He won't risk some innkeeper asking questions or spreading rumors about a lieutenant tracking down his runaway wife."

"Did you see Jan?" she asked Rico.

"Yes, he seems well, but now his feet are tied as well as his hands."

No one else said anything and, with little else to do, Julianna turned back to breaking out supplies while Rosario and Cadell moved away to pick a spot for a small campfire. Rico crouched beside Julianna.

"You can't blame Jan for being what he is," he said suddenly, catching her off guard.

Blinking a few times, she stared into his face. His features were so much Jan's, and yet... he didn't look like Jan. There was no humor in his face, no charm; it was locked in a perpetually serious state.

She suddenly became aware that all the others in the camp were either too busy or too far away to hear anything she and Rico might say to each other.

"I don't blame him," she whispered back, feeling defensive.

Rico studied her with his black eyes. "I picked Lydia because she is the only woman I've met who will never expect me to be anything other than what I am. She will not wake up in a year or two and expect me to be a man who laughs or to engage in long talks about feelings."

These last words made Julianna realize that in the time she'd known Rico—over three moons—he and she had never *talked* before. He must want to express something quite badly.

"Jan will always turn the heads and hearts of women," he continued. "It means little to him now, but it is part of who he is. He cannot help it."

Julianna dropped her gaze. "I want a husband, Rico. I don't want a prize that I'm going to have to defend or fight for again and again."

"I'm a year older than him and I've known him since he was born," he said softly. "I've seen him with other women, and I've seen him with you."

Rico somehow lowered his head in his crouch, staring at her as if the cat within now watched her.

"You'll never have to fight anyone for him," he murmured. "And he will never give you a reason to do so."

Without knowing why, Julianna gripped the fingers of his hand dangling over one bent knee, and she held them hard.

The following late afternoon, during the long day's ride, Jan let his gaze drop to his horse's mane as he let his mind drift. Between last night and today, he'd noted some things regarding the nine Äntes soldiers with Braeden.

Four of them appeared loyal to Giselle and unhappy with the treatment she was receiving. Sergeant Cullen and Corporal Rowan were the only ones openly attempting to care for—and protect—her as best they could without offending Braeden. But Jan was good at reading faces, and two other men made no secret of their discomfort with their weary lady being treated like a prisoner on a forced ride... wearing nothing but a nightgown and a loaned cloak.

However, the other five Äntes soldiers appeared fanatically loyal to Braeden and seemed to view Gisele as getting exactly what she deserved.

As of yet, Jan hadn't seen a way to use this divide among the men, but his thoughts kept turning.

The sound of a soft thump broke his concentration, and he looked up.

At first, all he saw was a riderless horse in front of him, and then he saw that Gisele had fallen from her horse onto the road. She'd been ill and exhausted when the journey started, and Jan had wondered how long she'd able to ride.

When she didn't move, he almost called out her name, but then stifled himself, fearing any open concern on his part might only make things worse for her.

The pockmarked Guardsman Günter was riding in front of her. He turned his horse and looked down in what appeared to be disgust.

"Sir?" he called.

Braeden pulled up his horse and glanced back, frowning. After hesitating a moment, he turned his mount and rode back, stopping a few paces from where Gisele lay and looking down at her.

"Get up," he ordered.

Her eyes were closed, and she didn't move.

Jan clenched his teeth to hold in a stream of profanity. Again, anything he tried to do to help Gisele would only make things worse for her.

"I said, get up," Braeden repeated coldly.

"Sir," a voice called.

Sergeant Cullen had been riding at the back. Now, off his horse, he strode up and dropped down beside Gisele. "She is too weary to ride, sir." He lifted her off the ground. "I can hold her in front of myself on my horse."

By then, everyone had halted, and a number of the men turned their mounts around and were watching.

Braeden stared down impassively at Cullen as if he didn't care where Gisele rode so long as the contingent moved on. Without a word, he wheeled his horse and headed back toward the front.

Cullen's eyes followed, glowing with anger.

Then Jan looked over at Corporal Rowan and the other two men who'd shown pity for Gisele. Their faces were tense, jaw muscles tight, in an effort not to betray open hatred for a superior.

The situation was heating up without Jan having lifted a finger yet. He began to think that a set plan might not be necessary. He would simply need to wait and watch and know when to act.

That night, not long past darkness, Julianna stood beside her horse with her hands clenched. They were hiding in the trees on the north side of the road, and their only light source was a single glowing candle lantern on the ground. A short while ago, Cadell had sent Rico to locate

Lieutenant Braeden's camp. She had no idea how what would happen then... but she knew tonight they would take action.

She barely caught the sound of soft footfalls before Rico emerged between two nearby trees. His black hair was a tangled mess and, like the previous night, he wore only his pants and carried his boots.

Rosario handed him his shirt. "Well?"

Cadell, Klayton, Logan, and Sawyer gathered around to listen.

"Their camp's not far," Rico answered, sounding slightly troubled, "on the same side of the road as us. But the arrangement is different. Two guards on watch are inside the camp instead of on its outskirts, so we can't take them out quietly. No matter what we do, all the soldiers will be alerted instantly."

Julianna breathed quietly, trying to stay calm. She knew Cadell had hoped to even the odds a bit before invading the camp.

"But you saw Jan?" she asked. "He's still safe?"

Rico nodded once.

Rosario crouched and drew a circle in the dirt. "Give us an idea of who is where."

Rico crouched as well. "The soldiers on watch are here and here." He pointed to the east and west sides of the circle. "Braeden is lying near the fire with three sleeping men close by. The other four are sleeping here around Gisele." He pointed to the camp's south side. "And Jan is not far from them, with his hands and feet bound again."

After hearing this, Cadell walked to his horse and pulled something from one of the saddlebags. When he came back, he held pieces of black fabric.

"We cannot let Braeden live. He will only come after Jan again and again. I saw madness in his face. But if we can cause enough confusion that the soldiers don't understand what's happening... and Jan just manages to escape, we might be able to avoid killing some of the others." He glanced around. "I don't like the idea of killing men who are only following orders."

"I don't either," Guardsman Klayton agreed with a sigh. "Though we must be prepared to kill if necessary."

"Of course," Cadell agreed impatiently, fiddling with the pieces of fabric. "We'll kill anyone we have to. They took Jan. But we can at least disguise ourselves. Rosario, take off that vest. It is too memorable." He paused. "Before we left home, Nadja made each of us one of these." Lifting a piece of the black fabric, he pulled it over his head.

Watching curiously, Julianna drew in a loud breath when she soon saw only his eyes. It was a black hood with two holes.

"Masks?"

"Like bandits," he answered. "But we need to do more than hide our faces. This cannot look as if we are attacking with the purpose of rescuing Jan."

"Who kills Braeden?" Klayton asked suddenly.

From his tone, Julianna thought he might be volunteering.

"I will," Rico answered, staring down the sketch in the dirt.

Julianna knew he meant to transform for the attack. She glanced at Klayton, Logan, and Sawyer, but no one else bothered to explain anything about Rico. She realized someone must have already told them about his... ability. Cadell and Rosario would never allow them to be surprised in the middle of the fight.

"Uncle Cadell," Rico continued, "I think you and Julianna should remain hidden in the trees. Just before the attack, you two can use your crossbows to wound the men on watch." He looked up at Julianna. "Can you aim well enough to hit a man in shoulder?"

"I think so." She nodded. "Yes."

"The instant that happens, I'll charge into the camp," he went on. "I'll kill Braeden first, if I can, and that will panic the rest. We cannot give them a moment to think. Klayton, Logan, and Sawyer, you follow once their attention turns inward on me." He looked to Rosario. "Father, run for Jan, cut him loose, and he'll know what to do. As soon as he is free, we need to break off and vanish... so long as we've caused enough wounds and terror that we won't be followed right away."

"What about Gisele?" Julianna asked.

"Without Braeden, she might be better off where she is," Klayton answered.

"You don't know that."

"Jan will know," Rico interrupted. "If she's in danger from the soldiers, he'll grab her before he runs."

"Oh..." Julianna began but didn't finish. She hadn't thought of that.

Rosario looked around. "We're in agreement then? We try Rico's plan?"

With his eyes on the dirt sketch, Cadell nodded. "Rico won't need a mask, but the rest of you take one now."

J an's wrists and ankles were bound tightly. He had no blanket or cloak where he sat on the cold ground. Thankfully, he'd been given a cup of water and a few bites of jerked beef earlier. Perhaps Braeden didn't wish him to die of thirst before he could be hanged.

Gisele lay near Sergeant Cullen, wrapped in his cloak, and she hadn't spoken all evening.

Jan wondered if she'd eaten anything, though in worrying about her, he was growing more concerned for himself. From bits and pieces he'd heard from the soldiers, they were about a day and a half from Enêmûsk, and so far, he'd seen no opportunity to escape.

Closing his eyes, he again saw Julianna's bleak, frightened face in the courtyard of the keep when he'd been taken. He couldn't allow that to be his last memory of her... nor her last memory of him.

There had to be *some* way out of this.

A part of him knew he should lie down and try to sleep. Around the camp, most of the men were lying on the ground, wrapped in their cloaks. Only Günter and another of Braeden's sycophants were standing watch, one on the west side of camp and the other on the east.

Jan found he was absently biting his fingernails and took his bound hands away from his mouth.

He wondered what Julianna was thinking, alone in her bed at the keep.

Suddenly, Günter cried out.

An instant later, so did the other guard on watch.

Jan's head swiveled back toward Günter as a crossbow quarrel appeared to sprout from the man's right shoulder, and he dropped to his knees with a shocked cry. The other sentry suddenly fell backward, flopping down with a quarrel protruding from his chest.

Braeden and the other seven soldiers all stirred in confusion and shouts when an ear-splitting yowl smothered all other sounds.

Two breaths later a roar followed, much closer, and a great black cat the size of a small pony charged out of the darkness straight at Braeden.

Jan almost couldn't believe the sight.

"Rico," he breathed.

J ulianna was hiding in the trees, waiting for Cadell to shoot. He was on the east side of the camp, aiming roughly in her direction at a pock-mocked soldier with a dour expression. She was on the west side of the camp, aiming her crossbow at the other soldier on watch. Then she realized she was holding her breath, unlike what Cadell had told her to do.

She'd tried to sound confident when she'd assured Rico she could do this, but she was not at all certain she could hit someone in the shoulder. The camp wasn't large, so the distance wasn't far, but she'd only fired a crossbow a few times in her life—and always in practice beside the zupan. She had a case with a few extra quarrels, and Klayton had helped to make sure she knew how to reload quickly.

She was determined not to miss on her first shot.

As she and Cadell had no way to signal each other, the plan was for her to fire immediately upon him hitting his target. They were both wearing their black hoods in case anything went wrong and they were seen.

With her crossbow cocked and aimed, she'd been ready when the pockmarked soldier cried out as Cadell's quarrel hit him in the shoulder. Julianna aimed as carefully as she could and fired. The quarrel struck the second sentry in the chest, and he fell backward.

Julianna felt a sudden chill that she might have killed the man, though she was simply relieved she hadn't missed. On instinct, she began cocking the crossbow to load another quarrel.

A yowling roar in the night made her flinch.

When a second roar came and faded, she had the crossbow cocked and reloaded. But when she looked up, too much was happening too quickly.

Rico charged into the camp in his great cat form. She'd seen him like this before, but the sight was still terrifying. When he snarled, his black fur blending with the darkness only made his fangs glow white. He went straight for Braeden.

The other three men sleeping nearby roused and tried to gather themselves, but it was too late. Men in black hoods rushed from the trees with swords drawn.

Klayton, Logan, and Sawyer charged in behind Rico at the soldiers around Braeden. And then... to Julianna's shock, the pockmarked man that Cadell had shot suddenly dashed between Rico and Braeden with his sword drawn. He swung hard, catching Rico's black form across the shoulder.

The blade instantly darkened in the night with blood.

An eerie, almost human cry of pain erupted from Rico.

He whirled on his haunches, stumbling on the wounded foreleg, and slashed up with his other paw. The pockmarked soldier's throat darkened like his sword and he fell instantly. Rico stumbled again in trying to twist the other way, and by the low fire-light, Julianna saw blood glistening on his wounded shoulder.

Klayton, Logan, and Sawyer had already engaged the three soldiers who'd been sleeping near Brae-den, and a cacophony of clanking steel and grunts filled the camp.

Rosario burst from the trees in his black hood, a dagger in his hand, and made a run for Jan.

Only the span of a few blinks had passed.

Julianna looked back to Braeden, who was on the ground and now crab-stepping backward away from Rico. Rico wobbled and stumbled, seeming disori-ented, and Braeden's head turned as he spotted Rosario running for Jan.

Even without his vest, few men were as large as Rosario, and Julianna saw recognition in Braeden's face... followed by a twist of manic rage.

The four Äntes soldiers who had been sleeping around Gisele were on their feet. But instead of rushing to help their comrades, they encircled her. Jan was tied near-by and Rosario was pounding in their direction on his large booted feet.

A middle-aged man with a close-trimmed beard among Gisele's guard was grabbing for a sheathed sword that had been lying on the ground beside him, but he didn't have time to pull the blade. So instead, moving almost faster than Julianna could see, he darted in front of Rosario, and using both hands, he swung hard with his sheathed weapon, catching Rosario across the face.

The impact snapped Rosario's head aside with enough force to knock him off his feet.

"No!" Jan shouted, jerking at his bonds.

Julianna wanted to shout in fear and frustration. This was all going wrong, and she quickly looked back to Braeden.

The lieutenant ignored the savage fighting taking place around him and the bleeding, wounded great cat attempting to struggle toward him... and he stared only at Jan in hatred.

Braeden's sword was on the ground, but he ignored it and jerked a dagger from its sheath on his hip as he ran toward Jan. Julianna's panic increased. Braeden truly was mad. He cared for nothing anymore besides punishing Jan.

Jan's eyes widened as he saw the crazed lieutenant coming toward him.

Without thinking, Julianna dashed out of the trees, running in behind the lieutenant as she shouted, "Braeden!"

Something in her voice must have struck him, for he skidded on one foot in looking back. As his head turned, she merely pointed the crossbow and fired.

The quarrel struck him in the right eye. His head snapped back. His body toppled and flopped upon the ground. Julianna stalled for one cold instant.

Braeden didn't move, and she didn't wait any longer.

Dropping the empty crossbow, she crouched and grabbed Braeden's fallen dagger before running straight to Jan. He stared at her, beyond speech, as she knelt beside him and began slicing at his bonds.

From behind, she could still hear cries and grunts and snarls and clashing steel. A scream sounded, followed by the clatter and a thud of a fallen blade and body. She finished cutting the rope around Jan's ankles and started on the one around his wrists. She had to get him free.

A woman's voice shouted in the night. "Stop this now!"

.　　.　　.

Jan still reeled in disbelief at everything happening around him. Even with the hood over her head, he recognized Julianna's form and voice, and she finally cut through the bonds on his wrists. When he got up, he saw Gisele standing on a fallen log with Cullen, Rowan, and her other two loyal guards gathered around her with their swords drawn.

Rosario was sitting up and groaning with one large hand against the side of his jaw.

Across the camp, Jan recognized his father's shape, though he wore a black hood and was holding an empty crossbow as he stood over a large black cat struggling to stay on all fours. Rico had been wounded.

Three men wearing the rough wool tunics of the keep's guard over their chain armor were panting and bleeding from various wounds, and the three soldiers who'd been sleeping near Braeden were now on the ground, dead or dying. One of them had a quarrel through his throat. Had Jan's father come in from the trees and shot him?

The two men who'd been on watch were also dead, one shot in the chest. The other had a quarrel protruding from his shoulder, but his throat had been slashed by Rico.

Braeden lay prone and still, not far beyond Julianna with a quarrel standing upright through his one eye.

As Jan absorbed this, he realized that Braeden and all five of his loyal men were gone.

Gisele, however, was still standing on the fallen log with her men at the ready.

"You will stop!" she repeated, and her voice had never sounded so strong.

Everyone still on his or her feet stopped moving. Instead of looking at her husband or the carnage around her, Gisele looked to Cullen.

"Sergeant, do you and your men still wish to serve protecting Braeden manor?"

This was the last thing Jan had expected her to

say, but it made sense. With their lieutenant—and lord—dead, their only other option would be to go to Enêmûsk and try to gain a place in one of Prince Rodêk's contingents. That was a far riskier life in Droevinka than protecting a manor now left to a dead officer's wife.

Without even looking at his men, or turning to face his lady, Sergeant Cullen nodded, though he kept his sword up, watching all those who had invaded the camp.

"Yes, my lady."

"Then when we are asked," Giselle added, "we will say that we were attacked by bandits along the road, and your lord was killed. We will take his body for proper burial, and you will resume your duties. Is this agreeable?"

Cullen turned hard eyes upon his fallen lord and then glanced around at those men who had stood with him in defense of their lady. Rowan nodded, followed by the other two.

"Yes, my lady," Cullen answered.

Giselle, wearing nothing but a nightgown and with her hair hanging in a tangle around her, still looked and sounded like the great lady of a manor.

Jan didn't have to wonder about the cause of this transformation. With Braeden dead, she was free.

Looking out over the camp, she called out, *"Bandits... if you know what is good for you, flee... now."*

She knew exactly what was happening here and who they were. She was giving everyone a chance at an outcome with no more bloodshed. No one needed to be told twice.

Jan's father reached down to help Rico, who struggled up, limping but able to walk on three legs. Rosario was on his feet next.

Everyone in a black hood began vanishing into the trees.

Jan felt someone grab his hand and pull him. Julianna led the way as they ran.

He believed that Gisele would be safe as the widowed lady of Braeden Manor with her own loyal guards. But he looked back one last time before the trees blocked his view, and he thought he saw one guard carefully assisting her down off the log.

Once he and Julianna were well inside the trees and alone, she slowed and pulled off her hood.

He could see the outline of her narrow face in the darkness, and he was still trying to take in the past few moments since the first Äntes soldier had been shot. Not only was Julianna here... but his father and Rosario and Rico.

Grasping Julianna, he held her in front of himself.

"You came after me," he breathed.

"Of course we came after you."

"You killed Braeden."

"He was going to kill you."

Jan didn't know what to say to that and blurted out, "Do you still want to marry me?"

"What do you think?"

She was suddenly in his arms, holding him tightly, with her face pressed into his neck.

"Jan," she whispered.

S ix days later, Julianna stood facing Jan with a purple silk ribbon binding their wrists together. As vassal of the fiefdoms, Zupan Cadell conducted the ceremony himself.

"Do you, Julianna, swear to care for Jan, to protect his heart, to cleave only to him no matter what comes, all the days of your life?"

"I swear," she promised.

"Do you, Jan, swear to care for Julianna, to protect her heart, to cleave only to her no matter what comes, all the days of your life?"

All humor and charm was absent from Jan's face as leaned closer to her. "I swear."

For an instant, with that utterly serious expression, he looked so much like Rico that it startled her. Then he smiled and was himself again. She smiled back.

"On this autumn day," Cadell called out to everyone behind them, "I pronounce them husband and wife."

Julianna turned to see the small crowd gathered under the canvas stretched between the two wagons. Among the guests were Nadja, Doreena, Rosario, Rico, and Belle. Rico's arm was in a sling, as the wound he'd taken had been deep and required a great deal of stitching, but she thought he would heal.

As Jan turned beside her, his face glowed. A first cheer went up, growing in volume, and Julianna's gaze turned to the tables set up with wildflowers. But all of the twelve small bells that had been placed there as well were already gone.

Julianna grasped Jan's hand as the cheers grew louder among the gathering, along with their ringing of the bells... no longer silent. ∎

THE END

CPSIA information can be obtained
at www.ICGtesting.com
Printed in the USA
LVHW031335181218
600931LV00016B/971/P